ROUX FOR TWO

Praise for Aurora Rey

You Again

"*You Again* is a wonderful, feel good, low angst read with beautiful and intelligent characters that will melt your heart, and an enchanting second-chance love story."—*Rainbow Reflections*

Twice Shy

"[A] tender, foodie romance about a pair of middle-aged lesbians who find partners in each other and rediscover themselves along the way…Rey's cute, occasionally steamy, romance reminds readers of the giddy intensity falling in love brings at any age, even as the characters negotiate the particular complexities of dating in midlife—meeting the children, dealing with exes, and revealing emotional scars. This queer love story is as sweet and light as one of Bake My Day's famous cream puffs."—*Publishers Weekly*

"This book is all the reasons why I love Aurora Rey's writing. It's delicious with a good helping of sexy. It was a nice change to read a book where the women were not in their late 20s–30s."—*Les Rêveur*

The Last Place You Look

"The romance is satisfying and full-bodied, with each character learning how to achieve her own goals and still be part of a couple. A heartwarming story of two lovers learning to move past their fears and commit to a shared future."—*Kirkus Reviews*

"[A] sex-positive, body-positive love story. With its warm atmosphere and sweet characters, *The Last Place You Look* is a fluffy LGBTQ+ romance about finding a second chance at love where you least expect it."—*Foreword Reviews*

"This book is the perfect book to kick your feet up, relax with a glass of wine, and enjoy. I'm a big Aurora Rey fan because her deliciously engaging books feature strong women who fall for sweet butch women. It's a winning recipe."—*Les Rêveur*

"If you enjoy stories that portray two gorgeous women who slowly fall in love in the quirkiest way ever coupled with nosy and well-meaning neighbors and family members, then this is definitely the story for you!"—*Lesbian Review*

Ice on Wheels—Novella in *Hot Ice*

"I liked how Brooke was so attracted to Riley despite the massive grudge she had. No matter how nice or charming Riley was, Brooke was dead set on hating her. A cute enemies to lovers story."—*Bookvark*

The Inn at Netherfield Green

"Aurora Rey has created another striking and romantic setting with the village of Netherfield Green. With her vivid descriptions of the inn, the pub, and the surrounding village, I ended up wanting to live there myself. She also did a fantastic job creating two very different characters in Lauren and Cam."—*Rainbow Reflections*

Aurora Rey "constantly delivers a well-written romance that has just the right blend of humour, engaging characters, chemistry and romance."—*C-Spot Reviews*

Lead Counsel—Novella in *The Boss of Her*

"*Lead Counsel* by Aurora Rey is a short and sweet second chance romance. Not only was this story paced well and a delight to sink into, but there's A++ good swearing in it and has lines like this that made me all swoony because of how beautifully they're crafted."—*Lesbian Review*

Recipe for Love

"[A] gorgeous romance that's sure to delight any of the foodies out there. Be sure to keep snacks on hand when you're reading it, though, because this book will make you want to nibble on something!"—*Lesbian Review*

Autumn's Light—Lambda Literary Award Finalist

"Aurora Rey is by far one of my favourite authors. She writes books that just get me...Her winning formula is Butch women who fall for strong femmes. I just love it. Another triumph from the pen of Aurora Rey. 5 stars."—*Les Rêveur*

"[*Autumn's Light*] was another fun addition to a great series."—*Danielle Kimerer, Librarian (Nevins Memorial Library, Massachusetts)*

"Aurora Rey has shown a mastery of evoking setting, and this is especially evident in her Cape End romances set in Provincetown. I have loved this entire series."—*Kitty Kat's Book Review Blog*

Spring's Wake

"[A] feel-good romance that would make a perfect beach read. The Provincetown B&B setting is richly painted, feeling both indulgent and cozy."—*RT Book Reviews*

"The Ptown setting was idyllic and the supporting cast of characters from the previous books made it feel welcoming and homey. The love story was slow and perfectly timed, with a fair amount of heat. I loved it and hope that this isn't the last from this particular series."—*Kitty Kat's Book Review Blog*

Summer's Cove

"As expected in a small-town romance, *Summer's Cove* evokes a sunny, light-hearted atmosphere that matches its beach setting... Emerson's shy pursuit of Darcy is sure to endear readers to her, though some may be put off during the moments Darcy winds tightly to the point of rigidity. Darcy desires romance yet is unwilling to disrupt her son's life to have it, and you feel for Emerson when she endeavors to show how there's room in her heart for a family."—*RT Book Reviews*

"From the moment the characters met I was gripped and couldn't wait for the moment that it all made sense to them both and they would finally go for it. Once again, Aurora Rey writes some of the steamiest sex scenes I have read whilst being able to keep the romance going. I really think this could be one of my favorite series and can't wait to see what comes next. Keep 'em coming, Aurora."—*Les Rêveur*

Crescent City Confidential—Lambda Literary Award Finalist

"This book blew my socks off…[*Crescent City Confidential*] ticks all the boxes I've started to expect from Aurora Rey. It is written very well and the characters are extremely well developed; I felt like I was getting to know new friends and my excitement grew with every finished chapter."—*Les Rêveur*

"This book will make you want to visit New Orleans if you have never been. I enjoy descriptive writing and Rey does a really wonderful job of creating the setting. You actually feel like you know the place."—*Amanda's Reviews*

"*Crescent City Confidential* is a sweet romance with a hint of thriller thrown in for good measure."—*Lesbian Review*

Built to Last

"Rey's frothy contemporary romance brings two women together to restore an ancient farmhouse in Ithaca, N.Y…[T]he women totally click in bed, as well as when they're poring over paint chips, and readers will enjoy finding out whether love conquers all."
—*Publishers Weekly*

Winter's Harbor

"This is the story of Lia and Alex and the beautifully romantic and sexy tale of a winter in Provincetown, a seaside holiday haven. A collection of interesting characters, well-fleshed out, as well as a gorgeous setting make for a great read."—*Inked Rainbow Reads*

By the Author

Built to Last

Crescent City Confidential

Lead Counsel (Novella in *The Boss of Her* collection)

Recipe for Love: A Farm-to-Table Romance

The Inn at Netherfield Green

Ice on Wheels (Novella in *Hot Ice* collection)

The Last Place You Look

Twice Shy

You Again

Follow Her Lead (Novella in *Opposites Attract* collection)

Greener Pastures

Hard Pressed

Roux for Two

Cape End Romances

Winter's Harbor

Summer's Cove

Spring's Wake

Autumn's Light

Written with Jaime Clevenger

A Convenient Arrangement

Love, Accidentally

Visit us at www.boldstrokesbooks.com

ROUX FOR TWO

by

Aurora Rey

2023

CREDITS
EDITORS: ASHLEY TILLMAN AND CINDY CRESAP
PRODUCTION DESIGN: STACIA SEAMAN
COVER DESIGN BY INKSPIRAL DESIGN

Acknowledgments

I've wanted to write a trans main character for ages. I introduced Bryce as Kate's brother in *You Again*, hoping to give him a story of his own but not entirely sure how. Getting to doing it in small-town Louisiana with a fat, queer femme who gets her own cooking show was even more fun than I could have imagined and, it turns out, completely on brand.

A thousand thank-yous to the spectacular trans guys in my life. You're smart, funny, and swoon-worthy. Knowing you and seeing the ways you live your lives—authentically and without apology—makes me a better and braver human. Particular thanks to Daniel for the sensitivity read and thoughtful feedback.

Thanks to Jaime and Leigh for the beta reads that up the ante of what I think I can do. Also, thanks to the usual suspects: Sandy, Rad, and the BSB team for supporting it. Ashley and Cindy, you make me snort-laugh—I mean a better writer—with every book. (I know I keep saying it, but it keeps being true.)

And maybe most importantly, thank you to everyone who reads these stories of mine. I'm so grateful you go on these adventures with me. Thank you from the bottom of my heart.

For Daniel
This one wouldn't have happened without you

Chapter One

Chelsea Boudreaux pulled her car to the side of the road and put it in park, letting her head fall back against the headrest. "You've got to be kidding me."

The popping sound had resembled a gunshot, or at least what she imagined a gunshot would sound like. The rumbling came hot on its heels, along with a heavy pull to the right. She cut the engine and got out to assess the damage. Not that she needed to. Flat tires didn't leave much to the imagination.

Sure enough, the rear wheel on the passenger side slumped, leaving her Fiat with a rather sad lean. "Fuck."

She returned to the driver's side and snagged her phone from the center console, only to find zero service. Not even one lousy bar. "Really, AT&T? I know I'm rocking some backroads, but Jesus. I'm not even an hour outside of New Orleans."

She turned a slow circle, arm thrust skyward, as though that might make a difference. It did not. Did it ever?

She dropped her phone onto the driver's seat and turned another slow circle, this time looking for any semblance of human activity. Sugarcane fields sprawled on one side of the road, soybeans on the other. A tractor that had seen better days with no one at the wheel. Signs of civilization, but none that would do her any good today. And if she'd done her math right, she was still at least thirty miles from Duchesne.

She planted her hands on her hips and kicked the tire for good measure, grumbling a few more expletives when pain shot through her big toe. After running through the usual suspects on her swear list, she stopped. It was bad enough to be stuck in the middle of Podunk south Louisiana with a flat tire. She didn't need to turn into one of those women who talked to themselves on top of it.

It was fine. It would be fine. She technically knew how to change a tire, even if she'd never been called upon to do it. And it was the middle of the afternoon. Hotter than Hades, but with a decidedly lower risk of being run over by a passing car or kidnapped.

The pep talk came to an abrupt halt when she realized that the spare—and the jack and that wrench thingy—were tucked away under the floor of the cargo area. The cargo area packed to the roof with boxes and bags of clothes, breakables, and everything else she didn't entrust to movers. "Son of a bitch."

She huffed out a second round of cuss words and stalked to the back of the car, popping the hatch and staring at the contents with dismay. Unfortunately, staring didn't get them out of her way any faster, so she started unloading. A suitcase and six boxes later, the sound of an approaching car caught her attention. Relief and reticence warred for top billing. Her day was about to get a whole lot better or a whole lot worse.

The car turned out to be a truck, a vintage Ford painted baby blue and white. Its driver was definitely male, and her anxiety ticked up a few notches. She reminded herself even assholes were rarely serial killers and tried not to think about the other stuff assholes got up to.

The guy approached slowly, like he could sense, or maybe even appreciate, her apprehension. He wore khakis and an LSU polo shirt. Not that such a dorky look made him harmless, but that combined with his body language managed to render him a lot less menacing.

"Car trouble or setting up camp?" he asked.

Since the question came out more comical than condescending, she tipped her head. "I'm attempting to dig out the spare."

He laughed. "It's nice in theory that they're tucked out of the way, isn't it?"

She laughed too. "In theory."

He stopped, still a good ten feet shy of where she stood. "I don't want to presume you need a hand, but I'm happy to offer one."

The last of her anxiety vanished. Well, anxiety related to her immediate safety at least. She still had plenty else to worry about, but that would keep for a couple of hours. "I wouldn't say no."

He smiled and something about it felt familiar. Not enough to place him, but considering how many people never left, it was entirely possible they'd crossed paths at some point in her childhood. "Anything back here breakable or otherwise you don't want me to touch?" His cadence felt familiar, too, though that likely had to do with where they were more than him in particular.

"A few are fragile, but they're packed well."

He nodded and grabbed a box, adding it to the pile on the ground. "Moving here or moving away?" he asked.

"Moving back." It felt funny to say. She never thought she would and even now that she was, she didn't think of it as coming home.

He moved another box and looked at her. Like, really looked at her. "To Duchesne?"

She narrowed her eyes. "How did you know that?"

He smiled again. "I knew you looked familiar."

She wanted to say the same, but he seemed to actually know who she was, and she had nothing more than a vague sense. "Really?"

"Chelsea, right? Chelsea Boudreaux?"

It was hard to say whether being recognized made her feel better or worse about standing on the side of the road with a man she couldn't place. "Yes, that's right. I feel bad that you remember me, and I can't place you."

He grabbed a duffel bag. "It's okay. I've changed a lot since you last saw me."

She racked her brain for someone fatter or skinnier. Or maybe nerdier. Despite the golf-playing, car salesman vibe of his attire, he was attractive. As in, really attractive. Intense blue eyes and brown hair, cut close on the sides but long enough on top to be a little wavy. Plus that five o'clock shadow stubble not every guy could pull off. But as much as she tried, she couldn't get any further than that fuzzy sense of having seen him before.

While she busied herself on a fruitless trip down memory lane, he cleared enough of her stuff to free the panel covering the spare. He looked to her, and she gestured for him to go ahead.

"What's your name?" she asked.

"Bryce. Bryce Cormier."

Her mind kicked into overdrive. She'd gone to school with the Cormier sisters. One in her grade and one a few years older. Maybe he was a cousin? God knew cousins crept up like crab grass around here.

"I transitioned. Didn't start until the end of high school, though, and you went away for college."

The fuzzy familiarity turned into a flood of memories. The tomboy she'd had a crush on but didn't recognize as a crush. Learning sophomore year of college that her attraction to masculinity didn't necessarily mean cis men. "Wow."

Bryce stared at the ground for a moment and ran a hand up the back of his neck. When he looked at her again, it was his eyes that held apprehension. "Not a bad wow, I hope."

It hit her that Bryce coming out to her had to be at least as much of a risk as her accepting his offer of help. Not physically, maybe, but some of the biggest risks never were. She offered what she hoped was a reassuring smile, even if the real cause had more to do with her newfound appreciation of the particular kind of man Bryce was. "Not bad at all."

"Oh, good." Bryce freed the spare from the latches holding it in place. "Now that we've got that out of the way, let's see what we can do about that flat."

In what felt like no time, Bryce switched the tires, letting Chelsea hand him tools so she didn't feel utterly useless. They reloaded the boxes and bags together, chatting about innocuous things like how stupidly hot it was. When they were done, the desire to get on with it got lost in how easy he was to talk to, on top of how nice he was to look at. "I really can't thank you enough. I like to think I could have managed that on my own, but I'm sure it would have taken me at least twice as long."

"A pleasure."

She attempted to wipe the sweat from her forehead gracefully. "I'm sure you're lying, but it's nice of you to say."

"How about I was glad to help?" He hesitated for a moment. "And I was glad to bump into you."

"Me, too." Because while she had faith in her intellectual ability to change a tire, the physical part would have been iffy. Also, how many hot trans guys were realistically cruising around these parts?

"And I imagine I'll be bumping into you again. Duchesne's pretty small," he said.

"You still live there?"

"I work in Baton Rouge, but yeah."

Her heart did a flip of happy, rather than nervous, anticipation. Sure, the prospect of running into him on the regular would be nice. But even more than that, she liked the idea of knowing someone—anyone—in town besides her mother. She wasn't scared to be back, but moments of doubt crept in. Even if the impetus for her homecoming was a point of pride, not knowing anyone could make for a rather lonely triumph.

"You going to be okay?" he asked.

"I'm great. I think the heat must be catching up with me."

If he suspected any artifice, he didn't let on. "It'll get to you, that's for sure."

As much as she wanted to ask what he did in Baton Rouge—or for his number or if he wanted to grab a drink sometime—she didn't want to seem desperate. And, like he said, they'd probably bump into each other soon enough. "Thanks again for coming to my rescue."

He smiled at that. He might have blushed, too. Or maybe it was the heat. "I'll be seeing you."

She went for a smile that Bryce could read as flirtatious if he wanted to. "I'll be looking forward to it."

He offered a friendly wave and returned to his truck. She got into her own car and started the engine, cranking the AC to full blast. After a minute, she realized he was waiting for her to pull out. She did, trying not to think about the fact that he'd likely be following her the rest of the way to Duchesne. Instead, she turned her attention to more pleasant things. Things like her very own house, about to be outfitted with a brand-new kitchen. Like finally accomplishing something that might actually impress her mother. Oh, and being weeks away from filming the first season of her very own cooking show.

❖

Bryce leaned on the kitchen counter and sipped an Abita Amber. "You'll never guess who I rescued today."

Kate, his sister, looked up briefly from the cutting board where she was chopping vegetables for a salad. "Delores Bourgeois."

"Who's Delores Bourgeois?" The question came in stereo—from him and from his niece, Harper, who sat perched on a stool at the island tearing lettuce into a large bowl.

Kate made a back-and-forth gesture with her hand. "You know. Mrs. Bourgeois. Eighth grade math. Kind of mean?"

"You had a mean math teacher?" Harper, who'd just finished sixth grade and took math very seriously, looked horrified.

Kate came around to Harper's side of the island and slid the piles of carrots, cucumber, and sugar snap peas onto the lettuce. She bumped Harper with her shoulder. "Don't worry. She retired."

Harper shook her head. "Still."

"Have you had any mean teachers?" Bryce asked.

Harper scrunched up her face. "Mrs. Picou wasn't mean, exactly, but she wasn't very nice either."

"That's a very generous assessment." Kate bumped Harper's shoulder again.

It was. He'd had Mrs. Picou for second grade back in the day when she was new to the classroom. Not a bad person, but not a personality suited to elementary education.

Harper shrugged before looking at Bryce with impatience. "Okay, it wasn't her, or you wouldn't have asked who she was. So, who did you rescue?"

The fact that the redirect came from Harper made him laugh. "Chelsea Boudreaux."

"Who's Chelsea Boudreaux?" Another case of question in stereo, this time coming from Kate and Harper.

"She was in my grade. Went away to college and never came back." He didn't mention the low-grade crush he'd had on her through the better part of tenth and eleventh grade.

"Huh." Kate angled her head and stared at the ceiling. "Any siblings?"

"Not that I know of. She kind of kept to herself. I think her mom was super religious."

Kate shook her head. "I got nothing."

"Well, she's moving back. And got herself a flat tire on Highway 90."

Kate let out a sniff. The stretch of road was a notorious dead zone for cell service and she had opinions about it. "She's lucky you came along."

He grinned. "She said the same thing."

That got him an eye roll. "Did you offer to welcome her back to town over drinks sometime?"

"Why do you assume I hit on every woman I come into contact with?"

Kate shrugged. "Not every. But single women don't move to Duchesne very often and even fewer move back. And that's pretty much your type."

"That's not true. The last two women I dated lived in Baton Rouge." Not that he wouldn't have preferred a woman from Duchesne. Or at least one who appreciated the kind of life Duchesne had to offer.

"Yeah, and we know how that turned out."

Bryce cringed. "Thanks for rubbing it in."

"Mama." Harper hit Kate's arm. "Don't be mean."

"Yeah, Mama. Don't be mean." Bryce didn't hit Kate's arm but only because he wasn't close enough.

The singsong echo of Harper's words got him a smack on the shoulder from Kate as she passed by on her way to the sink. "I'm not being mean. I'm simply pointing out that you're too charming for your own good and it gets your heart tangled up with women who don't want the same things as you."

As usual, his sister had his number. "So, you're saying I should have asked her out?"

"I don't know her from Adam. But if she's moving back to town after God knows how long, maybe she could use a friend." Kate opened the oven and pulled out the cast iron pot she used for only one thing.

"Are we having jambalaya?" he asked.

"Pork and andouille." Harper gave the salad a toss with the big wooden hands Bryce had put in Kate's stocking the Christmas before. "You're welcome."

Kate lifted the lid and steam wafted. Scientifically, the aroma couldn't have made its way to Bryce's senses at the exact same time, but he'd swear it did. "That smells amazing."

Kate's fiancée, Sutton, strolled in and made a beeline for Kate. After kissing Kate with the attentiveness of a woman madly in love, she slung an arm around Harper and planted a more affectionate peck on Harper's temple. "Hey, Bryce. You been here long?"

"Nah. Just long enough to get my daily dose of sisterly harassment." Sutton chuckled. "Sorry I missed it."

"We're discussing Uncle Bryce's love life." Harper shrugged with the practiced indifference of a preteen. "Or rather, his lack of a love life."

"Ouch." Sutton cringed.

Bryce merely shrugged.

"How was your meeting?" Kate asked.

"Good, good. We're doing their implementation next month."

Bryce, happy to shift the conversation from both his love life and Harper's pithy assessment of it, seized the moment. "Where are you jetting off to now?"

"Des Moines."

It was Kate's turn to cringe. "My condolences."

Bryce waved her off. "I was there for a conference once. It's a cool town, for Iowa at least. Drake?"

Sutton nodded. "Yeah."

Kate shook her head. "Harper, can you set the table while these two nerd out? Unless, of course, you'd like to learn about colleges in Iowa."

"No thanks." Harper made a face and hustled over to the utensil drawer.

Although their careers were technically very different—Bryce worked at LSU and Sutton implemented software at colleges and universities all over—he appreciated being able to talk shop with someone outside of work. One of the many things he loved about Sutton and Kate being married. Well, almost married. The wedding was just under four months away.

Sutton grabbed a beer from the fridge and leaned on the counter next to Bryce. "Same here. I'd much rather talk about Bryce's love life."

Bryce shot Sutton a look of betrayal. "Et tu?"

Harper put the salad on the table. "What's et tu mean?"

Kate lifted a finger. "Let's serve first, and then we can discuss."

They piled plates with jambalaya at the stove, then settled at the table, passing the green salad as well as a bowl of potato salad. Bryce shook a healthy dose of hot sauce on his and let out a happy sigh. "Thanks for the dinner invite."

Kate gave him an affectionate smile. "You're a pain in my ass but my favorite pain in the ass."

Bryce smiled. "Same."

Harper cleared her throat with the subtlety of a Mardi Gras parade float.

Kate gave a disapproving look, but Bryce couldn't help but laugh. "Right, right. Et tu," he said.

Harper scrunched up her nose. "It's French, right? Something you?"

Bryce nodded. "Close. It's Latin and means 'and you.'"

Harper looked even more confused than before, so Kate jumped in. "It's a line from a Shakespeare play. When Julius Caesar is assassinated, he sees Brutus, who he thought was his friend. So now people say it when someone betrays them."

"But not really betrays," Sutton said.

"Yeah, more like a joke," Bryce said.

Harper looked at Bryce. "So, when Sutton said she wanted to talk about your love life, you were mad but fake mad, not real mad."

Bryce grinned. "Exactly."

Harper shook her head. "Old people slang is weird."

He wagged a finger, channeling every ounce of old man he could muster. "You just wait, little missy. Pretty soon you'll be yelling 'get off my lawn' like the rest of us."

Harper narrowed her eyes, like she might ask for an explanation of that too, but seemed to think better of it. "Whatever. Would you pass the hot sauce, please?"

Kate opened her mouth but then closed it. As though she was having her own internal debate over whether to say something to Harper. But much like Harper, she seemed to reconsider and turn her attention back to Bryce. "So, you didn't ask her out, but are you going to see her again?"

And they were back to it. Bryce handed Harper the bottle before shrugging. "It's a small town. I'm sure I'll bump into her."

"Bump into who?" Sutton asked. "Oh, wait. Is whoever it is why we're discussing your love life?"

The question might not have been addressed to Harper, but that didn't stop her from answering. "Uncle Bryce helped a lady change her tire. She used to live here and now she's moving back. Her name is Chelsea."

Sutton chuckled. "Yeah, that definitely sounds like a love connection in the making."

"But they were in the same grade," Harper said, as though that one detail explained everything.

"But we never dated or anything. She knew old me and didn't even recognize new me." Not that it bothered him to be reminded of how much his outward appearance had changed.

Sutton nodded. "I think that earns you a pass from prodding."

Kate shot Bryce a wink and smirked. "For now."

Harper, never one to be left out, gave a decisive nod. "For now."

"Thank you."

"Besides, we have news," Kate said.

Harper bounced up and down in her chair. "Big news."

Bryce looked from Kate to Harper, then to Sutton before turning to Kate. "Well, what is it?"

Kate opened her mouth but didn't speak, ostensibly for dramatic effect. Harper continued to bounce. Sutton kept her gaze squarely on Kate. Eventually, Kate broke into a huge grin. "We're pregnant."

"You are?" He shouldn't be completely surprised, but he was.

They'd been planning for it, but had only made one attempt thus far. More a trial run than anything else, a turkey baster situation when Sutton's friend—and their chosen sperm donor—had been unexpectedly in town. Kate hadn't mentioned it since, so he figured nothing had come of it.

"I am." Kate looked to Sutton. "We are."

"That's awesome." He cleared his throat, a swell of emotion sneaking in. "Really awesome."

"Well, it's going to save us a fortune, but it means I'm going to be almost eight months pregnant at the wedding." Kate shrugged, like she'd decided on blue for her bridesmaid's dresses instead of green.

Bryce laughed. "Of course you are."

She rubbed her belly. "What can I say? I have a very hospitable uterus."

What ifs and what abouts swirled in his mind, but they all took a back seat to joy. He grabbed Kate's hand, then Harper's. He did his best to shoot Sutton a meaningful look. "I'm so happy for y'all."

Kate squeezed his hand back. "Good, because you're going to be on duty for all sorts of things."

If a tiny stab of envy poked in his chest, he ignored it. He'd get there, eventually. For now, celebration. And as Kate said, a whole lot of things to do. "Sign me up."

Chapter Two

Chelsea unlocked the front door but stood on the porch for a long minute, hand frozen on the knob. How ridiculous was it to buy a house sight unseen?

Well, not entirely unseen. She'd spent time there as a kid. It belonged to the family of Bethany Babin, the girl who'd been her best friend from the first day of kindergarten until the day her family moved across the state at the end of fourth grade. She'd been devastated and hadn't set foot in the house since.

And now it was hers.

When the network told her she was getting her own show, she suggested setting it in her hometown. Good for the narrative of the show, she'd said. After ten years in the business of food TV, she knew as well as anyone that the story mattered as much as the dishes cooked on camera.

They'd agreed. Then they asked about a kitchen—whether she'd be able to buy or rent or borrow a house that would feel homey and authentic. They even offered to front the cost of a remodel to make it all camera ready. Several hours on a house hunting site, a crap ton of paperwork later, and here she was.

She didn't put a lot of stock in fate or the notion of things meant to be. But finding this house on the market the day she started looking felt like a case of stars aligning and smiling down on her. Like the universe knew she needed a good omen to take the leap.

Would it look the same as she remembered? Smell the same?

As nice as that might be for a trip down memory lane, the photos she'd seen told her in advance the answer would be no. No more country blue carpet. No more floral sofa with matching chairs. No more sweeping swags of drapery on the windows. In fact, the house had been remodeled less than a decade ago, bringing the bathrooms and kitchen into the current century. Familiar, but not too familiar. Kind of like home, but not home. And again, all hers.

She pushed the door open and stepped inside. It looked and smelled clean—a total bonus in her book and better than a couple of the apartments she'd rented through the years. The beige carpet, while newer, had still seen better days. That would need to go. Along with some of the paint colors. Nothing she couldn't handle. Well, handle with professional help. She knew better than to think she could DIY her way out of a paper bag.

She'd no sooner wandered into the dining room when her phone rang. Jada. She swiped the screen with a smile. "How do you always manage to know when I need a vote of confidence?"

"Voodoo," Jada said without missing a beat.

"That's not what voodoo is."

"No?" Jada sighed. "I have so much to learn about the backwoods of Louisiana."

"It's a small town, not backwoods. Besides, it was your idea to come here." Not technically Jada's idea. But when Chelsea pitched her hometown to the executives, Jada jumped right on board. Producing a show shot on location would be a nice résumé bullet after all the assistant producing on one sound stage or another.

"And like I said when I signed on, I'm eager to learn." Jada waited a beat. "Why do you need a vote of confidence?"

"I'm walking through the house I now own."

"That bad?"

She strolled into the kitchen. Generic cabinets and appliances, but it had the beams and bones of an old creole cottage. "Not bad. Just still a bit surreal."

Jada let out a sigh. "It's all kind of surreal, isn't it?"

It was. They'd both spent the last five years hustling behind the scenes of *Charlie's Table*, the top-rated show of legendary Chef Charlie Paul. Chelsea had served as the show's off-camera sous chef and Jada had been assistant producer. It had been a great way to climb the ladder, even if the iconic host had been a raging asshole.

They'd kept that part to themselves until one allegation turned into twenty, and Charlie's culinary empire came crashing down in a sexual harassment scandal. But instead of being handed pink slips, she and Jada had been cherry-picked to reflect the network's renewed commitment to diversity and inclusion. In other words, the queer fat girl was getting her own show and the woman who'd put up with her fair share of Charlie's lechery was going to produce it.

"Do you have an appointment with the contractors yet?"

"Thursday. Dania sent me the specs she needs for the cameras and other equipment, and the set designer sent me some ideas." Pictures of kitchens she'd only dreamed of.

"Do you like them?"

"I mean, some are a bit curated for my tastes, but I'm not a girl who is going to turn her nose up at brand new professional grade appliances and quartz countertops." Things that would be hers even if the show got canceled after the first eight episodes. Well, hers to sell at least. No way she'd stay in Duchesne for the hell of it.

"A woman after my own heart."

Chelsea let out a snort. "You wouldn't know what to do with a six-burner stove if it bit you in the ass."

"If it bit me in the ass, I'd schedule an exorcism. Otherwise, I'd boil water for a lovely cup of instant noodles."

She appreciated Jada for her wit as much as her talent as a television producer. "Touché."

"Have your things arrived yet?"

"Sadly, no." That was the thing with moving companies. They couldn't be scheduled to deliver in advance, and the likelihood of them arriving exactly when desired was slim to none.

"Are you going to check into a hotel for the night?"

There probably was a hotel to be had closer than the hour-drive back to New Orleans, but certainly not in Duchesne proper. Thibodaux, probably. She'd already discovered it boasted the closest Target. "Eh?"

"I'm sure the network would cover it."

She snorted again. Not because of anything inherently funny in the observation. No, the very statement had become their shorthand for the network's efforts to cover its ass with, maybe not a blank check, but something not too far off. "Is it weird that I want to spend my first night here?"

"Not at all, but where are you going to sleep?"

She had a vision of knocking on Bryce's door and asking if he might be interested in a sleepover. She just as quickly brushed it aside. One, that sort of thing required a level of feminine confidence she couldn't even pretend to have. Two, she had no idea where he lived. "Um."

"Girl, you are too old to be sleeping on the floor."

She was. Not to mention too plump. Rather than cushion her bones and joints, being on the extra curvy side meant that hard surfaces put every part of her at a bad angle and she'd wind up sore and stiff for days. "Maybe I'll go buy an air mattress. That way you'll have something to sleep on when you're here."

Chelsea thought that might get her a snarky reply or at least a groan, but the line merely went silent. Like, all the way silent.

"Jada? Are you still there?"

"I'm here. I simply refuse to dignify that with a response."

She laughed. "Fine. You know I'm kidding. And I know you have a hotel room to yourself clause in your contract."

"Damn right I do." A muffled voice came through the background. "Chels, I have to run. Call me tomorrow?"

She wondered where Jada was, who she was with. Not jealous, just curious. And maybe missing knowing more than two people in a hundred-mile radius. "I will."

"Talk soon. Bye."

Chelsea got her good-bye in before the call ended, and the line went silent for real. She slipped her phone into the pocket of her paisley skirt and meandered through the rest of the house. She'd gotten a sense from the photos in the listing, but being in the actual space brought new floods of memories. Playing Sorry and Life with Bethany, sleepovers with pizza rolls and Blue Bell ice cream. Nothing luxurious by any means, but so different from her own house, where frivolity might as well have been one of the seven deadly sins. Along with fattening food.

She shook off the irritation that sparked and headed to the kitchen to make sure the fridge had been left on. She'd go shopping for that air mattress and get some spare bedding for good measure. And since she'd be out anyway, maybe she'd pick up some pizza rolls and a pint of butter pecan. For old time's sake. And because she wouldn't have so much as a spatula at her disposal until the moving truck arrived.

❖

"Thank you, Mr. Cormier." Marianna, Bryce's twelfth student of the morning, nodded with a combination of eagerness and relief.

"Please call me Bryce. And it's my pleasure."

Marianna continued to nod and looked down at the schedule he'd printed for her. "You're sure it isn't too many credits?"

"It's in the normal range for a first-year student. The higher end of normal, but normal. If you start the semester and it feels like too much, come see me and we can decide about dropping something."

"Right. Because it's easier to drop a class than to try to add something late," she said.

He loved when students quoted advising lines back to him. It made him feel like they were paying attention, but also like maybe they'd actually remember it after the info dump of orientation was over. "It most certainly is."

"I promise I will."

"But you can come see me for any reason, good or bad." Another of his lines but one he meant with his whole heart.

"Really?" Marianna seemed dubious.

"Absolutely. I'm here to help solve problems, but I'm also here to celebrate your success or brainstorm possibilities or just chat about how you're settling in." Marianna struck him as a rock star student, but she could still use a friendly face and some encouragement along the way.

"Okay." More nodding. "I'll do that."

"Remember you can check or change your schedule on Navigate, but let me know before you make any changes. Email me anytime with questions." A glance at the clock on the wall of his office told him he had exactly a minute before his next scheduled appointment. "And have a great rest of your summer."

Marianna stood. She picked up her bag but seemed to hesitate. "Do you know if there's like a GSA or an LGBT Resource Center on campus?"

It was probably cliché at this point, but having a student come out—in any way, shape, or form—gave Bryce a surge of pride and the sensation of a big hug at the same time. Especially new students who likely didn't read him as part of the queer community. "There are several student clubs and a whole bunch of other things available through the Office of Multicultural Affairs. They'll have a table at the Resource Fair this afternoon."

Marianna bit her lip. "Okay, cool. Thanks."

"But if you want to wait until you're on campus this fall, the meeting schedules and events and stuff are posted on their website and social media."

The eagerness returned to her face and she smiled. "Yeah. Okay. Thank you."

A dozen scenarios ran through his mind, from unsupportive

parents to run-of-the-mill shyness. He didn't have the time or rapport to inquire now, but hopefully Marianna would take him up on the offer to stop by. For now, he offered the best form of solidarity he could. "I go to Spectrum sometimes and usually Trans Advocates, too."

A flash of surprise in Marianna's eyes gave way to a glow of recognition. Followed by a blush that could mean any number of things.

"Take care, okay? I'll look forward to seeing you in August."

"Yeah. Me, too. Bye, Mr. Cormier. I mean Bryce."

He chuckled at the self-correction and offered a wave as she left, then spent a few seconds reviewing the schedule of his next appointment. Unfortunately, that appointment belonged to a frat boy in the making. The one after that belonged to an earnest international student and the last of the morning turned out to be the granddaughter of his high school algebra teacher.

He mentioned the last part to his colleague, Amy, as they ate lunch in the tiny break room of the Advising Center. Amy, the wife of a newly hired anthropology professor and a New Jersey transplant, shook her head and laughed. "Louisiana, man. You people don't leave."

He lifted a shoulder. "Some of us do."

Amy looked incredulous.

"My sister's fiancée went to college in Georgia and lived in Atlanta for like ten years."

"And?" Amy asked.

Bryce tipped his head. "And then she came back."

Amy lifted both hands. "I'm sure some people move away. But on the whole, more stay than anywhere else I've lived."

He shrugged. "It's home. Why would I want to live anywhere else?"

She made a sweeping gesture toward the window, where the almost daily afternoon storm seemed to be gathering itself already. "Do you know there are places where it's not ninety degrees and ninety-percent humidity for six months of the year?"

He feigned shock before polishing off his ham sandwich. "Say it isn't so."

Amy put the lid back on her salad container. "There's a whole wide world out there, Bryce. I'm not saying you're unhappy here, I'm saying there's a lot of it out there. Mountains, deserts, whole states that vote reliably blue."

"Now you're being mean."

"Just your favorite friendly pot stirrer." She offered him a wink and stood. "I'm going to go do twenty minutes of yoga with the rest of my lunch hour."

He had no plans to do yoga but returned to his office as well. Instead of attacking his inbox—the way he often did with his lunch hour—he propped his feet on the desk and stared out the window. The skies continued to darken, and thunder rumbled ominously. The rain came fast and heavy, falling in sheets along the sidewalk outside.

It made him smile, even as he experienced a stab of pity for the students running between buildings for one orientation program or another. He didn't envy them navigating the sauna that would follow, either. Steam rising from the asphalt, ensuring anyone not drenched in the downpour would end up damp with humidity and sweat.

He laughed. He didn't mind the heat for the most part, as long as air-conditioned spaces made up a significant portion of his day. Just like he accepted living in a conservative place because he was able to find enough open-minded and progressive people to feel like he had community beyond his immediate family.

Did Chelsea have that? Did she want it? Was that why she was moving back now?

His memories of her from school remained fuzzy, fueled by the fact that they hadn't been in many of the same classes or clubs. Well, that and his proclivity to steer clear of the fire and brimstone crowd. Not that Chelsea had been part of that. She hadn't really been part of any crowd. And he'd had enough going on in his own quest to find himself that he kept to his known support circles.

He sighed. No doubt he'd run into her. Whether anything became of that—friendship or otherwise—would sort itself out. He wasn't one to push, one way or the other. Even if he hadn't dated since Jasmine and missed the flirtation and physical connection of being in a relationship. Even if Chelsea, with her gorgeous curves and that flash of appreciation in her dark brown eyes when she realized who Bryce was, remained prominently in his thoughts.

CHAPTER THREE

B ryce shut down his computer at a quarter after five and decided to leave it in its docking station for the night. After making his way to the parking lot, he rolled down the window to chase away the worst of the heat, then rolled it up so the air conditioning could work its magic. After clearing the city, he relaxed into the bench seat and settled in for the more relaxing half of his commute.

When he got to the stretch of Highway 90 where he'd happened upon Chelsea and her little Fiat hatchback, he slowed. As though she might be there again, waiting for him to come along and save the day. Knowing it was silly didn't seem to stop him.

Of course, there was no Chelsea, needing rescue or otherwise.

He was being an idiot. If he wanted to bump into Chelsea, he'd need to do it in town. Like at the grocery store. Or maybe Clotille's. Hell, even the family hardware store. The latter was probably a stretch, but still a better choice than going home to his empty house. Not that he didn't love his house.

He drummed his fingers on the steering wheel, pulling together a plan. Clotille's on Friday, maybe. He could talk Kate and Sutton into coming out. Or maybe Melody. They didn't see enough of each other these days. And the Shur-fine Saturday morning. He specifically avoided getting groceries on Saturday because that's when everyone else seemed to, but if there was a chance that everyone included Chelsea, he could make an exception.

Feeling better—or at least less passive—about his chances of seeing Chelsea again, he decided to swing by the hardware store. It wasn't likely to earn him a chance run-in with Chelsea, but running into Kate and Harper would be the next best thing. And he could pick up some tomato food while he was there.

He parked and headed inside, surprised to see a half dozen customers milling around and several more standing in line. Owen manned the main register and Kate stood behind the customer service desk, ringing out plumbing supplies and flower pots and the other odds and ends that stores like Cormier's stocked. He offered a wave and headed to the garden section, where he stared at the various boxes and bottles and promptly forgot what he'd bought the last time.

Eventually, he grabbed two, figuring he'd let Kate tell him which to buy. He made his way back to the front, which had gone almost eerily quiet. Even Owen had disappeared. "Where is everyone?"

Kate shrugged. "Five o'clock rush."

He laughed. Using the word rush to describe anything in Duchesne felt a bit oxymoronic. "Come and gone, eh?"

"We handled our business," Kate said.

She had picked up the phrase from Harper, who'd gotten it from her softball team, which made him chuckle. "Speaking of, where's Cormier's customer handler extraordinaire?"

Kate cringed. "Poor girl's down with a case of killer cramps."

It was Bryce's turn to cringe. "God, I don't miss that."

Rather than smack him with a snarky comeback about the travesties of having a reproductive cycle, Kate's whole demeanor softened. "I'm glad you don't have to deal with it. I'm perfectly happy to have a uterus and the whole thing still makes me miserable."

He was very happy not to. "Should I swing by with ice cream or is it a please don't talk to me or even be in the same room as me kind of situation?"

"I think ice cream is always welcome when you're eleven." Kate waved a hand. "But don't feel like you have to."

"Yeah, but if I get ice cream for Harper, I can get some for myself and not feel bad about it."

Kate folded her arms. "You never feel bad about eating ice cream."

He nodded. "You're right. I don't. Food shame is one of modern society's worst inventions."

"Can't argue with you there." The comment came from behind him, the voice familiar but not one he could place.

Bryce turned and found himself face-to-face with the woman he'd been thinking about more than he cared to admit. "Chelsea. Hi."

"Hi." Chelsea smiled but then looked down before returning her gaze to Bryce. "I wasn't expecting to see anyone I know."

He tried and failed not to take in the length of shapely leg exposed by the athletic shorts she wore. "I told you we'd bump into each other."

"I'll have to remember that before running a quick errand without bothering to put on real clothes." Her smile seemed to hold more self-deprecation than true self-consciousness.

"Pretty sure that outfit is more than appropriate for a trip to the hardware store." He glanced back at his sister, knowing full well every ounce of her attention was on them. "Right, Kate?"

"Absolutely." Kate waited half a beat. "Welcome back to Duchesne."

To Chelsea's credit, the flash of confusion lasted no more than a second. Her gaze flicked to Bryce before returning to Kate. "Thanks."

Bryce had no doubt he'd get a full inquisition in due time but, for the moment, Kate's attention stayed on Chelsea. "Can we help you find something today?"

If Chelsea was flustered by people already knowing her business, she didn't show it. "Light bulbs. Many, many light bulbs."

Kate grinned, in full customer service mode now. "Well, you've come to the right place."

"Apparently, I have." Chelsea smiled at Kate, but she spared Bryce the briefest moment of eye contact.

Bryce cleared his throat, allowing himself to believe that her agreement had as much to do with seeing him as it did the lighting selections of the store. "I can show you."

Both Chelsea and Kate raised a brow.

"Since you're covering the front solo," he said to Kate, knowing full well the explanation would only fuel the ribbing he'd get later. "I might not work here anymore, but I do know where things are."

Whatever teasing he'd get from his sister, Chelsea seemed to take his words at face value. Either that or she liked the prospect of spending a few minutes with him. "That would be great."

Bryce bowed, happy to be helpful but even happier that Chelsea might like the prospect of a few minutes with him, too. "Right this way."

Chelsea followed Bryce down the lighting aisle, telling herself it was silly to feel practically giddy over seeing him. "So, this is your family's store?"

Bryce looked over his shoulder with a smile. "Third generation. Fourth if you count Kate's daughter, Harper. Though I have a feeling she's destined for bigger things."

"Like you?" She tried to sound casual—small talk curiosity more than the deeper curiosity she'd developed about Bryce and his life.

He chuckled. "I'm not sure telling college students what classes to take counts as bigger things, but it suits me."

"Is that what you do?"

He stopped in front of the light bulbs, put his hands on his hips, and sighed. But when he turned his gaze back to her, it felt happy and relaxed more than resigned. "I'm an academic advisor, so in its most rudimentary form, yes. I like to think I help them forge their path to adulthood. With academics, obviously, but not only that." That explained the car salesman attire from the other day. And today, for that matter. Though the sage green polo with navy pants came off as way more subtle.

"Do you like it?" she asked.

"Most days. Most days, it feels like work that matters but doesn't come with high stakes stress."

She smiled at the description. "That seems like a good balance."

"For sure. I try to hold on to that on the days that involve parents yelling at me for not making their kid go to class."

"Why does that both shock me and not surprise me at all?" Not that her mother would have done such a thing, but she'd been given enough interns on the show to know the type.

Bryce regarded her with curiosity. "Do you work with students?"

"Not primarily. We get our share of interns."

He turned toward the bulbs but almost as quickly turned back. "What is it you do?"

He was the first stranger—well, casual acquaintance—who'd asked since her job imploded. Imploded and then risen like a phoenix from the ashes of Charlie Paul's misogynistic empire. She opened her mouth to answer but nothing came out. Instead, a wave of emotion she absolutely wasn't expecting washed through her.

"Hey, it's cool if you don't want to talk about it. I always tell students it's bad form to start conversations with 'what's your major,' and I'm basically doing the same thing."

"No, no. It's fine. I'm happy to talk about it. It's, um…new. It's all feeling really new." As in, signed on the dotted line but still a tad unreal. As in, contracted for eight episodes but not actually done a minute of filming.

Bryce offered an encouraging smile. "Ah. I see. Is that what's brought you back to town?"

She imagined more than a few of his students came to see him just to get a dose of that smile. "Yes, in fact, it is. I'm launching my first show on Food TV."

Once the words were out, the swirl of emotion coalesced into pure joy. Joy laced with terror, but joy nonetheless. She had a passing worry of coming across as smug or self-important, but she couldn't help it. It felt really fucking amazing to say it out loud.

Bryce's eyes went wide. "Wow."

An undignified snort escaped—not her most elegant moment, but it did wipe away any semblance of conceit. "I know, right?"

"Like, it's going to be a cooking show? You in a kitchen, chopping and stirring and all that?" Bryce seemed surprised, but maybe also delighted, by the prospect.

"Yep. All that."

"That's like, insanely cool. So cool I can't seem to stop saying like." He ran a hand through his hair. "Sorry."

Did he have any idea how fucking charming he was? "No apologies needed. I'm living it and I'm still kind of gobsmacked."

"Part of me wants to know everything, but I'm sure you'd like to get on with your day." Bryce made a sweeping gesture with his hand. "And your light bulbs."

She laughed. "I'm not sure I have words for how much I don't want to get on with my light bulbs."

Rather than laugh with her, Bryce narrowed his eyes. "Is your place not okay?"

The genuine concern in his voice made Chelsea's pulse trip. Which was absurd, really. "No, no. Nothing like that. It's just that some of them are really high up, so I should also be buying a ladder, which is pretty much the last thing I want to do."

He nodded knowingly. "A decent one will cost you a pretty penny, but it's a good investment if you have your own place and want to be able to take care of things."

"There's also the matter of climbing it. And being terrified of heights."

"Oh." He frowned.

"Yeah. Standing on a kitchen chair pretty much pushes the limits of my comfort zone. But home ownership isn't for the faint of heart, right? That's what I keep telling myself." She squared her shoulders and tried to channel confidence. He'd already come to her rescue once. She didn't need him thinking she was some damsel in distress.

"You're allowed to ask for help, you know."

"Maybe for things like plumbing or the roof. But paying someone to change light bulbs makes me either pathetic or a diva, and I'm not interested in being either." Though she'd be lying to say she hadn't considered it.

Bryce ran a hand through his hair again. Such a sexy nervous tic. "Or you could ask a friend."

She'd had friends like that in New York. Not that she'd needed them for handy type projects in her well-maintained apartment building, but still. Would she find friends like that here? She hadn't given that part a lot of thought before buying a big old house. "I need to make some friends before I can impose on them."

"You've been out of the South too long. When it's a friend, it's not an imposition."

She tipped her head in concession. "Touché. But I still need to make them first."

"We could be friends, you know. I even have my own ladder."

"Oh, God. I hope it didn't sound like I was fishing." Realization hit and made her feel twice as dumb. "For friends or a ladder."

Bryce offered her an easy smile. "Let me try again. I'd like to be friends. And I'd be more than happy to come over with my ladder."

She could blush and be awkward. Something about Bryce threatened to bring that out in her—flirty but shy, giggling and doe-eyed. It wasn't her style, though. And as much as she might enjoy the feelings that came with it, she could use a friend even more than she could use a ladder. "Only if you let me do something nice for you in return."

He seemed to really consider it. "I suppose you could mow my lawn."

Forget blushing and awkward. She jumped right over those into stilted and speechless. "Uh…"

"Kidding. You're a fancy chef, right? Maybe you could invite me over for dinner. After you're all settled, of course."

"Yeah. Yes. That would be great. I'd love that." Okay, then. Back to blushing and awkward.

"Would Saturday be good? Late morning?"

She nodded. "Only if you're sure it isn't a bother."

He waved her off. "I like being handy and I love helping a friend."

Friend. Right. Because even though he'd invited himself over for dinner, that's the territory they were wandering into, nothing more.

"I'm free all day. All week, really. Just waiting around for movers and contractors and such. For the kitchen, I mean. Contractors for the kitchen. The network is paying for the reno to make it usable as a set."

Christ. Why couldn't she stop talking?

"How's ten?" Bryce either didn't notice she was rambling or didn't mind.

"That would be great." She bit her lip in a way she hoped came off as cute more than wishy-washy. "You're sure you don't mind?"

"I'm sure." He winked. "Especially if there's coffee."

"I may have had to go buy an air mattress to sleep on, but the French press made it into the car with the other essentials." Because a girl had her priorities.

"A woman after my own heart." Bryce nodded toward the front of the store. "Come on. Let's get you to the checkout before Kate sends a search party."

It was hard to know whether Bryce meant to poke fun at himself or his sister, but the easiness of his delivery softened the edges of her own self-consciousness. "We wouldn't want that."

He gestured for her to go first, so she did. Kate asked if she'd found everything she needed, complete with a knowing and somewhat suggestive look at Bryce. If part of her bristled on principle, the rest of her found the whole thing rather comical. She hadn't forgotten how small towns worked, but she'd somehow blocked out the fact that she'd be included in the tongue wagging and not simply observe it from the outside.

Again, it could have bothered her but it didn't. Maybe because she didn't have anything to hide anymore. And because perhaps for the first time ever, she'd paid her dues and put up with the bullshit and come out on top. And she didn't mind one lick if everyone knew it.

CHAPTER FOUR

Chelsea opened the door to find Bryce striding up the porch steps with a bright red, seemingly brand-new step stool. "Good morning," he said.

She folded her arms and didn't even pretend not to smirk. "You know, I pride myself on not being overly concerned with size, but I'm not sure your ladder is up to the task."

Bryce set the stool down, letting the folded frame lean against his thigh. "I'm glad to hear you're not one of those bigger is better types. But I assure you my ladder—which is still in my truck, for the record—is big enough to handle whatever you want to throw my way."

"I see." She didn't blush this time, but her stomach flipped in a way that had nothing to do with ladders.

"And I have an even bigger one at home should the need arise."

Okay, this was ridiculous. Even with the level of double entendre they were rocking, being turned on at ten in the morning while chatting with a virtual stranger made her feel borderline desperate. She didn't do desperate. She lifted her chin, not to be haughty exactly, but to make it clear she saw through the absurdity of the banter. "Good to know."

"This one is for you." He picked up the stool and held it out to her.

"It is?" She couldn't hide the surprise in her voice.

"A housewarming gift. It's more stable than a kitchen chair and it will reach most of the places you need to get to on a regular basis." He winked and she'd swear to God he was flirting with her. "And it seemed safely within your height limitations."

A snort of laughter escaped, but it gave way to feeling touched by such a thoughtful gesture. "You shouldn't have."

He smiled his easy smile. "I wanted to."

There was no pretense in his words or his body language. No machismo dressed up as chivalry. No quid pro quo. Just a genuine pleasure in doing nice things for people. It left her with more than a slight sense of wonder, which in turn made her feel silly and maybe the tiniest bit sad. "Thank you."

"I promise I won't make you use it today, though. I offered to help, and I want to earn that dinner you promised me."

And just as quickly as Bryce turned her into an emotional puddle, he turned the tables and made her laugh again. It proved equal parts lovely and unsettling. "I'm going to let you, but only because I plan to serve you lunch, too. Assuming, of course, you don't have other plans."

"Just supper at my mama's at six, so as long as you promise not to spoil my appetite too badly, I'd love to have lunch with you."

"I kept it super simple, I promise. I'm operating with very limited resources."

"Deal." He gave a decisive nod. "Let me go grab the real ladder and we can get to work."

He went back to his truck and she simply watched, enjoying the view of broad shoulders and muscular calves. Before he could catch her staring, she carried the stool in and leaned it against the bench-slash-coatrack she'd bought for the entryway. She held the door wide for him, then closed it to keep in as much of the air conditioning as possible.

"Okay, where do you want me?"

In my bed? Chelsea cleared her throat and pointed to the light fixture overhead. "The first one is right here."

"That's easy enough." He set up the ladder without fanfare or further innuendo. Clearly, she was the one lacking self-restraint. Or, maybe, he was making a point of keeping his R-rated thoughts to himself, too.

"I got one of those Edison bulbs, but I'm not sure it will fit," she said, mostly to have something to say.

Bryce freed one of the glass panels on the lantern-style fixture. "I think they're standard size. Let's give it a try."

She freed the bulb from its package and handed it to him. It fit easily enough and Bryce had the glass back in place in no time. In well under an hour, they'd made quick work of her entire list of ladder projects. Bryce asked for a tour of the rest of the house. They made their way through the rooms he hadn't seen yet and, without really intending to, she rattled off all the little projects she wanted to tackle—painting the bedroom—and those she intended to hire out—pulling up the carpet in the living room and refinishing the hardwood underneath.

He was so easy to talk to, offering friendly advice from his own home reno and additional help anytime she might need it. Friendly. Or, rather, like they were friends. She might not forget the moments of awkward semi-flirtation and blushing, but it situated them surely in the realm of wishful thinking.

"What about in here?" He made a sweeping gesture to indicate the kitchen where they now stood. "I'd think a chef would be all in on a primo kitchen."

She leaned in, to make it seem like she was sharing a secret but also to see what it would be like to get closer to him. "The network is going all out."

He laughed at the exaggerated grin she made when she pulled back. "Nice."

She shrugged. "I've decided it's the least they can do."

He looked duly impressed. "They must consider you their up-and-coming star."

She could maintain that illusion. Hell, she planned to with most of the people she encountered casually. But Bryce had been real with her and she wanted to return the favor. They were friends, after all. "It's more of an ass-covering PR campaign than anything to do with me specifically."

"I don't follow."

She had notions of crafting a ninety-second version of the story, one that didn't put too much emphasis on her ties to Charlie and his scandalous tumble from the pinnacle of celebrity chefdom. Only it was the sort of thing she'd have to write down and memorize to sound good, and she hadn't bothered to do that yet. "Have you heard of Charlie Paul?"

Bryce's lip curled. "Yeah."

His instinctive reaction gave her immense satisfaction. "I used to be the sous chef on his show."

"I'm sorry."

She laughed. "Well, it wasn't the most pleasant experience, but I was spared the worst of his lechery. He didn't come on to fat girls."

Bryce shook his head. "That somehow makes me feel better and worse."

"Thank you. But long story short is that the network is trying to prevent additional lawsuits and do some damage control, so I get my own show and Jada, his former assistant producer who blew the whistle on him in the first place, gets to produce it." She tipped her head. "I'm feeling pretty good about the outcome."

"You're right. A new kitchen is the least they can do."

"Right?" She stuck out her hands, wanting to keep the conversation from veering too far into the serious. "But if you want to think of me as an up-and-coming star, please don't let me stop you."

"I see no reason why you can't be the recipient of some good karma and a star in the making at the same time."

"I knew I liked you." Even if she wasn't ready to admit the full extent of said liking.

"Well, good, because the feeling is mutual." Bryce grinned.

The gleam in his eye gave her the sense he might kiss her. Or at least wanted to. Oddly, it gave her a confidence boost and a case of the nerves at the same time. "I haven't even served you lunch yet."

He waved her off. "Lagniappe."

The word—Cajun for a little something extra—was ubiquitous in south Louisiana. Yet, she'd sort of forgotten it existed. How many other things had she banished in her quest to put as much distance between herself and her childhood as possible? Rather than letting it make her sad, she offered Bryce a winning smile and promised to immerse herself in as much authentic Cajun everything she could get her hands on before filming started. Up to and including—if the stars aligned—Mr. Cormier himself.

❖

With Chelsea's kitchen still mostly in a moving truck somewhere between New York and Louisiana, Bryce's expectations for lunch were low. But apparently, she'd gone shopping for what she called the essentials, and whipped out a bowl of chicken salad. Super simple, she'd insisted, before confirming she'd roasted the chicken herself. She'd also added toasted pecans, red grapes, and flecks of what he learned was tarragon. And while she—almost sheepishly—confessed to buying pitas to stuff it into, she also whipped out a plate of decadent shortbread cookies, artfully drizzled with dark chocolate. Nothing store-bought about them.

He poked fun at Chelsea's definition of super simple, then poked at her until she promised to enlist his services for any and all odd projects around the house, particularly those that involved being more than three feet off the ground. Because that's what friends were for, after all. Plus, he wasn't the sort of guy to turn his nose up at free lunch. There was also the matter of wanting the chance to spend more time with Chelsea, sooner rather than later.

He went home and mowed his lawn, regretting not squeezing it in before going to Chelsea's—and before the temperatures climbed into the mid-nineties. He finished with enough time to take a cool shower and down one glass of water and one of iced coffee before heading to his parents' for supper.

He arrived just in time to see his mother pull a gorgeous pork roast from the oven. He closed the oven door behind her and, once the roasting pan sat safely on the stove, kissed her cheek. "I'm glad you taught me to cook, but I'm not going to lie. I love it when you feed me."

"And I'm glad you still come over, even when Sunday supper is on a Saturday."

"If you cook it, I will come. What can I do?"

She angled her head toward the dining room. "Help Harper finish setting the table and tear your father away from the riveting game of golf on the television."

"On it."

With his assignments accomplished, it wasn't long before the six of them sat around the table.

"So, how'd your morning with Little Miss Helpless go?" Kate batted her eyes in mock innocence.

"Who's Little Miss Helpless?" Harper asked.

Mama passed her the dish of succotash. "You took the words right out of my mouth."

All eyes turned Bryce's way. He spared a glare in Kate's direction before answering. "I assume my sister is referring to Chelsea Boudreaux, who I went to school with and who has recently moved back to town. I lent her my ladder and helped her change some light bulbs at her new house this morning, though I'd argue there's nothing remotely helpless about her."

Harper put a small pile on her plate before passing the bowl to Bryce. "Isn't that the lady you helped with her flat tire?"

"Would you rather I call her your damsel in distress?" Kate asked as she helped herself to a slice of pork.

He spooned himself a generous helping of succotash and passed it on to Sutton. "She's not that either. The tire was bad luck, and she probably could have managed it on her own. The ladder was to save her buying one for a couple of small projects."

"You mean a ladder she might have purchased from the family business?" Kate asked.

She was simply being obnoxious now. It had been her favorite pastime since they were kids. Usually, he gave it back at least as good as he got it, but something stopped him. Something that had to do with the look of genuine wonder in Chelsea's eyes when he gave her the step stool. A look that made him want to keep that memory to himself rather than use it as ammunition. "A ladder she'd never use on her own because she's afraid of heights."

Kate stuck out both hands. "What did I say? Damsel."

Sutton pointed at Kate with her fork. "I don't like heights. Does that make me a damsel?"

Kate didn't hesitate. "Absolutely."

Sutton grumbled about having other, underappreciated skills. Harper, with the sort of parental discountenance only a tween could muster, rolled her eyes and assured Sutton computer skills far outweighed ladder skills.

"I was kidding," Kate said. "Though I'm not technically disagreeing with you."

Harper turned to Bryce. "Does your lady have computer skills? What's her profession?"

Harper's utter fascination with careers had only intensified with her time in middle school. She seemed determined to know every job on the planet before being called upon to choose one for herself. As someone who advised college students who often had no idea what they wanted to do with their lives, he found the trait especially endearing. "She's a chef."

"Ooh." Harper's eyes got big. "I've never met a chef before."

"Want to know what's even cooler? She's getting her own cooking show on TV."

Harper's mouth fell open. A chorus of wows came from her parents and Sutton. Even Kate looked impressed. "Okay, I rescind my damsel comment. Not because of the TV part, but no woman cooks professionally without a spine of steel."

"Can I meet her?" Harper asked.

It hit him that perhaps he'd overplayed his hand. But after the morning he spent with Chelsea, complete with a box of homemade shortbread cookies for him to take home, he could probably deliver. Chelsea might not be attracted to him, but she seemed more than a little interested in being his friend. Surely a meet and greet with an eager kid wouldn't be too much of an ask. "I'll have to ask her, but I'm pretty sure she'll say yes."

"Yes." Harper pumped her fist.

He loved that for all the pressures to be cool that ramped up at her age, she didn't try too hard to be aloof. "It's going to be recorded at her house. They're turning her kitchen into a TV set."

Harper shook her head. "That's sick."

His mother, a fan of any cooking or house show not based on competition, nodded her approval. "I think that's wonderful. And based here, in tiny Duchesne."

"I know, right? She convinced the network it was a good angle and moved back here basically to launch the show."

Kate angled her head. "Okay, no more Miss Helpless for her. I'll just refer to you as her fan boy."

As far as he was concerned, there were worse things. "Go right ahead."

Harper turned to him with wide eyes, as though she'd solved a complex puzzle. "Do you like her, like her?"

His father, who'd stayed mostly quiet so far, chuckled. "I think that might be a new record for how quickly dinner conversation turned to your love life, Bryce."

He'd thought Kate being pregnant might have spared him, but no. "Not helping, Dad."

He shrugged and resumed eating. Bryce went to do the same but was cut off by an exaggerated cough and insistent stare from Harper. "Well? Do you?"

Before he could formulate an answer, Kate mimicked the sound. "Rude, Harper."

Her shoulders slumped. "Sorry."

Kate offered her a wink. "It's okay, because if you hadn't asked, I would have. You get leeway when it's family."

He looked to Sutton, since his parents had given up trying to wrangle him and Kate years ago. Sutton merely shrugged. He hung his head, playing the part of browbeaten more than feeling it.

"You don't have to answer." Harper gave him a gentle nudge with her elbow. "It's hard to have a crush sometimes."

She spoke with the wisdom of a young girl experienced in such matters. It melted his heart while smacking him with a dose of they grow up so fast. "I don't mind. I think she's pretty and I definitely could like her that way, but I want to be her friend, and that's more important."

Harper nodded, suddenly the sage. "Yeah."

CHAPTER FIVE

If Chelsea's first few days in town felt like tiptoeing into a new life, the next several came at her at a full sprint. A sprint that involved movers, all her earthly possessions, contractors, and the demolition of half her kitchen. After a full morning of banging and wondering why she'd held on to so many damn books, the need for a break won out.

Her first thought was Bryce. She told herself it stemmed from him being her only friend in town. A friend whose pants she'd like to get into perhaps, but a friend. Alas, it was a Tuesday, and he had a day job.

After some hemming, some hawing, and a fair amount of pacing, she steeled herself for what she'd been putting off since her arrival. Better to get it over with before a chance run-in at the Shur-fine or some old biddy she didn't recognize spilled the beans at some church function or other.

Right? Right.

A visit with one's mother shouldn't warrant full hair and makeup, but she spent a half hour making sure her appearance was just so. Another fifteen minutes picking out a dress from her freshly unpacked closet. Getting it right proved a tall order: casual but nice, flattering but not revealing, reasonably wrinkle-free. At least the ritual of getting ready gave her some joy. Along with some semblance of being in control.

She let the contractors know she'd be out for a few hours and made the short drive. The yellow house looked as it always looked— tidy row of azalea bushes, manicured lawn, and a fresh coat of paint. Irene Boudreaux did not mess around.

Chelsea strode to the front door with purpose, thinking maybe she should have called first. It had been a strategic decision not to, a vague notion of using the element of surprise to keep the upper hand. Though now that the moment had come, she realized it would simply be one more thing for Irene to find fault with. She rang the bell and waited, her pulse ratcheting as each second ticked by.

After what felt like an eternity, the door opened. To Irene's credit, her eyes lit up. "Chelsea."

"Hey, Mama."

Irene opened her arms and Chelsea stepped into the embrace. Brief and brisk, but a hug nonetheless. "Come in before we let all the air conditioning out."

She chuckled because, for all she used to hate her mother saying that, she now understood it.

"Did you just get in? Do you want something to drink?" Irene headed for the kitchen, not waiting to see if Chelsea would follow.

"Water would be great, thank you. And only a couple of days ago. I've been consumed with movers and contractors." Not a complete lie. And even if it was, some fibs fell into the better for everyone category.

"I still don't know why you had to buy a house sight unseen. You could have stayed here for as long as you'd like." Irene poured two glasses from the pitcher she kept in the fridge.

"Because the network needed to know the footprint for planning purposes. And because I need a kitchen that's ready for filming in less than a month." Also not lies. Even if they went hand in hand with her resounding refusal to spend more than a night or two under the same roof as her mother. "Besides, it wasn't totally unseen. I spent loads of time there as a kid."

"Right, right. Your little friend from primary school lived there. What was her name?"

"Bethany."

"I wasn't crazy about her parents. Christmas Catholics they were. And maybe Easter." Irene sniffed her disapproval.

She knew better than to argue, to mention how lonely middle school had been as a result of them moving away. "The house is in good shape. The kitchen is getting some work, but the rest is paint and a few cosmetic changes. Oh, and new floors in the living room."

Another sniff. "I was never one for that old Creole style."

One more thing they didn't agree on. "Well, I'm happy with it and I think it will be good for the show."

"They're really giving you your own show." It wasn't a question, but it may as well have been for the dubious tone in Irene's voice.

"They are." She resisted the urge to make a case for herself.

"Well, you're talented enough. I just never figured you had the right look for television."

The "right look" was code for skinny enough. One of many Irene employed to avoid the only F-word she found more offensive than *fuck*. "Mario Batali isn't thin. Neither was Paul Prudhomme."

"And they were both men," Irene said.

She'd promised herself she wouldn't be baited, but the ship of good intentions sailed with the last of her patience. "And women shouldn't be held to a different standard. The fact that someone who looks like me gets to be on TV is a good thing. It's something to celebrate."

Irene bristled at the disrespectful delivery more than the words. "I only thought they'd be worried about promoting an unhealthy lifestyle."

Chelsea took a deep breath, letting it out as slowly as humanly possible. She wasn't going to let Irene undo a decade of therapy in one afternoon, but neither was she going to spend her time arguing with a woman who bickered like it was a professional sport. "I guess you're wrong."

Irene shrugged. "I told the ladies at the last Catholic Daughters meeting and they were very impressed. You'll have to tell me when it comes on so I can tell them."

Like most things regarding her mother, it no longer surprised Chelsea that she bragged in public and saved her nitpicking for in private. Truth be told, she understood it. Or rather, understood it in the context of a woman who went through life with deep-seated insecurity and depression she refused to treat because it was the cross God had given her to bear. "If everything goes smoothly with filming, it will be early fall."

"Everything moves so quickly these days."

"Not everything." She bit the inside of her cheek. No need to be contrary on principle. "But life in general for sure."

Irene seemed to take that as sufficient appeasement. "How are you otherwise?"

Chelsea answered with her usual vague references to being busy but happy. It was their standard fare, more small talk among acquaintances than evidence of any true connection. She inquired about the rest of the family—births, deaths, marriages, and divorces. If they agreed on nothing else, the unspoken consensus not to discuss her father held. Last she heard, he was on wife number four and couldn't care less if it stuck.

They managed an hour with minimal discord, but it left Chelsea feeling like she'd run a marathon. She kept that opinion to herself as she said her good-byes. It was mean-spirited to be sure, but a running reference would also likely get her mother going on exercise talk. She'd been there and done that enough for several lifetimes.

Irene invited her to lunch the following week, like she might a church friend. Chelsea accepted, relieved that she didn't seem keen on trying for more. She returned the invitation, promising dinner as soon as her kitchen was done.

By the time she got home, Chelsea wanted nothing more than a glass of wine and an evening of peace and quiet. Fortunately, not a thing in the world prevented her from having both. She changed into a flowy tank top and a pair of pajama shorts and poured herself a nice glass of Chardonnay before curling up on the sofa with her binder of show notes.

It was productive. It was relaxing. And if she indulged in a couple of daydreams about Bryce along the way—ones that involved making out more than making progress on her house projects—no one but her needed to know.

❖

Bryce pulled into one of the few open spots in the parking lot lining the row of softball, baseball, and soccer fields that made up the majority of the Duchesne town park. He made his way to the small set of aluminum bleachers next to the dugout occupied by the Diane's Auto Repair Hornets, the team Harper had been assigned to for the current Lassie League softball season. Kate and Sutton were already there, Koozied beverages in hand. "Did I miss much?"

Kate smiled. "Just the first inning. Harper won't bat until the second."

Harper's team had taken the field for the top of the second and he spied Harper in center field. He waved, but her focus was squarely at home plate, which he respected. He returned his attention to Kate and Sutton. "I want to know how y'all are, but I want to know if there's something for me in your cooler first."

Sutton unzipped the insulated bag. "We're trying to cut back on

Coke, but I can offer you a sparkling water in pomegranate, hibiscus pear, or lime."

Kate laughed. "Honey, don't you know you're speaking his language?"

"Right, right. Mr. Health Nut." Sutton shook her head as Bryce fished out a can at random.

"I'm not a nut. I'm selective in my indulgences." He popped the top and took a long swig before sliding the can into a Koozie. He lifted it in a casual toast. "Thanks and cheers."

They clinked cans, but Sutton's phone rang, and she indicated she needed to answer it before stepping away. Kate shooed her with an air kiss, then looked at Bryce. "How's your chef, fan boy?"

"I haven't seen her. How's morning sickness?" he asked.

"Brutal but brief. Why haven't you seen her?"

Because he didn't want to come off looking like a stalker. Since he knew better than to say as much to Kate, he shrugged. Sutton returned, sparing him having to come up with another explanation.

Harper didn't see a lot of action in the outfield, but at bat, she got a base hit that turned into the Hornets' first run of the game. As the teams switched for the top of the third, Bryce's gaze wandered to the other set of bleachers. "Oh, hey. Melody's here. I'm going to go say hi."

"Tell her hey from me, too," Kate said.

"And from me, three." Sutton winked.

"Will do." Melody might have been his friend from second grade, but since everybody knew everybody, it was the way of it. He climbed down the bleachers and headed over to the other side.

Melody spied him about ten feet away and her eyes lit up. "Hey, stranger."

He smiled and sat on the bench seat beside her. "Fancy seeing you here."

"I could say the same. Harper playing?" Melody tipped her head toward the field but didn't break eye contact.

"Center field. Kayla?" Melody had two daughters, one a little younger than Harper and one who'd just turned six. He hadn't seen Kayla on the field, but between the uniforms and the ponytails and big bows most of the girls sported, they sort of blurred together after a while.

"Pitching the second half. It'll be her first time and I'm not sure which of us is more nervous." Melody laughed at the confession.

"Pitching, huh? That's fantastic."

"She's over the moon." Melody smiled, but it didn't quite reach her eyes.

"Is everything okay? You seem, I don't know, not quite you." They didn't spend much time together these days, but they'd known each other long enough that even subtle shifts showed.

Melody blew out a breath. "Keith and I are getting a divorce."

"Oh, Mel. I'm so sorry."

"It's been a long time coming." She shrugged. "I'm starting to think it's inevitable when you're dumb enough to get married right out of high school."

He hadn't been thrilled when it happened, but Melody had been so happy. And he'd been so wrapped up in his transition, it hadn't felt like the time or place to stick his nose in. "You weren't dumb."

Melody's features softened. "It's kind of you to say so. And I have two fantastic kids, so I can't bring myself to regret it."

He wanted to probe but didn't. At least not here. "What do you need? How can I help?"

"I'm okay, all things considered. It's a mutual decision."

That was a relief. Melody deserved better than some cliché affair or whatever. "What if I asked Kate to watch the girls, and we could grab dinner and hang out, like old times? Since we both have cars now, we could even drive somewhere."

"I'd love that." Melody nodded, then took a deep breath and blew it out. "What about you? What's going on in your world?"

"You know. Work, eat, sleep. Some family, some puttering. Living the dream." He said it jokingly, but to be fair, it wasn't so far off from his dream life. With one glaring exception.

"So, your love life sucks?" she asked.

He pressed a hand to his chest. "That hurts."

"I mean, takes one to know one?"

Sympathy took any sting out of the teasing, though there wasn't much of a sting to begin with. "Can something suck if it's nonexistent?"

"Of course." Melody patted his knee. "Especially if it's something you want to exist."

Although he'd spent maybe three hours in total with Chelsea, discussion of his love life—nonexistent or otherwise—had her face flitting around in his brain. "I'm going to artfully change the subject now. You'll never guess who I ran into."

She raised a brow, clearly dubious about his assertion of artfulness. "Who?"

"Chelsea Boudreaux. Do you remember her?"

"Of course I do. She was in our class. Went to culinary school, right?" Melody angled her head. "And never came back."

"That's the one."

Melody sighed. "I always felt bad for her."

"You did?" Not that he was surprised. Melody had that combination of intuition and empathy that made her see and feel things the average person might overlook. At least that had been his experience. She'd asked him if he was trans before he'd even admitted it to himself. Not in those exact words, but she saw him for who he was when no one but Kate even had an inkling.

"She always kept to herself, but I think it had more to do with her mother being strict than not wanting to be social or make friends. We had art and English together and she'd be super chatty and friendly, but never wanted to hang outside of school." Melody cleared her throat. "Anyway, you saw her?"

"Yeah. She's moving back to town. You'll never guess why."

The inning ended and, in between cheering for Kayla, he filled her in on the reason for Chelsea's return. After a walk and a hit, Kayla managed a strikeout. After a couple of ground balls that her teammates managed, the teams switched once again. He declared it a triumphant first time out and promised to stick around to congratulate Kayla after the game.

"You should be her friend," Melody said.

"Who? Kayla?"

Melody elbowed him lightly. "No. Chelsea. I bet it's scary coming home and not really knowing anyone anymore. Even if you've gotten fancy and famous."

"I don't think she's famous yet. Though I imagine she will be soon enough."

"All the more reason to need a friend."

He'd already planned to. And maybe more if the stars aligned. Melody didn't need to know that part. She'd be encouraging but also a bit mother hen and worry about him. Like his own mother. Or Kate but with less harassment.

For now he'd stick with the friend angle. Because even though they'd dabbled in flirting territory, he had no idea if he was her type. Or if she was looking for a relationship. Or if she really planned to stick around in the long run.

CHAPTER SIX

Chelsea gave Jada a long, tight squeeze. Jada held on just as long and just as tight. "I'm so glad you're here."

Jada released the embrace but grabbed both of Chelsea's arms. "I'm so glad you have air conditioning."

She laughed. "To be fair, it's all but universal down here."

"I approve. I also approve of your hair. What are you doing to it?"

She patted the curls she'd managed to tame with a conditioning serum and a soft-setting shaping gel. "It's a super-secret styling tool called So Much Humidity. I'd say you should try it, but you're going to whether you want to or not."

Jada winced. "That is not going to go well for me."

"I've got good product. I'll share." Though, to be fair, Jada's long hair—with just enough wave to give it body—didn't need a lot of help.

"You damn well better. Now enough about all the help my hair is going to need." Jada dropped her purse on the hall bench. "Give me the grand tour."

Chelsea twitched her lips back and forth. "Do you really want the grand tour or do you just want to see the kitchen?"

Jada seemed to mull her options. "Show me the kitchen first or I'll totally be distracted, but I do want to see the whole thing."

"Right this way." Chelsea thrust an arm in the direction of the kitchen and headed to it without bothering to see if Jada followed.

They'd no sooner rounded the wall that separated the living room from the kitchen and dining room than Jada let out a squeal of delight. "It looks so good. So much brighter and more open than it was. They're making good progress."

Chelsea didn't squeal, though she had a couple of times already. "It's the French doors. They let in a ton of light."

Jada nodded. "That and the lighter cabinets. World of difference. Once we get set lights in here, it'll practically glow."

She'd been summoned to Charlie's set enough to dread the heat and intensity of the lighting, but like so many aspects of this whole process, she filed it under Tiny Price to Pay for what was about to happen. "The contractors say they'll be done this week."

"That's perfect. It will give us a day or two to play before the crew arrives. And you can decide if there are any setups or design elements you feel strongly about."

Chelsea looked at the space that would soon hold the six-burner stove she never thought would honestly and truly be hers. "I feel strongly about the appliances. The rest is gravy."

That got her an eye roll. "Only you, Boudreaux."

"Uh-uh. Me and plenty of other people. Including all the talent on the network where you've chosen to make your career."

"Right, right." Jada continued to roll her eyes but grinned. "Damn chefs."

Chelsea kissed her noisily on the cheek. "You know you love us."

"I do. I particularly love the chef standing in front of me." Jada made little circles with both index fingers. "She's so flexible and adaptable. Never a diva."

While she might like to think she resembled that remark, the delivery gave her pause. "What's wrong? Or maybe a better question, what do you want?"

Jada took a deep breath and blew it out. "The network is pushing back on the occasion front."

She didn't even try to suppress a groan. "It's so schticky."

"It makes your dishes more relatable."

"It makes me more relatable, you mean. We have to prove the fat girl has friends." She'd resisted the idea when pitching her first eight episodes, choosing instead to focus on highlighting the differences between Cajun and Creole cuisine and offering a juxtaposition of classic, updated, and easy weeknight iterations of some of her favorite dishes.

"It has nothing to do with the fact that your flavor of gorgeous is full-figured. It's the tried and true formula for success, especially for shows set in a home kitchen. Think about it. Every single one brings in the husband or the sister or the sassy gay friend. It works because it gives you someone to interact with besides the camera."

She should have known it would come to this. The network was looking to cover its ass and save face, not reinvent the wheel. She might hit the wickets, but she was also an unknown. They weren't going to take any more chances on her than they had to.

"Why are you so opposed? Witty banter is your bread and butter as much as kitchen wizardry. You proved that the few times Charlie brought you on camera. Think about how much better it will be to interact with people you actually like."

It was a perfectly reasonable plan. With one glaring problem. "Where do you propose I get these family and friends?"

Jada's eyes narrowed, more confusion than suspicion. "What do you mean?"

"I'm all but estranged from my mother. My father is the devil knows where. I barely speak to the aunts, uncles, and cousins that live around here. And since I moved away like fifteen years ago, I'm not swimming in local friends." She pressed her fingers to her forehead before sticking her hands out in exasperation. "Now can we please change the subject before I feel like even more of a loser than I do already?"

"Babe, you are not a loser."

Chelsea shook her head and wagged a finger. "You're looking at me with pity, I can tell."

Jada's sympathetic look turned indignant. "No, I'm not. I'm thinking how fucking brave it was to leave your life and move back here to make this show exactly what you want it."

She couldn't help but smirk. "Brave sounds nicer than vindictive."

"Ha." Jada slowly walked the length of the kitchen and back, then started to pace in earnest. "We can do this. Let's think. We need guests for eight episodes. I can be one of them. You're introducing the Indian girl to all things Cajun. We can fake a housewarming easily enough. Oh, and I'm sure we can fly one or two of your friends in for a girls' weekend."

God, she loved this woman. "You're the best. You know that, right?"

Jada stopped pacing and planted her hands on her hips. "I do know. Oh. What if we did a thank you for the contractors?"

"For sure." The sinking feeling in her stomach gave way to cautious optimism. They might be able to pull it off without making her feel like a sad loner.

Jada resumed pacing. "And I know you're an introvert, but you're not completely antisocial. We can probably scrounge up a new friend or two for you, or wow one of those long-lost cousins with promises of being on TV."

She cringed. "Gee, thanks."

"You know what I mean." Jada once again stopped. "Hey, what about the hottie who fixed your flat? The one who came over with his ladder?"

To be fair, Bryce popped into her mind the moment Jada started talking about having people on the show. They already had the flirty banter thing going, even if it came with those awkward, are we really flirting moments. Only, she had no way of knowing if he'd say yes. And if he didn't, it would feel as bad as being turned down for a date. Well, almost as bad.

Still.

He did fall into the friend category. Currently, the only one she'd made since coming back to town. Maybe he'd say yes. And maybe she'd be able to segue that yes into a real date. Not that she was in the market for a boyfriend—or a girlfriend, for that matter—but a friend with benefits would be nice. She'd already had a couple of sex dreams about him, ones that left her more turned on than the last few months with her most recent real-life girlfriend.

"You're thinking about him, aren't you? What's his name again?"

No point pretending she wasn't. "Bryce."

"Mm-hmm. Mm-hmm. We should definitely get him on."

"I can ask."

Jada looked around the kitchen. "Grab a pen. We should write these down. I also want to get at least one obviously queer person on. No hiding your light under a bushel."

Chelsea lifted her chin. "You look pretty gay."

"Eh, not really. But if we can get Dev to come on with me. That's some Gen Z enby glory right there." Jada headed to the entryway and returned with a notebook.

She laughed at the assessment of their intern. "Just you saying that makes me feel old."

"Right? I might be a millennial, but I'm starting to understand where all the boomer whining about getting older comes from." Jada scribbled some notes.

Chelsea slung her arm around Jada's shoulder, feeling excited but also confident. She hadn't realized how much she'd been lacking the latter. "How about I take you to dinner and we can go through my episode notes and iron some of this out?"

"Will there be seafood and something fried?" Jada asked.

"I think we can make that happen for you." Most likely in the form of fried seafood.

"Well, then. What are we waiting for?"

Chelsea took a breath, and it filled her lungs all the way. "I'm really glad you're here."

"Me, too, babe. Me, too."

❖

When Bryce hadn't heard from Chelsea in almost a week, he sent her a friendly text offering company or a pair of hands to help with whatever she might be tackling over the weekend. She replied with enthusiasm, saying she had hopes of getting her living room and bedroom painted before filming started the following week. He offered his ladder, she offered lunch, and it was as simple as that.

She greeted him at the door in a pair of athletic shorts and a faded LSU T-shirt, dark brown hair pulled into a bouncy ponytail. As much as he considered himself a sucker for women in dresses and perfume, perhaps the occasional hint of cleavage, something about this more casual look got to him. Relaxed girl next door. And while there might not be any cleavage on display, her butt filled out the shorts nicely, and her creamy smooth legs made his fingers itch to touch.

"You're here," she said with a smile.

"I said I would be."

"Yeah." Her voice had an almost wistful quality to it, like his answer came as a pleasant surprise.

"I mean, I fully expect to be fed for my efforts."

That seemed to snap her back to a more playful state. "Oh, you will be."

She held the door while he maneuvered the ladder inside. Since she'd moved all the furniture to the middle of the room, he set it down along one of the blank walls. He turned a slow circle before leaning to peek at the kitchen. "I can't believe how much work you've gotten done."

Chelsea laughed. "Apparently, that happens when you hire professionals."

He did, for things like major plumbing and electric, but not stuff he could technically do himself. "I'll have to try that sometime."

She shrugged. "Honestly, I think it has more to do with refacing the cabinets instead of replacing them. That and going with a prefab, standard-size quartz for the counters."

"So, what's left to be done?" he asked.

Chelsea waved her hands back and forth. "Decorating and props and making it look pretty."

Since he couldn't tell if she was joking, he resisted the urge to laugh. "I get the sense you don't put a lot of stock in that sort of thing."

She sighed, like it wasn't the first time someone gave her a hard time about it. "It needs to look good. I get it. But I'm more in it for the cooking than the set dressing."

He folded his arms and leaned against the counter, giving in to curiosity. "Do you feel that way about parsley?"

"Parsley?"

He made a sprinkling motion with his fingers. "You know. Making the dish look pretty."

"Oh." Chelsea let the word drag. "Parsley is about flavor as much as flair if you're doing it right. Food should look enticing, but not like it was put on the plate with more attention than it was prepared."

"A very elegant answer." One that likely kept her from making enemies on both ends of the spectrum.

She shrugged. "Let's just say I've got practice hedging my bets and covering my bases."

She said it casually, but it made Bryce sad. Or, maybe more accurately, it made him grateful his career didn't call for such things. Diplomacy with irate parents notwithstanding. "Are you going to hold on to that trait now that you're the boss?"

Chelsea laughed and he tried not to notice how sexy it sounded. "I'm far from being the boss. I might have my show, but it's at the whim of network executives and audience ratings."

Again, she didn't seem bothered. Maybe she'd grown accustomed to the fickle nature of the entertainment industry. Play big or go home and all that. Ugh. "Well, I can't wait to see it and I'm sure you'll be a smashing success."

"I'm pretty sure you're biased, but I'll take it."

"Biased by how good your food is. Though I'd argue that's relevant." Along with being witty and gorgeous.

Chelsea offered him a sly smile. "Wait till you see what I made for lunch."

He went for a sly smile of his own. "Such a tease."

It could have been too much, but the look on her face told him it wasn't. "You like it."

"I do. I also like to earn my rewards, so put me to work." Not a lie, even if his brain conjured all sorts of rewards that had nothing to do with food.

"Happily."

They tackled the living room first, since it was larger and had a lot more edging work. Chelsea complimented his technique along the ceiling. It was all very innocent and innocuous, like two friends spending the day on a project together. Save, perhaps, the moments his gaze wandered to her legs when she stood on tiptoe to roll a spot out of reach. Or that inescapable urge he had to kiss her when she bit her lip in concentration.

After getting the first coat done, they moved to the bedroom. Closer quarters had them bumping into each other here and there. And after suggesting some tunes to set the mood, he caught her two-stepping between the tray of paint and the corner where she was working. "If you're not careful, I'm going to have to make you dance with me for real."

Chelsea blushed and covered her face with her hand. "Sorry. I forgot how much I like zydeco."

He rested his brush on the edge of the bucket and held out his hands. "Don't apologize. Dance with me."

She hesitated long enough that he figured she'd turn him down, but then she set down the roller and put her hands in his. He held one and put the other at the small of her back. Despite the initial reticence, she fell into step with him, and they circled the room together. The tempo kept him from pulling her too close, from turning the dance into the sort of sensual sway that practically molded her body to his. Still, there was something intimate about it, and he found himself a little sad when the song ended.

"I haven't done that in way too long," Chelsea said with a shy smile.

He wanted to ask about why she left, what made her decide to come home. Theoretically, she could have filmed her show anywhere. But for all his curiosity about who she was and what made her tick, it felt like a moment made simply to enjoy. "I consider dance breaks essential. Thanks for indulging me."

She picked up her roller. "I'm pretty sure you're the one who indulged me."

"Let's call it mutual." He hoped the attraction was, too.

"I like that." She gave a decisive nod. "Let's finish in here so we can call it lunch time."

Once again, she wowed him, though she attributed it to excitement over her kitchen being finished and needing to test recipes for the show. He'd eaten a lot of shrimp and grits in his life, but none compared to Chelsea's. And her salted caramel and pecan blondies were practically orgasmic. Despite vague longings for a nap, he rallied, and they managed to get second coats of paint in both rooms. Chelsea was effusive with her gratitude and insisted on sending him home with enough leftovers to last the week.

"I think I ended up with the better end of this arrangement." He lifted the canvas tote of plastic takeout containers.

She took it from him and carried it out so he could load the ladder back into his truck. "We seem to be rocking the mutually beneficial thing."

That was one way of putting it. "I hope you'll call me anytime you need a helping hand or a project buddy."

"You're at the top of my list."

He'd like to be at the top of another list. But if he didn't put out any feelers, there'd be no chance of that happening. "After all this work, I think you've earned some play."

"Play?" She lifted a brow like it was a novel concept.

"Yes. Adults are allowed to play, you know. You can't move back here and expect to be serious all the time."

She frowned.

Since he'd already opened the can of worms, he pressed on. "I mean dance breaks are great, but have you considered taking a day off?"

"Day off." She stared off into the distance, playing along.

"I mean it," he said with an emphasis. "Something tells me you're going to be even busier than you are now when the camera crew shows up."

"You're probably right." She lifted both hands. "Not that I mind. It's a dream come true."

"Even still." He hadn't meant to tee up an invitation, but since he had, he might as well use it. "You know, my family has a big cookout for the Fourth of July. Fireworks, the whole nine yards. I'd love you to come if you don't have plans."

"I…" Chelsea pressed her lips together.

"No pressure. I thought you might not have plans." Hoped she might not have plans. Hoped she might want plans with him.

She shook her head. "No, it's not that. I'd love to. It's just that my producer arrived yesterday because we'll start filming next week. She happens to be my friend, too, and I told her we'd do something together."

"Oh, well, she's absolutely invited, too. The more, the merrier."

"Yeah?" Chelsea asked, looking not at all convinced.

He chuckled. "You really have been away too long."

Chelsea made a show of grumbling and rolling her eyes before smiling. "Thank you. I'm sure she'd love that."

He lifted a finger. "It's not too rowdy by south Louisiana standards, but it is a big family party. I feel like full disclosure is in order."

She folded her arms, managing to look bossy and sexy at the same time. "Are you saying that for her benefit or mine?"

He imagined the flack he'd get from Kate for inviting her, but also what it would be like to spend a day with her that was about nothing but relaxing and having a good time. "I'll let you decide."

CHAPTER SEVEN

Chelsea opened the front door to find Jada, clad in a pair of cutoffs and a bright red tank top. She also wore a pair of red and white gingham wedges and had styled her hair in low, loose braids that draped over each shoulder. Jada stuck out her arms and turned a slow circle. "How do I look?"

Chelsea rolled her eyes but laughed. "Like an Indian Daisy Duke."

Jada's eyes narrowed. "Who's Daisy Duke?"

Jada's parents had come to the US for college and stayed, meaning many vintage American pop culture references were wasted on her. Even ones with ill-advised reboots. "Never mind."

"I'll just ask Bryce." She offered Chelsea a casual shrug and breezed into the house.

"Don't do that," she said to Jada's back. "It's a bad reference in the first place."

Jada ignored the warning. "You look pretty smokin' yourself. That dress puts the girls on display quite nicely."

Self-consciousness pulsed through her like a hot flash. She'd gone with one of those casual dresses that, in her book, were more comfortable than jeans or even shorts. But the neckline scooped low. "Is it too much? It's a family thing with kids. I don't want to come off like I'm looking to get laid."

Jada regarded her with curiosity. "Are you looking to get laid?"

"No." Her answer came a little too fast and a little too loud to be believable.

"Mm-hmm."

"I'm serious. Even if I was looking to get laid in the grand scheme of things, that's not on the table tonight. See above comment regarding kids." She angled her head and went for a withering look. "And you're going to be there."

Jada pointed to her chest. "Hey, I'm not a cock block."

She closed her eyes. "Could you not use that phrase please?"

"Wait. Why?"

"Because it reminds me of how long it's been since I've experienced a nice, you know…" She considered herself a reasonable person—someone who enjoyed sex maybe more than most but didn't think about it all the time. Unfortunately, the last couple of weeks had her ramped up like a horny teenager.

"Honey, if you're that susceptible to suggestion, I'm the least of your worries."

"Thanks for the reminder. Now, can we talk about something else, please?"

Jada turned. "Hey, the living room looks great. The color is subtle without being boring. We'll totally be able to film some nosh shots in here."

"Smooth. Thank you." She clapped her hands as realization hit. "And you haven't even seen the gorgeous kitchen table that got delivered now that the floors are done."

Jada's eyes lit up and she made a beeline for the kitchen. "Oh. Wow. I take it back. Between that and the French doors, all the eating will be in here. Or out on the deck."

She didn't really care where they filmed the requisite food on the table scene for the end of each episode. For her, it was all about what happened in the kitchen. Her utterly perfect, all but done kitchen. "The stove is here, too."

Jada shot her a look of exasperation but turned to study it. "Okay, I don't get feelings about stoves, but I respect that you do. And that one is pretty."

"High praise." She walked over and trailed her fingers over the brushed steel, as she'd taken to doing every time she set foot in the room.

"It'll look great on camera and I'm already daydreaming about the things you'll cook on it. How's that?"

"I'll take it." She touched the apron-front farmhouse sink with almost the same affection, but before she could draw Jada's attention to it, she heard a car in the driveway. "That must be Bryce."

"Can we discuss the fact that you live somewhere where you can hear cars pull in the driveway? Oh, and that you have a driveway."

She'd worried the quiet would be jarring after years in the city, but she'd settled into it with ease. And was already looking forward to fall when she could fall asleep with the windows open and a serenade of crickets. "Later. Right now, we need to go."

Jada smirked but didn't argue. Chelsea grabbed the tray of bite-sized strawberry tarts she'd made and they headed to the front door. Bryce had just gotten out of his truck by the time she and Jada made it down the porch steps. Too much or not, she couldn't miss the appreciative once-over Bryce gave her. The pulse of self-consciousness from before became a pulsing sensation of an entirely different kind.

Chelsea tipped her head toward Jada. "Bryce, this is my friend and producer, Jada. Jada, my newly reacquainted friend, Bryce."

They exchanged pleasantries and a handshake. Jada didn't waste a second asking, "Do I look like Daisy Duke?"

Bryce looked to Chelsea with panic in his eyes. Rather than let him squirm, she jumped in. "I told her she did, but I was teasing. Only she doesn't know who Daisy Duke is. I tried to tell her it was better that way, but she rarely listens to me."

"Ah." Bryce chuckled. "It is a uniquely Southern and rather fraught cultural reference, at least for anyone born after 1985."

Chelsea laughed. "Ouch."

Jada raised her hand. "I resemble that remark."

"I'll google it for you later." Chelsea shook her head. "Anyway. Thanks for being our chauffeur."

Bryce tapped the bill of his ball cap. "Happy to. That said, if you'd rather me drive one of your cars so we don't have to squish together on the bench seat, I'm still happy to be your designated driver."

Before she could get a word out, Jada waved him off. "Oh, no. We should go in your truck. It's more authentic."

Bryce didn't seem to take offense at that comment, so they piled in. Jada offered to hold the tray so Chelsea could scoot in, and it wasn't until she was sandwiched in the middle—with her thigh pressed against Bryce's—that she realized Jada had done it on purpose. And if she'd had any doubt, Jada's smirk confirmed it. She offered a quick eye roll before returning her attention to Bryce. "Thank you so much for inviting us."

Jada leaned forward and offered Bryce a genuine smile. "Yes, thank you. This Southern stuff is new to me. I'm trying to soak it all up."

"You might end up with more than you bargained for." Bryce

tipped his head at Chelsea. "Did this one explain what 'big family party' means?"

Chelsea shook her head. "I tried. But I'm not sure even I can do it justice. I'm not very close with my extended family."

"Well, watch your step or mine will pull you in and you'll both be honorary cousins before you know it." Bryce chuckled. "Especially if you make the mistake of letting on that you're single."

"Really?" Jada shot Chelsea a knowing look. "Even if we're queer?"

Bryce tipped his head back and forth. "We have a few closed-minded jerks in the mix, but they're outnumbered enough to keep their opinions to themselves. At least at family functions."

Jada beamed. "How refreshing."

A pang of sadness pricked Chelsea's chest. She shook it off before it could take root. She'd made peace with not having a supportive family years ago. No need to get glum about it now. "Yes. How refreshing."

Bryce cleared his throat and kept his gaze on the road. "So, y'all both identify as queer?"

Jada gave her a not even remotely subtle elbow to the ribs. "I'm pretty straightforward bi, but I like the queer umbrella."

"And you?" Bryce made eye contact for the briefest of moments.

"I call myself a queer femme." Chelsea wanted to elaborate but without being overly obvious. Too bad she couldn't think of a way to do that.

Maybe Bryce would have asked for clarification; maybe he wouldn't have. She'd never know. Jada didn't give him the chance. "That means she likes women who are masc of center and trans guys, but not so much cis unless it's Ryan Gosling."

"Yeah?" He glanced at her for confirmation.

She smacked her lips together to show her discomfort with the situation. "Pretty much."

Bryce nodded with about as much subtlety as Jada a moment before. "That's cool."

Well, at least they were even. And on the same page. Almost the same page. "You? I mean, since we're apparently disclosing things today."

Bryce laughed. "Fair's fair, I suppose. I'm attracted to women. I've dated both gay and straight, but I've had better luck with those who have some queer sensibility. If that makes sense."

She took some consolation in the fact that he looked as uncomfortable as she felt. But that didn't hold a candle to the delight she took in his answer. Maybe all that pseudo-flirting they'd done wasn't so pseudo after all. "Totally. Perfect sense."

Bryce continued to nod, and it was kind of adorable. He pulled up behind a row of cars parked along the side of the road. "There's a ditch, so if y'all don't mind scooting to my side, that's probably easiest."

Jada leaned forward. "We don't mind at all."

❖

Bryce grabbed a box of sparklers from the communal pile and bummed a lighter off Uncle Loic. He found Chelsea watching a couple of the kids already swirling them around, making zigzags and hearts and squealing with glee. Jada was nowhere in sight, leaving him unsure whether to be concerned or grateful. He settled on the latter, at least for the moment. As glad as he was for Chelsea to have someone she knew besides him, he'd wished more than once for a few minutes just the two of them.

"There's no age limit, you know." He held them up. "Can I convince you to play?"

Chelsea's smile came slow and seemed to imply meaning beyond the offer of some fireworks. "You could."

He slid a pair from the box and offered her one. "Or are you a double-fister?"

"Oh, yes. Go big or go home."

He took out a second pair for himself. "Where's Jada disappeared to?"

"I think she cornered Kate and Harper about appearing in an episode of the show." Chelsea shrugged like it was no big deal.

"Really?" Kate might not be game, but Harper would be over the moon.

"She'd have pounced on you already, but I told her I'd take care of it."

"Wait. Take care of what? Me being on your show?" The idea of Chelsea wanting him proved more thrilling than the prospect of being on television.

She tipped her head back and forth, like she was trying to downplay it. "I don't know how many cooking shows you watch, but it's a thing.

The host is cooking for a reason, an occasion. For other people. Those people come over and there are a few shots of them, sometimes helping in the kitchen but always enjoying the food at the end."

"You're right. I never really thought about it, but it is a thing." How weird.

"Makes the chef more likable. Builds rapport with the audience." Chelsea slapped air quotes around each statement.

"I take it you're not a fan."

"I'm not against it, but since I just moved back, my pickings are slim, and Jada has been giving me a hard time about it." She rolled her eyes. "You may have picked up on the fact that she's highly opinionated and used to getting her way."

He'd only known Jada for a few hours, but the description fit. "So, you're desperate."

"I wouldn't go that far." She lifted her chin and smirked.

The gesture might be playful, but something told him he'd touched a nerve. It made him wonder again about her family and what, if any, relationship she had with them. "I'm sure you don't need me, but I'd be honored if you wanted me."

Given how often their conversations strayed into flirtation and innuendo, he expected an appreciative once-over and a cheeky reply. But her features softened and he'd swear there was a shyness in her smile. "I'd like that."

Maybe it was because he'd used the word *honored*. Or maybe it came with not having a slew of people she could count on since moving home. Whatever the reason, that smile had him melting faster than an ice pop in August. And had him wanting to help. Even if it meant embarrassing himself on camera. "Just tell me when. Oh, and what to wear."

That got him a laugh. "Deal. And thank you."

"Now, where were we?" He pulled the lighter from his pocket and flicked it to life. Chelsea held her sparklers to the flame until they caught, then he did the same. He put the lighter away so he could hold one in each hand, but really, his gaze fixed on Chelsea.

Her eyes reflected the light, but they seemed to sparkle all on their own, and she grinned with delight. She zipped her hand this way and that, traced her initials, then held perfectly still. Bryce's own body stilled. His breath held.

He didn't spend a lot of time thinking about having a sense of wonder. He spent even less imagining it as an essential element in finding a woman attractive. But in that moment, Chelsea radiated wonder. And he couldn't fathom anything more appealing.

Chelsea's sparklers fizzled first. His followed seconds later. Chelsea's gaze caught his and held. Kids continued to run around, streaks of sound and glittery light. Their conversation on the ride over—awkward yet confirming everything he'd hoped about Chelsea's inclinations when it came to attraction—echoed in his mind.

"Thank you." Chelsea's smile lost that sense of awe, but it radiated both challenge and promise. The combination proved no less compelling. "I haven't done that in far too long."

She could be talking about sparklers, was likely talking about sparklers. The way she'd talked about dancing. But Bryce couldn't help but think—hope—she was talking about more than that. That what she really meant was a flash of mutual attraction: that elusive mix of physical longing and infinite potential that could take them anywhere. "Stick with me and I'll remind you of all the things Duchesne has to offer."

Chelsea didn't reply. Not with words at least. But her eyes reflected back everything Bryce felt and her body leaned ever so slightly into his. So subtle he might have missed it, but so obvious there was no way it was a figment of his imagination. She licked her lip, swallowed. "I'll remember that."

The real fireworks started. A pop followed by a sizzle and a cheer. A sudden flow of people and energy toward the field where the big ones would be set off. But his own energy remained fixed on Chelsea, on how badly he wanted to kiss her. Did she feel the same?

It wouldn't take much to convince himself the answer was yes. That her longing mirrored his, and that the chemistry between them was its own sort of firework, a bundle of pent-up energy just waiting to dazzle. But even if it was, she might not be inclined to kiss him so publicly. He cared too much about consent to test those waters tonight. He angled his head in the direction of the crowd. "Shall we?"

Chelsea sucked in a breath before nodding. She seemed relieved to have the spell between them broken, but disappointed, too. "Sure."

They stepped through the fresh-cut grass under the intermittent glow of fireworks in red, gold, and blue. He resisted the urge to take her hand, but as they walked, Chelsea's shoulder bumped his. Such a subtle move, but it said so much.

Bryce guided them to the blanket he'd put out earlier. Jada wasn't there, but he spied her sitting with his cousin Billy. Chelsea must have seen them, too, because she shook her head and chuckled. Chelsea sat first and he followed, situating himself so they were almost touching but not. She gave him another smile before turning her face to the sky. He, somewhat reluctantly, did the same.

He didn't regret the decision not to kiss her, mostly because it felt like a delay more than a closed door. Something told him the opportunity would present itself again. He could wait. After all, plenty of things worth having were worth waiting for. But damn if he'd be able to stop thinking about her mouth anytime soon.

CHAPTER EIGHT

Chelsea blinked a few times, willing the mascara to dry before it smudged. She contorted her lips this way and that, trying to follow Vivian's directions and thinking how little the whole process resembled doing her own makeup and how strange that was. When Vivian stepped back and nodded her approval, Chelsea turned to study herself in the lighted mirror that had been set up on the desk in the office-slash-guest-room. "Wow."

Vivian nodded. "You have amazing cheekbones."

She did. They gave her otherwise round face distinction and she didn't take them for granted. Still. "Yeah, but they never look like this."

"Just a little contouring. I can show you next time if you'd like." Vivian, whose body type resembled Chelsea's, winked.

"Yes, please." She angled her face this way and that. "This is more than my everyday look, but I'd love to be able to pull it off on my own."

Vivian slid brushes into a case. "We gotta work with what the good Lord gave us, right?"

She took one more appreciative glance before standing. "Apparently, we do." She headed to the kitchen, which had been turned into a television set in the hour it took for hair and makeup. She'd been on enough sets that she shouldn't be startled, but seeing it all in her own house—cameras, lights, reflective screens, boom mic—stopped her in her tracks. For the second time in as many minutes, all she could manage was a breathless "Wow."

"All for you, hot stuff." Jada came from behind one of the cameras and looked Chelsea up and down. She let out a whistle that would rival the crassest construction worker. "Damn, girl. You're hot."

They traded compliments and come-ons all the time; it was a

fundamental element of their friendship. But with the camera crew milling around and absolutely within earshot, it made her blush. "This hot stuff is ready to roll. Are we good?"

Jada made a bowing gesture. "Your kitchen awaits."

They'd gone over the recipes and the show script at least a dozen times, but they did it again with the full crew. The food prep team walked her through how things had been arranged in the fridge and what parts would be done on camera. Knives, cutting boards, utensils—everything had been carefully arranged so she could cook without pulling attention from her one-sided banter with the theoretical audience.

She'd managed to keep her nerves in check, but the carefully cultivated calm evaporated all at once. For all the prep and planning, it was like she was learning for the first time she was no longer part of the behind-the-scenes crew. The mere thought had her pulse ratcheting.

She was about to be on camera. Recorded. For television.

Layla, head of the film crew, stepped forward. "So, the first take will be mostly about you. Think interactive, like you're showing your best friend how to do it and why they'll love eating it when they're done. We'll do all the closeup food shots in the second take and can record any voiceovers we need."

Chelsea nodded and tried not to show the terror threatening to zip up her spine and squeeze the life out of her vital organs. It would be fine. She'd seen this exact process a thousand times, including the flubs and swearing and retakes when Charlie was having a bad day. "Got it."

Layla returned to her spot behind the main camera and Jada, who'd vanished briefly, appeared at her side. "You got this. And if you don't, we'll have a do-over. It's not live TV. You can't fuck it up."

She knew this. Deep down in the depths of her heart, she knew. Hearing it out loud helped. "Thanks."

"Now." Jada gave her one of those chin down, super serious stares. "Look delicious, cook pretty, and let's kick some ass."

She didn't stand a chance against the snort of laughter. She poked a finger at Jada's chest. "One, please say that to me every day we're in production. Two, you got it. And three, do not make me do that on camera."

"I'll do my best." Jada winked before taking a step back and saying in a much louder voice, "Let's do this, people."

Chelsea stepped behind the counter and took a deep breath. She adjusted the plum-colored swing dress she'd selected for the first episode. Then she tugged at the knot of the vintage hostess apron she'd tied around her waist.

"Stop fidgeting, hot stuff," Jada said.

She growled. "Yes, ma'am."

"Let's start with the episode intro. We can do a few takes of that to get you warmed up, then we'll start cooking." Jada shifted her attention to the camera crew. "Layla, it's all you."

Layla took over, running through a series of signals and directions for lighting and angles. The next thing she knew, the production assistant hopped in front of her with the slate and an announcement for take one, and they were off.

The next several hours passed in a blur. Cooking, smiling, talking. Cooking more, saying different things, even more smiling. She'd been on sets long enough that the pace didn't surprise her, but being the one on camera was definitely a different animal. More energizing but somehow also more exhausting. And despite her nerves, utterly thrilling.

After the last dish of the day had been photographed within an inch of its life, Jada emerged from behind the cameras and into the light. "All right, kids. I think that's a wrap."

The crew clapped, as was custom. Before they could disperse for cleanup and breakdown, Chelsea stuck her arm in the air, sort of like a kindergartener trying to get the attention of the teacher. No one was paying her much attention at this point, so she had to call out a rather ungraceful, "Hey."

The set went silent, and everyone looked at her expectantly. That was a first.

"Sorry. I don't want to keep y'all from your evenings, but I had to say thank you. This still feels a little unreal, but today went better than I could have imagined. I have each of you to thank for that." She imagined the beers and TV and calls home that awaited most of the people in the room. "I know this is the middle of nowhere for most of y'all and I want you to know how much I appreciate you being here."

Gio, one of the sound guys carried over from the *Charlie's Table* days, lifted his chin. "Happy to be on set with someone who isn't an asshole."

Murmurs of agreement followed. Chelsea nodded and willed herself not to get choked up. So many people standing in her house right now had suffered the bullying of Charlie Paul. "Thank you."

Gio offered her a sly grin. "Even if we are stuck somewhere between the backwoods and the bayou."

That got Gio a laugh and pulled her back from the edge of big feelings. "Don't get eaten by an alligator tonight."

Everyone laughed except Dev, the intern. They were barely out of culinary school and hadn't set foot below the Mason-Dixon line before this week. Their eyes got huge and they looked genuinely alarmed. Jada slung an arm around their shoulder. "Don't worry, Dev. She's just yanking your chain."

They nodded but their face said they remained unsure who to believe. She took pity but not enough to spare them the requisite newbie hazing. "You're not likely to find one walking down the street, but I'd stay away from any bodies of water you happen upon."

"Yes, Chef."

The title softened her, but her advice wasn't without merit, so she didn't take it back.

Jada gave them a firm pat on the back. "Let's plan to start food prep in the morning at eight and have cameras rolling at nine. Y'all have a good night."

It took about an hour for folks to wrap up their end-of-day tasks, meaning it was after seven before she and Jada stood alone in the kitchen. Chelsea put her hands on her hips and turned a slow circle. "Well, we did it."

Jada gave a satisfied nod. "We did. And you kicked ass. Like, seriously kicked ass."

Despite the exhaustion, Chelsea's insides buzzed with the remnants of adrenaline. "We both did. We should have ditched Charlie a long time ago."

"Truth." Jada put a hand on each of Chelsea's shoulders. "I know you were nervous, but you're a natural."

She laughed. "I'm not sure about that, but I had more fun than I was expecting. That has to be a good sign."

"It absolutely is. The camera loves you." Jada dropped her hands and smirked. "You know what it's going to love even more?"

She didn't like to give in to suspicion immediately, but it was Jada she was dealing with. "What's that?"

"You flirting with Bryce while you cook."

Chelsea rolled her eyes and groaned. She even gave Jada's arm a backhanded swat. But as she imagined bantering back and forth with him, standing hip to hip at the counter and feeding him the first bite of whatever they'd cooked together, she couldn't quite bring herself to disagree.

❖

Bryce considered driving by Chelsea's house on his way home from work but decided it veered too close to creeper territory. Besides, she'd started filming, so it wasn't like he could stop by unannounced. Besides, he had company coming and dinner to make. By the time Melody arrived, he'd changed out of his work clothes, fired up the grill, and opened a bottle of wine. It might not be the date he'd been wishing for, but it came in a reasonable second.

"A girl could get used to this," Melody said after hugs and hellos, when Bryce suggested she relax on the deck while he finished slicing zucchini, summer squash, and peppers to go with the chicken he'd marinated that morning.

He brought everything out to the deck, including the wine, and poured a glass for Melody to enjoy while he cooked. "Does Keith seriously never make dinner?"

Melody offered a shrug and a smile. "Honestly, he tries. Tried. You know what I mean."

It was hard to tell if she meant it or was being generous. "You don't have to paint a rosy picture for me."

"I'm not. He does stuff around the house. He's good with the girls. It's just, I don't know. We have no passion, nothing in common." She shook her head. "We were practically children when we got together."

He turned from the grill so he could make eye contact. "It happens. I respect you for admitting it instead of pretending for the sake of the kids."

She blew out a breath. "Oh, I considered it. Especially after my mother laid a guilt trip on me."

He grimaced. "You don't deserve that."

"She gave it up when I countered with wanting to set an example for the girls that they shouldn't settle for a life that doesn't make them happy."

That was one of the reasons he loved Melody. She took no shit. Not from him, not from her parents, and apparently, not from an unsatisfying marriage. "Well played."

Melody grinned. "I may not have made it to law school, but I wasn't a debate team nerd for nothing."

He laughed at the assertion as much as the memory of her taking down Preston Ardoin in front of the whole school on the matter of trans kids using the bathrooms that matched their gender identity. School policy hadn't changed during his time, but he credited her with getting the ball rolling. "You were a debate team queen."

"Thank you." Melody blew out a breath and took a sip of her chardonnay. "Now, could we talk about something other than my divorce?"

Bryce flipped chicken and winced. "Crap. Sorry. Of course."

"What about your love life?" She made a sweeping motion with her hand. "It has to be better than mine. Let me live vicariously through you."

Of course, his thoughts went right to Chelsea, to that spark of potential at the Fourth of July party. Not that he'd seen her since. "Like I said, it's nonexistent. There's nothing to tell."

Melody set down her glass and gave a terse shake of her head. "Unacceptable. I deserve something juicy. Make it up if you have to."

He piled everything on a platter and brought it to the table. "Have I told you lately that you're one of my favorite people?"

"No, you haven't. Thank you. But also, don't change the subject." She motioned to the food. "This looks fantastic, by the way. Plenty good enough to get you laid."

He shut off the grill and joined her, motioning for her to help herself. "Even if my love interest is a professional chef?"

Melody filled her plate and took a bite. She tipped her head back and forth while chewing, as though trying to decide if it passed muster. Then she pointed at him with her fork. "Absolutely. Besides, I'm guessing if she's a professional chef, she'd appreciate someone cooking for her once in a while."

"Noted."

"But you can't drop a line like that and leave it." She wagged the fork before stabbing another bite. "Tell me everything."

"Remember me telling you about Chelsea Boudreaux coming back to town?"

Melody's eyes lit up. "Oh, right! Is she your chef?"

He relayed the highlights of their reconnection, from the flat tire to helping her with house projects to the almost kiss over sparklers. "She started filming this week, so I haven't seen or talked to her. I got roped into being in one of the episodes, but I don't think we're going to have a minute alone."

Over the course of his story, Melody finished eating and pushed her plate away, propping both elbows on the table and resting her chin on her clasped hands. When he stopped talking, she waited a beat, then sat back. "You definitely need to make her dinner."

"You make it sound so simple."

"Isn't it?" She seemed genuinely confused that it might not be.

He wasn't one to overthink. And he hadn't exactly started overthinking with Chelsea. It was just—what? He wanted to respect her work and the enormity of what this week meant to her. Give her space to lean into that, focus on it. But that flash of potential hadn't gone anywhere. He hadn't seen her in a few days but had no reason to believe it any less real, or any less mutual. "You're right."

Melody smiled. "Thank you. Why do cis men have such a mental block with that phrase?"

"To be fair, it's not a trait unique to cis men." He pointed at his chest. "I just happen to have a sister who put me in my place early and often."

She angled her head, conceding the point. "So, what are you going to make her?"

Impressing her probably wasn't an option, or at least not with anything fancy. "Thanks to my mama, I can knock a pork roast out of the park, but that feels kind of intense for a date night, especially in the summer."

She crossed her arms and nodded slowly. "Yeah, nothing too heavy if your hope is to get laid."

"Who said anything about getting laid?" he asked.

"You didn't have to. It's implied."

He could have argued, but he'd be lying if he said his thoughts hadn't gone there. But he could still qualify. "We haven't even kissed yet. Some of us have to build up to getting laid."

"Thanks for the lesson, serial monogamist. The soon to be divorcée is taking notes."

Bryce pinched the bridge of his nose. "I'm sorry. I'm being completely self-absorbed."

Melody reached across the table and gave his hand a squeeze. "No, you're not. I asked about your love life. At first, I wanted a distraction, but now I really am going to live vicariously through you. I haven't been laid in months, and I don't even want to think about how long it's going to be before I have the chance again."

He frowned. "Okay, at least let me be sorry about that."

She smiled. "Token sorry because you're my friend. It's not like you can do anything about it."

For all the years they'd been friends, nothing romantic or physical had ever happened between them. Probably because Melody was already with Keith by the time Bryce figured out who he was and took steps to bring his physical self into alignment with that. Not that he was complaining. Having Melody as a friend—one who saw him and supported him during that whole figuring-out phase—had been better than any hookup.

"You're thinking about having sex with me right now, aren't you?" Melody leaned back in her chair, arms folded.

"What? God. No." Sure, he'd had a few fantasies back in the day, especially when he first started T and couldn't seem to go thirty seconds without thinking about sex. But he respected and cared about her way too much to ever admit it, much less act on it.

"Oh, so you don't think I'm attractive, then."

He knew from the twinkle in her eye she was baiting him, but he didn't mind. "Girl, if I saw you alone at a bar, I'd be hitting on you faster than the Beat Bama signs go up the week the Tigers play the Crimson Tide."

Melody tapped a finger to her lips a couple of times before making little circles with her finger. "Such a sweet sentiment. Such a terrible line."

Bryce laughed. Other than Kate, no one kept him in line better than Melody. "Yeah."

She let out a sigh. "But thank you. I love you too much to want to go to bed with you, but my ego appreciates the stroking."

"You know how bad I want to make a stroking joke, right?"

She tutted. "I hope you have better game with the women you actually want to sleep with."

He shrugged. He wasn't a Casanova by any means, but he did all right. Well, with getting women to go to bed with him at least. It was all the rest of it that seemed to trip him up. The fact that they never seemed to want the life he had to offer. "How do I get marry me and grow old together game?"

She squeezed his hand once again. "I think you've got the game, my friend. What you need is the right girl to play it with."

CHAPTER NINE

B ryce strode to Chelsea's front door, glad Harper's filming day came before his. And glad Chelsea had given him permission to stop by and watch. Maybe it was a silly use of vacation time, but knowing exactly what to expect would calm his own nerves the next day. And the last thing he wanted to be in front of Chelsea was a bundle of nerves.

It was weird. He spoke in front of groups all the time. He'd been interviewed for the campus TV station once, too. And, as he'd told himself more times than he cared to admit, Harper was doing it, too. Not to knock the bravery of eleven-year-old girls, but if Harper could do it, he could do it.

He didn't even get the chance to knock. The door swung open and someone he hadn't met stood on the other side, finger pressed to their lips. They had an edgy, nonbinary aesthetic—green hair and black clothing—but the look was softened by a wide-eyed, enthusiastic vibe. Bryce pressed his own lips together and nodded. He stepped inside and they all but body-checked him, ensuring they both remained just inside the door. It was awkward enough to be entertaining more than annoying. He'd begun to contemplate some combination of mime and mouthed words to ask how long they'd be stuck like that when Jada called "cut" from the other room.

And just like that, the ad hoc bouncer relaxed. "Sorry. Jada said you were on your way and stationed me here to intercept you."

He laughed. "No worries. I don't even work for Jada and I'm pretty sure I'd do whatever she told me."

That got him a laugh. "You can go on in."

"Thanks. I'm Bryce, by the way."

"Right. Yes. I'm Dev." Dev made a sweeping gesture, as though Bryce might not know the way.

In the kitchen, cameras and lights were set. Harper stood with Chelsea behind the counter and Kate hovered in the shadows, looking a little awestruck. Bryce sidled up and leaned close to Kate's ear. "I can't believe she gets to be in an episode before I do."

Kate, whose gaze didn't leave Chelsea and Harper, whispered back, "Harper has more stage presence than the two of us put together."

It was true, but that didn't mean he had to admit it. His own stage fright notwithstanding. "I present in front of groups all the time."

Kate turned to him then, brow raised. "With PowerPoint?"

"What's wrong with PowerPoint?"

"Nothing. But I'm pretty sure it doesn't contribute to your stage presence." She raised a brow. "Or your cool factor."

Even in the land of sibling quibbles, he couldn't argue that. "I guess you're—"

"Quiet on set." Jada's command spared him the full admission, but Kate gave him a victorious smirk nonetheless.

Bryce turned his attention back to Chelsea and Harper. Chelsea said something that made Harper laugh, then nod with enthusiasm. Harper stood up a little straighter and smiled at the camera. The lighting guy gave the all clear and someone darted in front of the camera with one of those movie things and rattled off the take. He stepped aside and Jada called, "Action."

The take only lasted a couple of minutes. Chelsea introduced Harper as her friend and the two of them discussed how cocoons, the crumbly little cookies with pecans, went by at least a dozen other names in different parts of the world. Whether genuine or affected, Harper shook her head in disappointment, but agreed they were delicious regardless of the name. Harper helped to measure ingredients for the dough and reminded Chelsea to start the mixer on low so she wouldn't wind up wearing the powdered sugar.

Jada cut the take and members of the crew scurried around to make adjustments and they did the whole thing again, this time bringing the dough together and getting it wrapped and in the fridge to chill. The take after that involved rolling the dough and getting it in the oven, but not before the woman who did hair and makeup zipped in to tame some wisps that had escaped Harper's French braid.

"She's a freaking natural," Kate said.

Bryce chuckled. "I'm a little worried about what this is going to mean for her teenage years."

"Please don't remind me we're starting those soon." Kate shook her head and patted her belly. "Especially since I'm about to start the whole process over with another one."

Bryce kissed her cheek. "She's going to be a great big sister."

Kate nodded, her features softening. "She is."

Jada directed a few more takes, then the kitchen crew swarmed the kitchen to reset the second run-through, the one that focused more on the food shots than the people making the food. Released from the spotlight for the moment, Harper bounded over. "What do you think? Did I do okay?"

Kate switched from sentimentality to proud mama grin. "You were fantastic."

"A total natural." Bryce resisted giving the top of her head a rub. One, Harper was getting to the age where she didn't find it funny and two, he didn't want to face the wrath of the hair and makeup woman.

"Chelsea said I did good. Did well. I messed up my lines a couple of times, though." Harper wrinkled her nose, but the smile never left her face.

"That's why they do more than one take," Bryce said.

Harper nodded. "And Chelsea messed up once, too."

Because her back was to the set, Harper didn't see Chelsea approaching from behind. "Don't you know it's bad show biz etiquette to point out your co-star's mistakes."

Harper whipped around, mortification written all over her face. "Oh, my God. Chelsea, I'm so sorry. I didn't mean it like that. I was talking about how I messed up and how it made me feel like less of a dork when you did, too. You're, like, so good at—"

Chelsea raised a hand. "Relax. I was teasing you."

"Oh." Harper blinked a few times, clearly unsure if she was supposed to play it cool or tease back or apologize more.

Bryce chuckled, glad he never had to be that age again. "I think you're both fantastic. It has me rethinking whether I can pull it off when it's my turn."

Chelsea gave his hip a bump with hers. "No way. No backing out now."

"I'm not. I'm just warning you I might not be a natural like this one." Since hip bumps were going around, he nudged Harper's with his.

Chelsea turned to Kate. "What about you? I could probably

convince my producer to put you on instead of my mother. I'm pretty sure we'd both have more fun."

The comment was flip, but it made him wonder again about Chelsea's relationship with her. He didn't want to pry, obviously, but he made a mental note to ask when it was just the two of them.

Kate shook her head. "I'm flattered, but that's a hard no from me."

Chelsea laughed. "Can't blame a girl for trying."

"You'll have plenty of fun with this one." Kate hooked a thumb in Bryce's direction.

Chelsea looked him up and down. "Oh, I'm planning on it."

It might have been flirting or it might have been teasing. Either way, Kate would undoubtedly harass him about it later. "But in the meantime, don't let us keep you," he said.

Chelsea smirked. "Trying to get rid of me?"

He glanced at Kate, fully expecting a pithy comment. She merely tucked her tongue in her cheek. Since that left him to reply, he went with the obvious, "Of course not."

"Mm-hmm."

Okay, that really felt like flirting. He poked his fingers to his chest. "I'm simply trying to be respectful of the fact that you're, oh I don't know, in the middle of making a television show."

"Is he always this conscientious?" Chelsea asked Kate.

"Only when he's trying to impress a girl."

He looked from Chelsea to Kate, then Harper. "How am I this outnumbered?"

Harper cleared her throat with the subtlety of a linebacker. "So, do we do that part again or do we do the whole episode, then start again at the beginning?"

He made a mental note to thank her for rescuing him, even if she hadn't done it elegantly.

"We do the whole thing, then do the whole thing again." Chelsea made an arc with her hand. "That way Jada can review the footage and make decisions about what needs extra attention the second time."

"I can't believe you do it all twice," Kate said.

Chelsea shrugged. "It makes for less work overall, I think. Fewer cuts and retakes along the way. Oh, and the fact that I don't walk off set and leave the crew to piece together all the food shots and cooking sequences."

Bryce had read enough of the headlines to connect the dots. "Like your former boss?"

"I don't know what you mean." Chelsea smirked.

"Oh." Kate let the word hang, putting the pieces together.

"Wait." Harper, who did not like being left out, frowned. "Who was your former boss?"

"Someone who used to be on TV and isn't anymore because he was a jerk to a lot of the people who worked for him," Chelsea said.

"Misogynist?" Harper's voice dripped with the sort of world-weary disdain that came with being the sort of girl who'd learned the word *feminism* from day one but also learned the whole world didn't work that way.

Chelsea chuckled, either at the tone or the fact that an eleven-year-old was using the word. "Something like that."

Harper shook her head. "Men."

"Some of them, at least." Chelsea gave Harper's shoulders a squeeze. "Good thing we've only got good ones here."

Harper nodded. "Yeah."

"Okay, we're ready for the next segment. Chelsea and Harper on set, please." Jada didn't bark the command, but everyone in the room snapped to. Well, everyone except Chelsea. She simply gave Harper a conspiratorial wink and sauntered back to her place.

They recorded and broke a few more times, then started the episode again from the beginning. Chelsea was an absolute pro, making Bryce wonder if she'd spent a lot of time on camera before or was simply born for it. Harper held her own, only flubbing a line here and there and never losing her cool.

When they wrapped, everyone gathered around the table and devoured the food that had been made over the course of the day. Without meaning to, Bryce managed to talk up the head camerawoman, the intern, and the boom operator. One was a Trekkie, one literally wanted to make pickles for a living, and one was married to a trans woman and was practically beside himself over Bryce being both on the show and unabashedly out. Even more than getting to see how things worked, the quirky relatability put him at ease. He headed home, complete with instructions to fall asleep with a cold compress on his eyes, genuinely looking forward to his turn in front of the camera with Chelsea.

❖

"Knock, knock. I hope it's okay I'm letting myself in." Bryce's voice carried down the short hallway.

"Back here," Chelsea called, delighted by his arrival even though she'd been expecting him.

A moment later, he appeared in the doorway. "Good morning."

"Good morning." She offered him a smile before resuming the open-mouthed vacant stare she'd learned made a makeup artist's job easier.

"So, the bedroom you converted to an office is now hair and makeup?"

Vivian finished glossing Chelsea's lips and gave her nod of approval. Chelsea returned her attention to Bryce. "Something like that."

"Well, I'm pretty sure half the salons in Duchesne are run out of people's houses, so it's not that much of a stretch."

"Maybe I'll stick around," Vivian said. "Hang a little sign on your front door."

Chelsea traced a circle in front of her face with her index finger. "You make me look like this on a daily basis and you can set up shop rent free."

Vivian gave a dismissive wave of her hand. "You have to stop saying that. You're a natural."

Chelsea shook her head. "You're a goddess."

"And you're gorgeous." Vivian looked to Bryce but used both hands to indicate Chelsea. "Isn't she gorgeous?"

"Total knockout."

Vivian gave him the once-over. "You're not too shabby yourself."

Chelsea stood, grateful Vivian laid it on thick across the board. "Careful, she says that to everyone."

Bryce shot Vivian a wink. "I don't mind."

"Peas in a pod." Chelsea left them to their own devices and headed to the kitchen. She'd abandoned food prep to have her own hair and makeup done, and it appeared that the crew had finished in her absence.

Jada stood in front of one of the cameras, clipboard in hand. She waited for Layla to nod before turning her attention to Chelsea. "Who's ready for a day of cooking and flirting with the hometown hottie?"

Chelsea winced and stole a glance behind her to make sure Bryce couldn't be in earshot. "Could you go easy on that?"

"It's too late. We're already referring to this as the Hometown Hottie episode. Bryce seemed completely on board."

Heat rose in her cheeks over the possibility he'd think it was her doing. "You didn't actually say that to him. Call him that."

Jada looked equal parts smug and entertained. "Of course I did. I can because I'm not trying to get in his pants."

"And I can't because I am?"

Jada shrugged. "I mean, if the shoe fits."

She sighed, if for no other reason than she wasn't a fan of arguing with the truth. They went over the script, including a few notes and some tweaks Jada wanted. Chelsea nodded because Jada was always right when it came to that sort of thing and filed the details in her mind.

They'd just finished when Bryce strode in. Well, swagger might have been a more accurate descriptor. He struck a Superman pose—legs apart, fists on hips, chest puffed. "Good-natured guest on set. Where do you want me?"

Chelsea took a moment simply to appreciate the way his shoulders filled out the Cormier Hardware T-shirt and how his stance made the shirt ride up slightly, revealing a glimpse of the brown leather belt threaded through the loops of his jeans.

"And what a handsome guest you are." Jada stepped from behind the camera. "Let me walk you through some basic blocking."

Chelsea cleared her throat. He'd clearly been talking to her, but she'd been too busy drooling to form a coherent sentence. Hopefully, Jada cutting in came off bossy producer more than tongue-tied host. She scurried to join them in the kitchen. "Thank you again for agreeing to this."

"Are you kidding? I wasn't about to let Harper be the only one in on the fun."

"Not to make you nervous or anything, but she's kind of a rock star. The bar is high."

He laughed. "I'm sure it won't surprise you to know it's not the first time I've heard this."

They got into position—Bryce in front of the stove set with her new Dutch oven and Chelsea at the cutting board primed with a peeled onion, stalks of celery, and a seeded bell pepper. Jada cued the room and Chelsea launched into her intro, complete with an explanation of the different forms of gumbo and her personal loyalties to team Cajun. Bryce agreed and the line flowed flawlessly, without either of them sparing a glance at the cue cards Dev held.

"And how do we start?" she asked, teeing up the truism of Cajun cooking that had inspired the name of her show.

Bryce gestured to the pot. "First, you make a roux."

They cooked and laughed, bantered and ate. Harper might have been a natural in front of the camera, but even she had nothing on the chemistry Chelsea had with Bryce. Flirty but not over-the-top, witty, and with timing so perfect it couldn't be faked. She might not be in the market for a cohost, but damn. Bryce could show up on her set anytime. She told him as much. Jada did, too.

Bryce rocked an aw, shucks vibe like it was his job before promptly changing the subject. "Now what?"

"Now we shoot the last two episodes for the season and spend a couple of days filming promos and B-roll." She went for an over-the-top smile. "Oh, and try to manage my anxiety until the first episode airs."

"You have nothing to be anxious about."

She appreciated the sentiment, even if it wasn't true. "It's TV. I have everything to be anxious about."

"Okay, I'll admit there's no accounting for taste, but your show is going to be fantastic. I don't even watch cooking shows and I'm going to watch it."

"You're sweet. Incredibly biased, but sweet."

"I am, but it's still a fantastic show. You're going to be a bigger star than Charlie Paul ever was." He lifted a finger. "Assuming that's what you want, of course."

Did she? It wasn't really about being famous. Not that she'd turn her nose up at gaining a modicum of celebrity. But mostly it was being the kind of chef she was—queer, fat, and more interested in food than showmanship. Oh, and getting to do that on a national stage over the likes of someone like Charlie. "I don't think whether or not I want it has much to do with things."

She'd been trying to make a joke, but Bryce frowned.

"I just meant that fame is fickle. People like what they like until they don't anymore." With or without a scandal.

"That's depressing."

She shrugged. "I'm not really in it for that, though, obviously, I hope the show does well."

That seemed to mollify him. "I have every confidence people will love you."

"We'll see in a couple of weeks, I suppose." They'd set her debut for mid-August since cooking shows didn't really follow any rules when it came to seasons.

"Really? That fast?"

"The show got fast-tracked given it's part of the network's attempt at damage control. The first episodes went right into post-production while we were filming the rest. And the first season is only eight episodes." The network's way of testing the waters and having something diverse to point to even if it didn't last.

"I'm glad you don't have too long to wait, then. Are you having a viewing party?"

"Um." She hadn't thought about it. Jada would be back in New York, and the prospect of sitting around while her mother nitpicked wasn't her idea of a good time.

"Let me rephrase. Can we throw you a viewing party?" he asked.

"We?" She had this flashback of her pawpaw asking if "we" meant her and the mouse in her pocket.

"Well, I want to, but Kate's better at entertaining. And she has a larger living room. I'm sure she and Harper would love to help you celebrate."

The idea of making it a real celebration set a swarm of butterflies flitting around in her chest. Still. "I'm not sure she'd appreciate you volunteering her."

"I'm pretty sure she would. But if for some reason she isn't available, will you at least let me celebrate with you?" he asked.

Like so many of their interactions, it could have been a friendly offer. Hell, it could have been one based in pity. But she couldn't shake the feeling that Bryce was interested in her. Interested in the way nice guys were—flirty but with this deep undercurrent of kindness. Like he genuinely cared about her feelings, her happiness. She didn't have a lot of experience with it herself, but she'd seen enough romcoms and read enough romance novels to recognize it.

"It's okay to decline. You might hurt my feelings a little, but I'm tough. I won't cry into my pillow for too long."

Even without that last bit, his playful smile told her all she needed to know. "If you must know, I wasn't trying to come up with a reason to say no."

"No?" His eyebrows rose. "What were you doing?"

"Overthinking. If we're going to spend time together, you should know it's one of my preferred pastimes."

He laughed. "I can't say I prefer it, but it's a hobby I've been known to pick up on occasion."

"You're funny." And not that clever sort of funny that came with an edge. Or an agenda.

"My sister would beg to disagree, but thank you." He waited a beat. "So, is that a yes? To a viewing party for your first episode? Even if it's a party of two?"

She wanted to say something about especially if it turned out to be a party of two, but she didn't. Though at this point, she wasn't sure why. "Yes. I'd love that. Thank you."

"Do you know when it comes on yet?"

"Sunday at eleven."

"Ooh, nice slot. Wait, in the morning, right?"

"Yes. Morning." Jada had teased her about losing the church crowd, and she'd wondered if that had been an intentional move on the part of the network to minimize any backlash. But in the end, she'd let it go because it was a great slot. And as much as she wanted to be out and fat and proud, she already had a simmering dread of the inevitable haters and trolls.

"I'm sure your calendar is already marked, but mark it again because we have a date."

Not exactly the date she most wanted when it came to Bryce, but she'd take it.

Chapter Ten

Chelsea balanced the crumb cake in one hand and knocked on the door with the other. It was silly to be nervous. She'd spent time with Kate and Harper, had at least met Sutton. And, well, she wasn't entirely comfortable around Bryce, but that came from unresolved sexual tension, which was another matter. Maybe it was that more than the prospect of a social engagement with new friends. Or maybe it was all that and knowing her face was about to be flashed on thousands of televisions and computers across the country. Yeah, definitely that.

Harper opened the door, wearing cutoffs and a Cormier's Hardware T-shirt. "Hey, Chelsea." Harper stepped back in lieu of inviting her in.

Chelsea willed the relaxed vibe to rub off on her as she crossed the threshold. "How's school?"

Harper groaned.

"That bad?" If her own memories of middle school were anything to go on, the groan might actually be an understatement. Especially the first week or two of a new school year.

"Not really." Harper shrugged. "I just feel like that's what I'm supposed to say."

Had she been that funny at eleven? Doubtful. "Well, better than the other way around, I guess."

Since the living room of the house opened to the kitchen, she offered hellos to Kate and Sutton and brought her cake over to the island with the rest of the food. Sutton eyed it and grinned. "That looks amazing."

"Not as amazing as that." Chelsea pointed to what looked like a ham and cheese quiche.

Kate shook her head. "Sutton's sweet tooth would beg to differ. Coffee?"

"Oh, yes, please." She'd had two cups at home, but what were a few more jitters at this point?

"Got it." Sutton grabbed a cup from a cabinet near the stove and filled it from the pot. She handed it to Chelsea and tipped her head. "Cream and sugar and such are there."

"Thank you." She'd no sooner stirred in a splash of cream than Bryce walked in without knocking.

"Good morning, fam." He came to the kitchen and set down a plate of berries, pineapple, and sliced melon. "And our favorite celebrity chef."

He kissed Chelsea on the cheek with the last bit, making her blush. Harper narrowed her eyes slightly, but no one else seemed to be paying attention. Chelsea bit her lip and the nerves she'd begun to banish returned. "Good morning."

Bryce surveyed the spread. "Is that crumb cake? Please tell me it's crumb cake. And quiche? Do we get to eat now?"

Kate gave him a friendly elbow to the ribs. "We were waiting on you, stud."

Bryce reached for a plate, but Harper swatted his hand. "Wait. We have to do mimosas first so we can have a toast."

"Mimosas, huh?" Bryce hip-checked Harper. "You think you're getting a mimosa?"

"Mama said I could have hers since she can't drink as long as it was mostly orange juice." Harper stuck out her tongue. "So there."

Bryce lifted both hands. "Oh. Well, then. I stand corrected."

"Wouldn't be the first time." Harper shimmied her shoulders with attitude.

The exchange struck Chelsea as more affection than sass. She laughed, enjoying a tween keeping pace with Bryce. But also because she couldn't remember the last time she'd thought or said the word *sass*. The South was rubbing off on her quick this time. Though maybe it was more accurate to say the South was rubbing off whatever veneer she'd put on when she left.

Since that felt way too philosophical for ten thirty on a Sunday morning, she set it aside. Much easier, not to mention more fun, to focus on the mimosa Kate handed her. That and realizing she'd made the kind of friends who would make mimosas to celebrate her first show.

Bryce made a toast—nothing sentimental, but it didn't stop all manner of emotions from bubbling up. She nodded too much and smiled too big, loving the attention but squirming under it all the same. Kate seemed to pick up on that and slid into mom mode, corralling everyone to fill their plates and get settled in before the show started. It might be weird, but she had as much gratitude for that as the party itself.

Chelsea sat on the couch, sandwiched between Bryce and Kate. Sutton took one of the cushy chairs adjacent to the sofa and Harper sat cross-legged on the rug with her plate balanced on her lap. "Frances, you have to wait," she said to the beagle eyeing her quiche hopefully.

Sutton turned on the TV but set the volume low. Everyone talked while they ate, like they'd been friends for ages and just needed to catch up on all the things. Harper taking up clarinet, Kate's latest sonogram, the wedding that would cut unexpectedly close to her due date, Sutton's dad making it through his second knee replacement. They made it easy to ask questions and deflect attention from her, which was exactly what she needed. Even if she caught Bryce giving her curious stares now and again.

"Oh, I think it's almost time," Sutton said before Chelsea had the chance.

Sutton turned the volume up, and everyone's attention shifted to the television. Like they cared about her show almost as much as she did. Chelsea tried to soak it in and not let on that her insides practically vibrated with anticipation. The show ahead of hers ended and a teaser came on. Her name. Her picture. World premiere.

Forget vibrating. She needed to keep herself from passing out.

"You okay?" Bryce's hand rested on her leg.

She nodded, not entirely trusting herself with words.

"It's a really big deal," Kate said.

More nodding. Still no words. What was wrong with her?

Fortunately, the skillet commercial ended and her voice filled the room from the television. "I'm Chelsea Boudreaux, and I make modern takes on classic Cajun and Creole cuisine." After asking people to come cook with her, the music Jada had picked for the theme song came on and the montage of pictures and takes they'd meticulously curated flitted across the screen. The intro ended and the screen cut to her standing in the kitchen. She'd seen the entire episode start to finish twice, but still. There she was. On TV. "Holy shit."

Harper giggled and Bryce gave her thigh a gentle squeeze. Her gaze darted from Bryce to Harper to Kate. "Sorry," she added.

Kate grinned. "We make exceptions for swearing when the situation calls for it."

The room fell silent, and everyone simply watched. Well, watched for the seven or so minutes it took to get to the first commercial break. The Chelsea on screen promised to finish the étouffée and make a marinated artichoke salad to accompany it. Then a dish detergent ad came on and everyone started talking at once.

"That was so cool," Sutton said.

"You look amazing," Kate added.

"I can't believe a kitchen I hung out in is on TV." Harper set her plate on the coffee table and looked right at Chelsea. "And you're on TV."

Bryce was the only one who didn't speak. But when Chelsea stole a glimpse of him in between her replies to everyone else, he had this smile—a mix of excited and something she couldn't quite identify. Proud, maybe? Whatever it was, it had an unmistakable boyfriend vibe.

"You're great," he said eventually. "Really, really great."

The next two segments passed in a blur, and before she knew it, the episode was over. For a group of people she didn't know all that well, they piled on the compliments and congratulations. But it all felt so genuine, Chelsea didn't get that fidgety, uncomfortable feeling that usually came with being the center of attention. Okay, maybe she did a little. But Bryce and his family made her feel like family, too, in ways her family never did. Maybe not as big a deal as seeing her show air for the first time, but it came a pretty close second.

❖

Bryce knocked on Chelsea's door, flowers in hand. He hadn't been certain she'd say yes to dinner, especially after celebrating earlier in the day. But he'd convinced her a fancy supper out was a different sort of celebration entirely, and one she more than deserved.

She blushed and turned bashful over the bouquet, making him doubly glad he'd stopped and picked it up. He got the impression she was unaccustomed to being spoiled and made a mental note to do something about it. Whether or not they ended up in bed together.

After giving her a moment to put them in water, he escorted her to his truck. She didn't blush when he opened the door for her, but she did bite her lip. "So, where are you taking me?" she asked as he slid into the driver's seat.

He buckled his seat belt and started the engine. "I made reservations at Palace Café, but now I'm second-guessing myself."

She gave his hand a squeeze over the gear shift. "Why second-guessing?"

"Because it's my favorite fancy place in the Quarter, but not the fanciest. And maybe you won't think it's worth the drive or that I don't have very good taste or—"

"Bryce, I was prepared to eat leftovers on the sofa tonight. Anywhere would be a step up. This? An absolute treat." She shrugged. "Besides, I'm in it for the company more than the food."

That last bit smoothed away the worries flitting around his mind. The real worries, the ones that had nothing to do with the caliber of the restaurant and everything to do with wondering whether or not this counted as a date. "To be honest, I've been hankering for a reason to ask you out."

"What made you think you needed a reason?"

He stole a glance and liked what he saw: bottom lip caught between her teeth, corners of her mouth turned up in a flirty half-smile. For the life of him, he couldn't fathom why he'd waited so long. "I have no idea."

"Well, I'm glad you did. And I don't really care about the reason."

Bryce kept his eyes on the road but let his imagination wander. To the dinner and conversation that awaited them. To having Chelsea's gaze locked with his. To what it would be like to pull that luscious bottom lip of hers into his mouth.

"Do you get to New Orleans often?" she asked.

"Not as often as I'd like. I confess commuting to Baton Rouge every day makes me a homebody on weekends." Plus the reality of most of his friends getting married and raising kids.

Chelsea laughed. "I imagined myself going at least once a week and I've only gone once, to play tour guide to Jada."

"I can't decide whether to ask why you haven't or why you thought you would." Though, really, he wanted to know both. To know everything she was willing to share.

"Turns out, settling into a house and making a TV show are time consuming." She took a deep breath, blew it out. "And, honestly, I was worried I'd be bored. You know, staring at my walls or enduring yet another afternoon with my mother."

At least a dozen more questions popped into his mind, but he bit them back. "And you haven't been? Bored, that is."

"No. I've managed to make some friends."

"Friends make all the difference." Was it too much to make a joke about being more than friends, and how that could make even more of a difference?

Chelsea lifted a shoulder. "Plus this really hot guy keeps showing up at my house, and tonight he asked me out on a date."

Well, that answered that. "He's probably really into you."

She offered a playful smirk that had him half-tempted to pull the truck over so he could kiss her. "I sure hope so."

Bryce cleared his throat. "Then I should have been more clear. He's really, really into you."

The playful smirk became a knowing smile and dinner became the absolute last thing on his mind.

That being said, dinner was amazing. He wasn't sure why he'd been worried. They shared dishes and talked and laughed and at one point played actual footsie under the table. Any lingering trace of will they, won't they disappeared faster than the sweet corn crème brûlée they ordered to close out the meal. In its place, a sizzling sense of when and what will it be like made the air between them feel genuinely alive.

"That's the best meal I've had in a long time," Chelsea said as they walked to where he'd parked.

"Come on. You must go to swanky places all the time."

"I really don't. Sous chefs on cooking shows aren't making the big bucks, you know."

"Okay, okay. I stand corrected." He unlocked the truck doors and opened the passenger side.

Chelsea stepped into the space but didn't get in right away. "It's hot when a guy can admit he's wrong."

"Is it? In that case, I'm wrong a lot. I could give you some examples."

"You could." She shrugged. "Or you could kiss me."

Bryce swallowed. Little turned him on more than a woman who was direct about her desires. Save, perhaps, that exquisite balance of direct and demure—things that shouldn't go together but somehow did when a woman made it clear she wanted him but also wanted him to make the first move. "Well, if those are my choices."

Her smirk hinted at triumph even as her eyes held invitation. Bryce took a step closer and pressed his lips lightly to hers. It started that way at least. But then her lips parted and the desire he'd been holding since that first afternoon on the side of the road swelled, taking up all the space in his brain.

She slipped her arms around his neck, a move that brought their bodies close and had her breasts pushing into his chest. Without thinking, he slid both hands into her hair. Chelsea's tongue teased his and he had a passing thought of how long it had been since he'd had sex in a vehicle.

The thought popped like an overinflated balloon when a loud whistle came from the opposite side of the street. Chelsea sprang away, practically falling into the truck, and Bryce's eyes darted around to assess its source and the level of danger that came with it.

"Don't let us stop you." The stranger's voice was slurred with alcohol but affable.

Chelsea giggled and gave him a knowing look but slid the rest of the way onto the seat. He closed the door behind her and rounded the hood. The mood might have been broken, but the promise it held pulsed through him. "You okay?" he asked.

She smiled at him. "More than."

He started the engine and began the drive home, already thinking about kissing Chelsea again. About a whole lot more than kissing. On the dark roads, they fell into comfortable quiet. Her hand came over to rest on his thigh, soothing his raging libido into a low-grade simmer of arousal. By the time he pulled into her driveway, he'd settled into an unlikely combination of turned on and relaxed.

"Would you like to come in?" Chelsea smiled, but the come hither look got lost when she stifled a yawn.

"How about a rain check?" Because his body might be thrumming with lust, but he wanted it to be mutual.

She looked up at him through her lashes. "Do you mean that or are you just being nice?"

He covered her hand with his and gave it a squeeze. "I absolutely mean it. You've had a pretty intense day."

She nodded. "I didn't realize it would all catch up with me at once."

"And not to be too forward or cocky, but if we get up to half of what I'd like to do with you, you're going to want to be well rested." When Chelsea's eyes went big and her lips parted, he winced. "Assuming, of course, you would want that."

"Oh, I want." She reached across the console with her free hand and put it on his chest. "I want very much."

"So, not to spoil the spontaneity or anything, but can we make plans for that soon?" Because at this point he'd be able to think of little else.

"Spontaneity is overrated, at least sometimes. I like knowing what's coming. Wanting it." She looked down at their joined hands, then into his eyes. "The anticipation."

His pulse already had a heavy thud going, but it tripped nonetheless. "Yes. Anticipation is good."

"Tomorrow too soon?" Chelsea laughed. "I know you have to work. The weekend would be fine—"

"Tomorrow would be perfect." And not only because he wasn't sure he'd make it through the week without seeing her again. Getting his hands on her. His mouth.

"How about you come over after work? I'll make dinner."

"This is sounding better and better," he said.

"You're sure?" A trace of worry still shadowed her eyes.

"Absolutely. Now, if you don't mind, I'd like to walk you to your door and give you a respectable good night kiss."

She pressed her lips together, looked him up and down. "Not too respectable, I hope."

Instead of answering, he got out of the truck and rounded the hood. It clearly made her squirm, but she waited for him to open the passenger door and take her hand. It took mere seconds to make their way up the walk and the low steps to her porch. Even as his hormones raged, he found pleasure in the moment. In the decision to slow things down ever so slightly.

"Thank you again for helping me celebrate," Chelsea said.

He tucked a stray strand of hair behind her ear. "Thank you for celebrating with me."

She looked at him, all deference now. He trailed a finger from the edge of her brow down her cheek before cupping her neck in his hand. Her lips parted again. No surprise this time, only invitation.

All the invitation he needed.

A brush of lips. A taste of what was to come more than an onslaught of pent-up desire. Chelsea's mouth warm under his, soothing him even as it seared, and with a lingering sweetness that reminded him of the bourbon his grandfather gave him when he graduated college. It warmed him from the inside, sharpened his senses and smoothed out his edges at the same time.

With that taste, he knew without a doubt he could lose himself in Chelsea. Lose himself but maybe find himself, too. Or at least find a part of himself he'd tucked away, waiting for the right woman to come along.

Chapter Eleven

*M*eeting with the execs at 11. Link in your email.
Chelsea willed her eyes to focus and read the message from Jada again. Then she looked at the time. Just after eight. Phew.

Or maybe not phew. What if the show was a bomb? What if viewers hated it and companies were pulling their ads and she was getting canceled after a single episode?

No. That wasn't how it worked. The network paid for eight episodes. They weren't going to flush that money down the toilet without giving her a fair shot.

Even if they did hate it. Even if everyone hated it.

Have you been online yet? So much love. Jada punctuated the second text with a string of heart emojis, every color of the rainbow.

Yeah?

Despite the desire to immediately google herself, Chelsea crawled out of bed and padded to the bathroom. She peed and brushed her teeth, noting her hair had worked itself into a particularly impressive frenzy in the night. Then, since she was naked, she went back to her room for a nightie before heading to the kitchen to start coffee.

She went for the pot instead of the pour-over, thinking it would probably turn into a multi-cup sort of morning. Meetings with the execs usually did. Once it started to burble and waft delicious caffeine aromas, she returned her attention to her phone. A half dozen more texts from Jada, mostly links but with a few phrases pasted in like review teasers on a movie poster. Words like *refreshing* and *fun. Full-bodied* and *joyful.*

She started clicking and reading and scrolling and toggling. She continued through her first cup of coffee and into her second. One critic dismissed her as too perky and a blogger she'd otherwise liked wondered about her credentials—ha!—but otherwise, the feedback was good. Like, really good. Like "after the fiasco formerly known as Charlie Paul, Food TV might be getting one right" good.

Chelsea set down her cup and pulled up the thread with Jada. *They like me. They actually like me.*

That got her an *Obvi* and an eye roll. Then, *This one is my favorite.*

The link led her to a short blurb on the website for *Q* magazine. It seemed to take more delight in her queerness than her culinary skills, but she didn't even care. Because it meant that people were reading the press kit. And the press kit was gay, gay, gay. Well, at least one gay. It referenced her identity as fat and queer and femme. The other reviewers might not be pinging it, but chances were they weren't oblivious, either. And she wouldn't have it any other way.

She said as much to Jada, then begged off to take a phone call from one of her culinary school buddies. Then it was a scramble to shower and get herself presentable for the conference call with the network people. Oh, and breakfast. Because girls gotta eat.

The conference call ran over an hour, though the gist could have been delivered in about five minutes. They likely wanted a second season but wanted to give the first one a few weeks on the air to get its legs and consider any potential format tweaks. In the meantime, they wanted her on the TV equivalent of a book tour.

"A junket," Jada had exclaimed with delight.

It was all she could do not to laugh in their faces. Well, not in their faces specifically. Just at the zaniness of it all. A junket.

Turned out this junket would include a couple of local TV spots, the NOLA Food and Wine Festival, and a guest editor role for an issue of *Food TV Magazine*. Nothing that should surprise her, really. Charlie did those sorts of things all the time. So did the other Food TV hosts. She'd been around TV production and promotion enough to know the drill. But for all the hours she'd spent daydreaming about doing it herself—making her own mark—she hadn't gotten much past the cooking.

By the time the call ended, she had a to-do list a mile long. Not to mention more than a hundred texts, emails, and voice messages from friends and former colleagues. Even a few other show hosts from the network sent well-wishes.

She made it out the door to buy groceries for her dinner with

Bryce, only to be stopped by at least a dozen people at the store. People she'd just met, friends of her mother from church or the salon, and a few childhood acquaintances she hadn't seen or spoken to since coming home. It might be low-level fame in the grand scheme of things, but she'd never felt like such a celebrity in her life. Much like the first day of filming, it was exhausting but thrilling.

At home, she threw a pasta salad together and did a quick marinade for the pork loin before getting it under the broiler. With about ten minutes to spare, she tossed some sugar snap peas in olive oil to go in with it and hightailed it to the bathroom. Even with the two-minute shower and not washing her hair, she was still tugging clothes over damp skin when the doorbell rang. She opened it with a smile, trying not to look frazzled or out of breath. "Hi."

The quizzical look from Bryce told her she hadn't quite managed it. "Did I catch you at a bad time?"

The silliness of the question helped her relax. "I'm the one who invited you over."

"Still. You're allowed to change your mind."

"No, no. I'm really glad you're here. Come in." She threw the door wide and stepped back, dabbing at the skin over her lip and willing her boobs not to sweat. "It turned into a busier day than expected."

He handed her the bottle of wine he held. "Fans already beating down your door?"

She smiled. "You know, you're not too far off."

"Ooh, tell me everything."

The sincere delight he took in her success was unexpected and its own source of delight for her. Paired with the encouraging words and appreciative looks he gave her the entire time they ate, she had a hard time being anything but starstruck. An odd descriptor given her day, perhaps, but there it was.

"So," she said after he'd polished off a second helping of pasta salad.

"So, are you going to let me do the dishes?" he asked.

She picked up her plate and his and carried them to the sink. "That would not be my preferred use of our time."

The mix of stuffy and suggestive earned her a sly look. "Yeah, but if we do them together, it will take five minutes and then it will be done."

She accepted the salad bowl he brought with him and covered it with a silicone lid before sliding it into the refrigerator. "This might be the first time in my life a guy, or anyone for that matter, pestered me about doing the dishes before having sex."

Bryce lifted a finger. "I need to make it clear, for the record, this is a matter of manners and not how much I want to have sex with you."

Chelsea laughed. "I wasn't feeling insecure about that, but thank you all the same."

When she turned from the fridge, he was there, deliciously taking up all her personal space. "You have nothing to feel insecure about."

"I have plenty, but I try not to lose sleep or obsess—"

His mouth covered hers, swallowing her words and any chance at a coherent train of thought. His hands came up to either side of her neck. "You are gorgeous." Kiss. "And I want you." Kiss. "Rather desperately."

"In that case, I'm going to insist that the dishes wait." She grabbed his hand and dragged him in the direction of her bedroom.

"I'd also like to state for the record that I find it immensely attractive when a woman knows what she wants and doesn't hesitate to ask for it."

She turned then, pressing her body to his. "I find it immensely attractive when it's mutual."

"Chelsea?"

Just the way he said her name made her pulse thud. "Yes?"

"Take me to bed."

She gave his hand a squeeze and quickened her footsteps. "I thought you'd never ask."

❖

"You'll tell me what you like, yes?" Chelsea worked at the buttons of Bryce's shirt. "What's off limits, what words to use. I want to know everything."

The very fact that she knew to ask put her light years ahead of some of the women he'd dated. "Guy words. No penetration. I try to be easy."

Her hands stilled and she looked into his eyes. "You don't need to be easy. I want you to be you."

He told himself the tightness in his chest came from desire even if he knew better. "I'm a guy on T. I get off lots of ways. Literally, easy. I want to know what does it for you."

Chelsea finished unbuttoning his shirt and pushed it from his shoulders. She ran her hands over his chest, tracing his scars with her thumbs. "I'm not on T, but I like all sorts of things, too."

He wouldn't be able to explain it if pressed, but her touch registered more appreciation than curiosity. It made his pulse trip and his dick throb. "Like what?"

She arched her back, pressing her breasts into him. "Having my nipples played with."

He cupped them briefly, appreciating the fullness and the weight, before pinching her nipples lightly through her clothes. "Yeah, I can get behind that."

Chelsea's head fell back, and she let out a little moan. "You're damn good at it."

He pinched harder and her breath caught. "Too much?"

She lifted her head and shook it slowly. "Just right."

He let go long enough to pull the dress over her head, to reach behind her and flick open her bra. She shimmied her shoulders, helping him slip it down her arms. After tossing it aside, he returned his hands to the impossibly soft undersides of her breasts and dipped his head to pull one of her nipples into his mouth. He sucked and made circles with his tongue, realizing it would be all too easy to lose hours to the worship of Chelsea's breasts. Since he wanted a hell of a lot more tonight, he reluctantly eased away. "How about that?"

Chelsea's eyes fluttered open. "Yep."

"Now who's easy?" He winked. "Though I feel like we should have the safe sex talk before going much further."

Chelsea nodded quickly, leaving him to wonder if she was unused to partners broaching the subject. "Yes, for sure."

Since she seemed amenable but slightly uncomfortable, he decided to go first. "I had my annual testing a few months ago. I was with someone at the time and haven't been with anyone else since it ended."

Chelsea continued to nod but more slowly. "I got tested after my last girlfriend cheated on me and I haven't been with anyone in over a year."

He cringed before he could stop himself. "Sorry about the cheating."

She waved him off. "She should have ended it instead of cheating, but I was a pretty terrible partner."

"Why do I get the feeling you're being too hard on yourself?" He hoped it was that more than imagining Chelsea to be something she wasn't.

"I was working obscene hours, miserable but stubbornly holding on to working for a toxic boss."

"Ah." That made sense and made him feel better. "Well, I'm still sorry it happened."

Chelsea smiled. "All for the best, I'd say. Now, where were we?"

If part of him wanted to press, to know the inner workings of Chelsea's heart and how he might be able to make her happy, the rest of him knew it was neither the time nor the place. And that part sided with the part that had a massive hard-on for the gorgeous, half-naked woman in front of him.

"Here, I think." He took the nipple he'd yet to taste into his mouth and sucked it.

Chelsea slid her fingers into his hair, scratching his scalp and the back of his neck and sending his system into overdrive. The need to feel all of her usurped his appreciation of her breasts. Since they stood a mere foot or two from the bed, he wrapped his arms around her waist and lifted her onto it. He covered her body with his own, nudging one thigh between hers. She looked at him with something resembling wonder, but before he could ask why, she grabbed the back of his head and pulled him in for a kiss.

Even as her tongue teased his, her body moved under him. The restless undulations pressed her breasts into his chest, and her hips rose to meet the thrust of his. Her hands roamed his back, grabbing and scratching with just the right amount of abandon.

The fact of the matter was he could come like this. But he didn't want to. He wanted more. He wanted everything.

He braced himself on one elbow and used his free hand to slide into the lace panties that matched her bra. She spread her legs wider, invitation tumbling into urgent request. The first touch, realizing she was that hot and that wet for him, had Bryce fighting for restraint. Chelsea gripped his shoulders and let out a moan, and suddenly touching her was no longer enough.

"I'm sorry, but these have to go." He got onto his knees and worked the fabric down her legs. The position gave him a moment to take in the whole of her—lushly feminine and full of brazen desire. Did she know she was the stuff of fantasies?

Chelsea bit her lip. It might have been coy, but something told him it came from nerves, from the intensity of his stare. Something to explore another time, perhaps. For now, his only agenda was to make her feel amazing. "Tell me what you like most."

She wrinkled her nose. "Honestly?"

Bryce laughed. "Yes, honestly."

"Hands. Fingers. On me, inside of me. All of it."

He resumed his position braced over her, his hand between her legs. "Why did you make a face?"

Chelsea tipped her head back and forth. "Everyone is all, 'ooh, oral,' and for me it's kind of meh."

The pithy assessment had him laughing out loud. "You get to like what you like."

She took a deep breath, let it out slowly. Like the idea was a revelation. "Right."

He didn't know the whole of her sexual history, didn't need to know. But he hoped he might be able to chase away some of the ghosts she seemed to carry. He slipped his fingers back into her wetness, sliding over her clit slowly, then along either side. "Like this?"

Chelsea let out a soft moan. "Uh-huh. Yeah. That's good."

He increased the pressure slightly, along with the speed. "What about this?"

Her body bucked. "Yep. Yes. That's nice, too."

Bryce continued like that for a few minutes, changing the speed and angle every so often and reveling in the way Chelsea's body responded, the noises she made. It struck him that he could touch her for hours and never get bored. It made him wonder if she'd let him.

"Oh. Just like that. Please." Chelsea's movements matched the urgency of her words and the grip she had on Bryce's shoulders tightened.

Bryce stayed with her, matching her pace and thinking how much he'd like to be inside her when she came. The thought vanished when her body arched, then tensed. She clung to him, cried out.

When she let go, she seemed to melt into the mattress, limbs limp. Her eyes opened and she blinked, as though willing them to focus. Then she smiled. "Fuck, that was good."

He kissed her. "I'm glad. Though I hope it's okay to say I'm really hoping you're not a one and done sort of woman."

She smirked. "Not when I'm with the right sort of guy."

"Oh, good. Because you made that comment about being inside you and it's pretty much all I can think about."

"I like the way you think." She trailed a finger down his torso, swirling briefly through his chest hair. "But I'm also hoping you're the sort of guy who likes to take turns."

Her meaning was clear. Still. It didn't hurt to hear exactly what she had in mind. "Take turns?"

"Yeah. Take turns." She took his cock between her finger and thumb, squeezing and tugging it gently.

"Fuck." Who needed to hear when they could get a live demonstration?

"I'd like a turn with you." Chelsea smiled, a glorious expression of confidence and desire. "How do you feel about blow jobs?"

Most of the blood flow to his brain had already diverted to his dick, so it took effort to form words. "Good. I feel very good about them."

Chelsea nudged him and he took the hint, rolling onto his back. She got onto her knees and continued to stroke him. "How's that? Are you comfortable?"

He didn't attempt more than a nod this time. Well, a nod and shifting of his body so she could situate herself between his legs. She did, making eye contact and licking her lips in a way he was pretty sure he'd remember until the day he died.

She remained on her knees, hinging her torso and resting a hand on either side of his hips. She swirled her tongue around the tip twice, then wrapped her lips around him entirely. "Mm-hmm."

The hum—of approval or appreciation or whatever the hell it was—reverberated through him. She sucked his cock slowly, using her lips and tongue in perfect unison. "You're really good at that," he managed between increasingly ragged breaths.

She lifted her head enough to make eye contact. "I love how hard you are."

She didn't wait for a reply, resuming her attentions with increasing pressure and speed. Bryce let his head fall back and his eyes close. A lot of the time, watching did as much to get him off as the actual touch. Not with Chelsea, though. She looked absolutely exquisite, but he meant what he'd said. She was damn good and it was taking considerable effort not to come immediately.

Despite those efforts, the quiver in his abdomen took hold before he could stop it. He slid a hand into her hair and let the fire spread through him like a shot of whiskey. The gesture seemed to spur her on. She rode the orgasm with him, head bobbing as his hips bucked.

When the surge of it subsided, leaving him loose and limber and satisfied, she crawled up the length of his body and curled against his shoulder. "That was hot."

He nodded slowly. "Massive understatement."

"Not now necessarily, but I'm open to pointers." She kissed his bicep. "If you have any."

He let out a happy sigh, sated but also seen in a way the last few women he dated never seemed to manage. "Only a request."

She lifted her head and regarded him with curiosity. "What's that?"

"That this, all of this, isn't a one-time thing." Not something he'd normally say right after hooking up with a woman for the first time. But he could already tell Chelsea wouldn't be like other women. He wanted more. More tonight and a whole lot more nights just like this.

She smiled, as though she'd been expecting something bad and his admission was a pleasant surprise. "Tonight or in general?"

He nodded. "Yes."

Chelsea licked her lips. "I think that could be arranged."

He rolled, covering her body once more. "Oh, good."

She tapped out a little after midnight, citing concerns of death by orgasm and needing to use her hip flexors to walk the next day. Bryce acquiesced, confident it truly wouldn't be a one-night thing. He extended his arm and she snuggled into the crook of his shoulder. "How annoyed are you going to be when my alarm goes off at five thirty?" he asked.

Chelsea groaned. "Why five for the love of all that is good and holy thirty?"

"Because forty-five-minute commute. But you're right. Six. Because being in bed with you is a totally legit reason to skip my run."

Chelsea groaned again.

"Would you rather I didn't stay?"

"No, no." She gave him a squeeze. "I definitely want you to stay. I was groaning over the fact that you're a runner."

He chuckled. "Fatal flaw?"

"Just my own baggage."

"I promise I'll never make you run," he said, even as he wondered who had, or who'd tried.

"I'll hold you to it." She gave him a kiss, which seemed like a way of closing the conversation more than starting one, and flicked off the lamp next to the bed.

He wanted to say more but didn't want to poke at something sensitive, or imply a can of worms that may not exist. So he kissed the top of her head and pulled her tighter against him and went with the sure bet. "Good night, gorgeous."

She wiggled against him deliciously. "Good night, handsome."

CHAPTER TWELVE

Despite grousing about Bryce's six o'clock alarm, Chelsea woke before it went off. She found herself half on her stomach and half draped over Bryce's naked torso. She'd never been a sleep cuddler, thanks to one too many comments about her limbs being heavy. But this? A girl could get used to this.

If by this, she meant anything and everything to do with Bryce.

Chelsea sighed. Then she stretched and smiled and indulged in a few flashbacks from the night before. Like how Bryce picked her up like it was nothing. The way his hands held her hair while she sucked him off. And, dear God, the feeling of him inside her—those long, strong fingers and the fact that he knew exactly what to do with them.

She clenched her thighs at the memory, which promptly made her wonder when she'd last had sex good enough to leave her sore. Doing the math could easily leave her depressed. Fortunately, being sex sated and still in bed with Bryce seemed to make her immune.

She'd almost forgotten it could be that good. Or, maybe, it was good with Bryce in ways it never quite managed to be with other partners. Which was dramatic, probably, but whatever. What mattered this morning was that Bryce was hot. And really good in bed. And, best of all, completely into her.

She could revel in that without getting precious about it. Acknowledge it was the first time in ages she wasn't overworked, overtired, and overstressed. Give a nod to the slower pace that came with being in Duchesne, even while filming a show. Be rational and sensible about how all that played together.

And maybe, rational or not, talk Bryce into a quickie before he left.

"Why do you look like the cat that ate the canary?" Bryce asked. His look of sleepy amusement only reinforced that plan as a winning strategy.

"Because I'm having impure thoughts."

"Why are they called impure thoughts? I think sex is one of the purest things humans can do with each other."

She lifted her head. "Because our culture is deeply rooted in Puritanical values that privilege deprivation and suffering over pleasure."

"Right, right. Damn Puritans. I'm glad at least some of us have shed that mantle." He kissed the top of her head. "I liked getting pure with you last night."

"I did, too." Although the desire for a quickie didn't abandon her entirely, the snuggly banter had lots to recommend it.

"It was okay, then?"

She liked that he would check in after the fact, not simply assume. "It was a hell of a lot better than okay."

"Oh, good."

"And you?" she asked, also not wanting to take anything for granted.

"Spectacular." He gave her a squeeze. "And I don't throw that word around lightly."

She smiled, more charmed than the moment warranted maybe but not caring enough to check herself. She traced the line of his scars. "When did you have top surgery?"

"When I was nineteen. The summer after my freshman year of college."

She tried to conjure memories from senior year. She and Bryce hadn't run in the same circles, mainly because she didn't run in any circles. But Duchesne High—with its graduating class of fifty-three that year—left little room for anonymity. Bryce hadn't openly started his transition, but he'd definitely started to change. She'd noticed and done her best to ignore it, along with all the other feelings and desires she didn't know what to do with. "Was it hard?"

"What? The surgery? Or transitioning in general?"

She looked from his chest to his eyes. "Either. Both. Neither if you'd rather not talk about it."

"I won't say it was easy because it's not. But I had supportive parents and Kate and decent insurance that covered the financial part.

I was never not Bryce with my college friends and professors, so that helped, too."

"I'm sorry we weren't friends then. In high school, I mean. I was so focused on keeping my head down and getting out as quickly as possible." It didn't feel selfish or self-absorbed at the time. She knew it closed her off from having friends, had decided to be okay with that. It only occurred to her now that it also closed her off from being a friend.

"I'm sorry, too. Mostly because I always thought you were pretty."

She propped on an elbow. "Stop."

"I won't. My hormones might have been raging and confused, but I wasn't dead. I would have to be dead not to notice you."

Life could be so strange sometimes. "I noticed you, too. But I couldn't make it make sense in my poor repressed little mind."

"Maybe I should be the one asking you about things being hard."

He looked at her with such tenderness it put a tremble in her chest. She sat up. "You absolutely should not."

Bryce sat up as well, but the compassion on his face didn't fade. "Hey, no pressure."

Realizing her refusal sounded harsher than she meant, she went for a smile. "Maybe sometime."

His expression made it clear he didn't believe her.

"I mean it." She'd done enough years of therapy that she could, even if she'd rather not. "For now, you need to get to work, and I should at least send you out the door with coffee."

Bryce waved her off. "You make exceptional coffee, but I have to go home anyway to shower and change, and I keep a pitcher of cold brew in the fridge."

She frowned before she could stop herself.

"Maybe if I play my cards right, we could do this again and I could bring that change of clothes with me. Then I'd have time to stay for a cup in bed."

Desire slicked through her, instant and hot, wiping away any weightiness lingering in the conversation. "I mean, it would be a kindness to my bruised hostess sensibilities."

Bryce made a tsking sound. "Can't have that. What are you doing tonight?"

Was it as easy as that? Apparently so. "Making dinner for you if you'll let me."

"I feel bad having you cook for me so much, especially if I'm not returning the favor."

"I won't have the bandwidth when we start filming again." She grimaced. "If we start filming again."

"You absolutely will. So I'll say yes if you promise you'll let me cook for you and take you out and bring over takeout when that happens."

Her stomach did a flip at the sweetness of his offer. But also because it implied they'd be spending more time together. Implied he wanted to spend more time with her. "I agree to these terms."

"Good because, sadly, I should get going." As if on cue, his alarm went off. He snagged his phone and silenced it, then kissed her before climbing out of bed.

She indulged in the view of his backside for a moment before joining him, slipping on a summer robe while he was in the bathroom. She went to the kitchen to start coffee. He might not have time for a cup, but she did. And as much as she might like to spend the day lounging and basking in the three orgasms he'd coaxed from her, she had things to do.

He came into the kitchen wearing his clothes from the night before, and she abandoned the coffee pot to walk him to the door. He kissed her like he wasn't in a hurry. "I'll see you later."

She watched until his truck disappeared down the street before closing the door with a sigh. Since she had a video chat with Jada already scheduled for ten, she resisted dropping hints—or more—over text. Instead, she indulged in a long shower, complete with her early aughts power jams and an all-over exfoliation. Sure, she'd wished she'd had the time to do that before going to bed with Bryce, but he hadn't seemed to mind her imperfections. She clutched the loofah against her breasts and closed her eyes.

It wasn't that he didn't mind. It was that he seemed to find her perfectly attractive, imperfections and all. Stretch marks, cellulite, all of it. It was funny. She could get on the body positivity, self-love soapbox six ways from Sunday, but it never failed to catch her off guard when someone—especially someone who looked like Bryce—found her sexy.

She resumed scrubbing. No point picking it apart. No, she spent years doing that and it never did her any good. Ruined a few things before they even got off the ground and didn't spare her the disappointment wrought by the occasional douchebag. This time would be different. This time, she would simply enjoy. Enjoy and, hopefully, enjoy again and again.

❖

Bryce strode into the hardware store, iced coffees in each hand. He found Kate at the register, ringing up a plethora of plumbing fittings and connectors for Ralph Bourgeois, his parents' next-door neighbor. He lifted one in Kate's direction. "Hey, Mr. Ralph."

Ralph looked up and smiled. "Hey, hey. If it isn't the second most famous member of the Cormier clan."

He set Kate's coffee down and gave a nod in response to her mouthed "thank you." "Who's the first?"

"I'm thinking that title goes to Miss Harper. No offense, son, but that girl's got sparkle."

"None taken. And no argument. I forget people have, you know, seen the show." Or that the two-second splices of each of them in the opening credits would even be noticed.

"Wait till you see her episode," Kate said.

"We can't wait." Ralph slapped a hand on the counter. "It's all Marsha's been talking about. *First You Make a Roux* this and Chelsea that."

Kate took a sip of her coffee and gestured with the cup. "But he's already gotten a pie out of the deal, so he's not complaining."

"No complaints whatsoever. I think our little town is more than deserving of some fuss and fanfare." He accepted the canvas tote Kate had filled with his purchases. "If only someone from one of those house shows wanted to come take care of the leak under my kitchen sink."

Kate swiped his credit card and handed it back to him. "It's good to have dreams."

"True story, young lady. Y'all be good and I'll see you 'round." He offered a parting wave, leaving Kate and Bryce alone at the front of the store.

Kate picked up her coffee, this time letting out a satisfied sigh after taking a drink. "God, this is good. Thank you."

"My pleasure, young lady." Bryce tipped an imaginary hat.

"Do you think he'll call us that until we're sixty?"

He shrugged. "Probably. Just like we'll call him Mr. Ralph until we're sixty."

Kate chuckled. "Old habits, I suppose. Anyway, to what do I owe this pleasure?"

"I had a doctor's appointment, so I left work early." At Kate's raised brow, he added, "Routine bloodwork."

She smiled. "I'm glad you don't have to be nagged about that sort of thing."

It was required for his T prescription, but he was enough of a health nut that he'd probably do it anyway. "Are you, though?"

Kate didn't miss a beat. "Of course. There are far more entertaining things to nag you about."

"Such as?" It was invitation as much as challenge. He'd take whatever she dished out and give it back twice over.

"Hmm." Kate made a show of considering her options.

"You snooze, you lose, sister."

"Not snoozing, just choosing." She rapped her knuckles on the counter. "Eh, let's go for the big one."

"What's the big one?" Not that he needed to ask. He knew. He always knew. When it came to Kate, there was little she enjoyed more than giving him a hard time about his love life.

She laced her fingers together, as though insulted by the question. "How's Chelsea?"

"She's fine. Or at least she was the last time I saw her." Naked save for a flimsy robe and sexy as all get-out.

"And when was that?"

He'd walked right into it, but he didn't really mind. He was more excited about Chelsea than he had been about a woman in a while. The sex, obviously. But more than the sex, too. The possibilities. The fact that she got him. And wanted him exactly as he was. Oh, and the fact that she already lived in Duchesne. Honestly, he knew it was too soon to use phrases like "meant to be," but his brain already had.

"Uh, earth to Bryce."

"I'm sorry, could you repeat the question?" Not stalling, just making her work for it.

Kate folded her arms, indignant on principle if nothing else. "When did you last see Chelsea, Bryce? Because I'm guessing it wasn't yesterday when you left my house."

"Oh. Right. This morning when I left her bed to go to work."

"You didn't."

"I did. I couldn't very well call in sick to snuggle and have sex all day." Though the idea had merit.

Kate's shoulders dropped. "That's not what I meant."

He grinned. "I know. But I spilled the beans pretty easy there, so I'm entitled."

"You do look awfully pleased with yourself. I figured it was the caffeine." She looked him up and down. "I take it things went well."

"They did." Not that his sister needed explicit details. "Fantastic, in fact. Like, in every way. Chelsea is amazing."

Kate's eyes narrowed slightly, the way they always did. She'd heard him say something similar enough times that she brought a healthy dose of skepticism to the table when he started seeing someone new.

"I'm not hearing wedding bells, if that's what you're worried about. It's just, I don't know. She's different."

Kate nodded, a small show of concession. "She does seem great. And she's from here, so that counts for something."

"But she's also seen more, done more, than if she'd never left." Professionally, sure, but personally, too.

"Hey, some of us never left and turned out okay," Kate said.

"And you are exceptional, in every possible way."

Mollified, Kate smirked. "I do like her. And I like that she's already spent time with us, with the family."

It was his turn to smirk. "And if that doesn't send her running for the hills, nothing will."

"Ha ha."

"I'm serious, though. She gets the small-town thing. Even better, she gets our small town." And why he loved it and why he'd chosen to build his life in it.

"I know it's a top-ten criteria for you." Kate sighed her big sister sigh. "Just don't let it be the only criteria."

He frowned. "I wouldn't."

"I'm not saying it's going to go south."

"What are you saying?" he asked even though he already knew.

Kate chewed her lip. "Maybe give it a hot minute before getting your hopes up."

"Yeah, yeah." He didn't have the heart to tell her that ship had sailed.

"Like, she is from here and she's here now, but she also left for more than a decade."

"But she bought a house and the whole premise of her show is here." Maybe not a rock-solid reason for her to stay, but a hell of a lot more than a couple of his recent girlfriends. Girlfriends who had, in fact, not stayed.

"Hey, don't get defensive."

"I'm not defensive." He scowled.

Kate blinked.

"Okay, fine. I won't get defensive and I won't get my hopes up, either. Am I at least allowed to revel in the fact that I got laid last night?"

By a woman who didn't need a trans guy tutorial.

"You can always revel in getting laid. Especially if you bring me iced coffee to do it." She punctuated the statement with a long swig.

"Even if it's decaf?"

Kate eyed the cup and set it on the counter with a sigh. Limiting caffeine was proving a harder pregnancy commitment than giving up alcohol. "Even if it's decaf."

He tapped his now-empty cup to hers. "Deal."

CHAPTER THIRTEEN

Chelsea's head pivoted at the knocking sound. "Someone's at the door. Can I call you back?"

Jada let out a squeak. "You mean like an unannounced visitor? Yikes. But yes. Hope it's a delivery. Love you."

"Love you, too." She ended the call and hurried to the front door, wondering if it might be her mother and also hoping it wasn't.

"Hi." Kate stood on the other side, offering a slightly sheepish smile.

"Hi." Chelsea returned the smile, hoping it read as welcoming more than worried. "Is everything okay?"

Kate winced. "You didn't see my text, did you?"

Panic swelled. "I didn't. I was on the phone with Jada. What is it? What's wrong?"

Kate did one of those back and forth gestures with her hands. "Oh, God. Nothing, nothing. I texted you to say I was being that obnoxious friend who drops by unannounced."

"Oh." The panic subsided, but confusion set in.

"I come bearing gifts, at least." Kate lifted the jars she held in each hand. "I pickled okra this weekend."

"Ooh. Thank you. And sorry. Come on in." She stepped back and Kate followed her inside.

"I really am sorry for dropping by unannounced. But I was hoping to pick your brain while Harper is at school, and I have work in a bit and it's kind of urgent. So, here I am." Kate rolled her eyes and shrugged.

"Honestly, I miss the casual drop-in. Especially from people who aren't my mother."

Kate laughed. "That's fair. Are you sure it's an okay time?"

"It really is. I just poured a glass of cold brew. Can I offer you one? Or something else?" She glanced at Kate's emerging baby bump. "Are you off caffeine?"

"Cold brew sounds fantastic, and I'm allowed one more cup for the day." Kate followed her into the kitchen. "I love it, but I'm terrible at remembering to filter it before it becomes rocket fuel, so I'm not allowed to make it at home."

It was her turn to laugh. "I've been guilty of that myself a few times."

"I confess the pitcher of cold brew in the fridge is the main reason I show up at Bryce's unannounced. I promise I won't inflict the same on you."

She imagined having friends who'd pop over to drop off treats or raid her fridge. It was the sort of thing she hadn't had since college. She hadn't expected to find it in Duchesne, hadn't been looking to, but she warmed to the possibility. "For the record, I will always trade coffee for pickles."

"Noted."

Chelsea poured a glass, adding simple syrup and a splash of milk at Kate's enthusiastic nod, and gestured to the kitchen table. "So, what's up?"

"Harper's birthday party is this weekend. Well, parties. Slumber party Saturday night with her friends from school and family party Sunday."

"Okay." She couldn't fathom what that had to do with her, save perhaps a last-minute invitation. Or maybe invite and request to bring something.

"We were all set to do 'make your own pizzas' for the girls Saturday night because it's fun and easy and everyone can have what they like, but Harper has decided she wants something fancy." Kate threw up a pair of air quotes. "More sophisticated."

"Ah." She chuckled at the memory of her own childhood longings for such things.

"And I think we're friends enough that I can say I hold you at least partially responsible, so I'm hoping you'll help come up with something that won't make me want to tear my hair out or down a bottle of wine trying to pull it off."

She might not spend a lot of time entertaining, but she spent plenty of time thinking about it. "You've come to the right place."

Half an hour later, they'd come up with what Chelsea would call pizza party, elevated. Snazzier toppings, individual crusts that could be baked ahead of time, and voila: flatbreads. Old school cheese and pepperoni would cover the pickier eaters and things like pesto, prosciutto, and figs would make even the chaperones feel fancy.

"Seriously, thank you," Kate said. "This will be perfect. I'm not sure why I couldn't come up with that myself. I blame pregnancy brain. I don't know if it's really a thing, but I'm going with it because I've been kind of a mess and it makes me feel better to have a reason."

"I totally think it's a thing. It takes a lot of energy to grow a human. That energy has to come from somewhere."

Kate's brow furrowed. "Thanks. Sutton has been super sweet, but I worry she's being indulgent."

"And why shouldn't she be?" In her mind, the partner carrying the baby deserved to be spoiled every which way.

"Did Bryce tell you our history?"

"Some." She assumed he wouldn't have if it wasn't public knowledge, but it still felt weird to admit.

Kate blew out a breath. "Sutton has this thing about making up for everything she missed the first time I was pregnant. Only we weren't together then and I'd majorly fucked up, so it doesn't feel fair that she should be carrying around any guilt or baggage or whatever from that."

Chelsea tried to imagine being in either of their shoes back then, and her heart broke a little for both of them. Fortunately, they'd managed to forge something real and solid in the now. Something that made them both happy. "She might just enjoy taking care of you."

"Yeah." Kate smiled but then swiped at her eyes. "Damn hormones."

If they hadn't crossed the line into really being friends before, they had now. "From what I can tell, you take care of each other. It gives the single among us hope."

"You sound like Bryce."

There were worse things in her book, though it hit her she'd been close to sharing the longings of her heart with the sister of the guy she'd just started sleeping with. "Is that a compliment or an insult?"

"Depends on the day. Speaking of you and Bryce." The look on Kate's face was anything but subtle. "You and Bryce."

"Yep." Was she supposed to say more?

"Things going well?"

Pregnancy brain her ass. How did Kate manage to be so pointed and so vague at the same time? "I think so. I'd say so."

"He seems to think so. Or at least that's the sense I get. And I've got a pretty good handle on him." Kate winked. "Though not as good a handle as I think you've been getting."

If her brain had been a gym rat on a treadmill, it would have tripped, done a faceplant, and been deposited in a heap off the end. "Did he tell you we slept together?"

Kate smiled. "Not on purpose. I backed him into a corner and he's not one for lying."

She frowned before she could help it. "Oh."

"I figured it was only a matter of time. He merely confirmed that said matter of time had passed," Kate said.

"Really?" She'd already told Jada, so maybe it shouldn't be all that shocking. Only Jada wasn't knocking on Bryce's door to discuss the situation.

Kate's eyes got big. "Not because he hooks up with a lot of people. I meant, he's been into you since you got back to town, and seeing you with him at the house the other day made me think the feeling was mutual."

"Ah." Should she confirm that, since Kate already knew what had come of it?

"Don't get me wrong. I think it's great. He doesn't always have the best taste in women as far as I'm concerned." Kate rolled her eyes like they were in on a private joke.

"Thank you?"

"Yes. Sorry. I meant that you seem like an exception to that." Kate paused, pursed her lips. She rolled her eyes again, though this time it seemed directed at herself. "He's a good egg, you know? He deserves someone who gets that, appreciates it."

It was hard to tell if Kate meant the comment as a pep talk or a daddy with a shotgun and a shovel insinuation. Either way, she couldn't decide whether to be offended or flattered. "I do appreciate him." Realization dawned. "All of him."

Kate nodded. "Good."

Now that she understood it wasn't a matter of her intentions, but rather her character, she relaxed. "Is he this protective of you?"

"He can be. Though, mostly, he just gives me a hard time."

She'd always wanted a sibling, hard times and all. "I don't suppose those are mutually exclusive."

Kate smiled, all affection now. "Good point."

"Can I ask you something?"

The smile became a smirk. "Considering I pried into your sex life, it only feels fair."

"Did you even need help with Harper's party?" she asked.

Kate tipped her head back and forth. "I mean, I probably could have come up with something, but I'm one hundred percent using your idea."

"So, not really." She respected Kate for telling the truth.

"How about, not mutually exclusive?" Kate eyed her hopefully.

"I can live with that." Since it felt like they'd become better friends in the process, she added, "The question is whether or not I tell Bryce that I got the visit from the overbearing big sister."

"How many jars of pickles for your silence?"

Chelsea laughed. "I'm sure we can come to some agreeable terms."

Kate stood from the table. "I'm telling Bryce to invite you to Harper's family party. If you're not busy, I hope you'll come."

Funny how that sort of thing always had to mean something. Not that it didn't mean anything now, it was—what? Easy. Bryce, his family, all of it. Hell, just being in Duchesne was turning out to be a whole lot easier than she'd allowed herself to hope. "If he invites me, I'll be there."

"I have no doubt he will, so I'll see you on Sunday." Kate picked up her purse and made her way to the door. "Thanks for the coffee. And for the talk. Talks."

Chelsea opened it. "Thanks for stopping by."

Kate offered a parting wave and Chelsea closed the door behind her. She sucked in a deep breath, blew it out slowly. She'd mostly wrapped her head around taking things with Bryce to the next level. The sex, but also the fact that they seemed to be slipping seamlessly into relationship territory. Was she really ready for all the rest? Only one way to find out.

❖

Bryce opened the passenger door for Chelsea, happy that she seemed to be getting comfortable with the gesture. "You didn't have to get a gift."

She spared him a withering stare before climbing in. "Yeah, I'm going to crash a kid's birthday party and show up empty-handed."

"One, you were invited so it's not crashing. Two, don't let Harper catch you referring to her as a kid."

"Okay, fine. Two points for you. I'd still never dream of showing up without something."

Bryce closed the door and went around to his side. "So, what did you get her?"

Chelsea chewed her lip in this really adorable way. "I'll tell you if you promise not to make fun."

"Hmm. Tough call. I'm not sure I can promise that until I know what you got." Though, short of a baby doll or something comparably age-inappropriate, he wouldn't. He was a firm believer in the thought counting for a lot.

"A set of prep bowls and silicone spatulas." Chelsea narrowed her eyes, as though scrutinizing his features for any sign of mocking.

"You know, for a kid like Harper, that's pretty on point."

Chelsea smiled, not quite smug but not far off. "I thought we weren't supposed to refer to her as a kid."

"Oh, you can refer to her as one, just not to her face."

She laughed. "Touché. Anyway. When we were on set together, she was kind of obsessed with the mise en place. I figured she'd get a kick out of being able to do her own as she's learning to cook. They're also great for sprinkles and stuff when you're decorating cookies or cupcakes or whatever."

"I take it back. That gift is completely on point." And it melted his heart a little that Chelsea would pay attention to details like that and remember them.

"I hope Kate doesn't find them fussy and a nuisance."

He grinned. "She won't."

"How do you know?"

"Because Harper learned how to do dishes way before she got run of the kitchen privileges." Just like their parents had trained the two of them.

"I should have known."

He pulled into Kate's driveway and put the truck in park but didn't cut the engine. "What do you mean?"

"Only that Kate strikes me as really smart. And a damn good parent."

He reached across the bench seat and gave her thigh a squeeze.

"Compliment her parenting to your heart's content. Just don't call her smart in front of me or she'll be insufferable about it."

Chelsea shook her head. "Y'all and your sibling rivalry."

"We'd all but kill for each other. But it doesn't mean we haven't also all but killed each other in the process."

"Right."

They headed inside. His parents were already there, along with two of Harper's cousins who'd stayed over the night before for the slumber party. Technically, Chelsea had met them—his parents—at the Fourth of July party, so he didn't think much about introductions. Chelsea, on the other hand, was almost formally polite, and uncomfortably bashful when they gushed over her being there.

Bryce searched the room for a diversion, but before he could, Kate swept in and asked her for a hand in the kitchen. Chelsea pounced on the out, smiling profusely but hightailing out of the conversation as fast as one of his students caught lying about whether they were going to class.

"She's truly lovely," his mom whispered when Chelsea was safely out of earshot.

He sighed. "She is. I'm not sure why she's so nervous, though. She's met you before."

Mom gave him a gentle nudge with her elbow. "Yes, but she wasn't your girlfriend then."

"I'm not a hundred percent sure she's my girlfriend now." Though he'd certainly like her to be.

That got him a knowing look. "She's here, isn't she?"

"Well, yes." And there was the whole date in New Orleans, epic sex, staying over three nights in one week part. Not that he planned to advertise that to his mama.

"And Kate mentioned you two had, you know."

Really, Kate? "Of course she did."

She patted his arm. "Oh, don't worry. Not in a TMI way."

What slayed him more: his mother knowing he and Chelsea had slept together or having her use TMI correctly and in reference to his sex life? Hard to say.

"What's TMI?" His dad, who'd stepped away to pour himself a glass of sweet tea, rejoined them.

Mama shot him a look of exasperation. "It means too much information."

He gave her a bland look in return. "I know what it means. I wanted to know who you're TMI-ing today."

Bryce snorted in spite of himself, and Mama narrowed her eyes. "It's a noun, Chuck. Not a verb."

"I think you can make anything a verb now. Can't you, Bryce? Like adulting."

He'd take a slang lesson over a conversation about his sex life any day. "I do believe that's the case."

"Fine." Mama huffed. "I was simply assuring Bryce that I wouldn't TMI him about the fact that he and Chelsea have, you know."

"Ah." Dad seemed neither surprised nor bothered by this declaration.

Bryce pinched the bridge of his nose. "Okay, yes. We're dating now. I'm still not sure about calling her my girlfriend, but it might explain why she was a little skittish around y'all. Hell, at this point I'm feeling skittish."

"That's just silly. We ―"

"Where's the birthday girl?" Uncle Loic called from the front door instead of a hello.

Bryce glanced heavenward. Saved by the big family who didn't believe in doorbells. Mama and Daddy went over to say hello and he scooted to the kitchen to check on Chelsea. Having a task and a minute to herself seemed to have done the trick. He considered sharing the exchange with his mother but decided it might make things worse rather than better. Fortunately, a flood of relatives arrived, bringing too much noise and chaos for Chelsea to be the center of anyone's attention.

Which wasn't to say Chelsea went unnoticed. No, Duchesne was a small enough town that Chelsea being on TV was big news, whether people were into cooking shows or not. She seemed to bask in that attention, though. Which made sense. It had everything to do with her accomplishments and didn't get too personal. He fared better with that sort of praise himself.

The party passed in a blur, as big family parties often did. Harper had enough kid in her still to be genuinely delighted by the presents and singing and being the queen of the hour. Chelsea's gift proved a hit, as he knew it would, giving the new softball glove and bat he'd picked out a run for its money.

When guests began to trickle out, he started to excuse them both, but Chelsea had already volunteered for cleanup duty and stood happily at the sink rinsing Solo cups for the recycling bin. By the time he drove Chelsea home, it was nearly six and he was torn between calling it an early night and asking Chelsea if she wanted some company for the evening.

"I know you have work in the morning, but do you want to hang out? Have a chill evening in, maybe?"

He smiled. "You took the words right out of my mouth."

She smiled in return, tucked her hair behind her ear. The move managed to be shy and suggestive at the same time. "And since we seem to be doing this, I wondered if you might want to be my date for the NOLA Food and Wine Festival."

He wanted to ask exactly what she meant by "this," but it was enough in the general direction of what he had in mind that he didn't want to change the subject. "I'd be honored. It's soon, right?"

"Next weekend. I have to be there the whole time. The network is setting me up in a hotel and I'd love you to stay with me, but I understand if you have other things to do. The opening night gala is the main thing." She tipped her head back and forth. "The main thing I'd love a date for, I mean."

It might make him sound boring and a little desperate to say yes to the whole weekend, but the prospect of Chelsea, what he imagined would be a relatively posh hotel, plus two days of foodie heaven was about the most fun his imagination could conjure. "I'd love to join you for the whole weekend. I'm sure you'll have appearances and stuff and I promise I'm capable of entertaining myself when you're busy."

"Yeah?"

"I can probably swing Friday off, too, so we can head up whenever." LSU had a rare Friday home game instead of Saturday. Students would be tailgating and his office would be dead.

"Really?" Chelsea looked as giddy as Harper with her pile of presents in front of her.

"Do we get to dress up?"

She wrinkled her nose. "It's black tie. Is that okay?"

He'd never want to wear a suit and tie to work every day, but swanky on occasion had its appeal. And he could count on one hand the number of times he'd had the chance to wear a tux. Well, two maybe, given the number of his friends who'd gotten married in the last couple of years. But still. "Definitely okay."

She did this little back and forth bouncing thing in the passenger seat. It made him glad she'd asked him to stay the night. Or, she'd implied it at least. Either way, he was in. At the rate things were going, he'd be in for just about anything that involved more time with Chelsea.

Best of all? It was looking like she felt the same about him.

CHAPTER FOURTEEN

Chelsea cruised along Highway 90, trying—and failing—to remember a time she'd been in a better mood. "Okay, since I'm commandeering your entire weekend, you get to pick where we go to lunch."

"Yeah, but I picked the last place we went to eat, so by rights, it's your turn." Bryce offered an affable shrug.

What a delightfully silly non-argument to have. "I mean, I've been NOLA deprived for a long time, so if you're abdicating your say in the matter, I'll take it."

"I happily defer to whatever sounds good to you."

Well, that was fun. "Watch out now. That's the kind of thing a girl could get used to."

He gave her a quizzical look. "Are you not used to getting your way?"

She chuckled even as her grip on the steering wheel tightened. "Loaded question much?"

Bryce laughed in earnest. "I didn't mean it to be. But now I want to know."

"I'm mostly kidding." At least since she left home and lived on her own.

"Are you, though?"

"You're worse than Jada." She released the steering wheel long enough to point at him. "And that's saying something."

Bryce pouted like a little boy. "I'm curious is all. I want to know everything you want to share."

The nice thing was, she believed him. It helped that the pout came off playful more than passive-aggressive. "I'd say I didn't get my way much growing up and maybe I overcompensated as an adult."

"Overcompensated?"

She didn't relish having this conversation, but better to own her shit now than have it spill out later. "I told you my last girlfriend cheated because I was a workaholic, right?"

Bryce offered an encouraging smile. "You mentioned it."

"I wasn't only a workaholic. I was stubborn about it, to the point of being rigid." She refused to admit it at the time, but it was easier in hindsight, when her pride had time to settle.

"Were you rigid or just really passionate about your work?" Bryce asked.

She blew out a breath. "I told myself I was passionate, but I was a jerk about it. And it had more to do with digging my heels in, and not answering to anyone but myself, than any noble pursuit."

"I don't know. I think figuring out how to answer to yourself can be noble. Especially if it's not something you were allowed, much less encouraged, to do."

"You don't have to be so unflinchingly nice, you know." It made her even more antsy than his unflinching assertions that she was beautiful.

Bryce frowned. "I'm not."

"You are."

"Maybe you need to adjust your standards of how people treat you."

She curled in on herself as though wounded, then pretended to pull a knife out of her gut and hand it to him. "Here, you might need this later."

He took her outstretched hand and brought it to his lips. "I'll apologize for poking at you, but I stand behind the sentiment."

"You don't need to apologize. It wouldn't feel like a knife to the gut if it wasn't true." She'd yet to find that middle ground that would make her a mature, well-adjusted adult, but she was working on it. Having some say over her schedule helped. So, ironically, did living in Duchesne.

"You deserve someone who is invested in your dreams, who wants to support you chasing them."

"I do." She knew that now. "But I have to be willing to offer the same, and to navigate compromises along the way."

He kissed her knuckles again. "That's something we could all stand to work on."

"Yeah?" From where she sat, he seemed to have his end of the equation all sorted out.

"I've had more than one relationship end because I wasn't willing to flex on where I live or the kind of life I want to have."

It was her turn to offer him an encouraging smile. "That sounds pretty essential."

"I guess that's one way of looking at it." Despite the agreement, he got a faraway look in his eyes.

"Well, here's to finding the happy middle." Because looking on the bright side felt less daunting than picking apart all the ways it was too easy to fuck up relationships.

He nodded, like he agreed with her words but like he sensed and shared the stuff she hadn't said aloud, too. And then he changed the subject. Whether he needed that or simply thought she might, she didn't know. But she'd take it.

They rolled into New Orleans in time for a late lunch. She decided to go old school with her pick, which meant chargrilled oysters at Drago's. The perfect balance of a lot and not too much, which seemed fitting given their conversation on the drive.

By the time they checked into the hotel, it was time to get ready for the gala. Well, get ready while having a quickie in the shower. And maybe one after the shower. She hadn't intended such a hedonistic day, but as she did her hair and makeup and her nerves began to ratchet, she realized it was exactly what she'd needed.

Bryce got dressed quickly and situated himself on the small sofa with the LSU game, promising to stay out of her way. She appreciated the few minutes to herself to do some breathing exercises and remind herself she'd been to events like this before. And even if she wouldn't be utterly anonymous this time—didn't want to be—it wasn't like she'd turned into some A-lister that would be swarmed by paparazzi.

She stepped into her dress and slipped it up her body. "Could I trouble you to zip me?"

He clicked off the television without hesitation and stood. "Only if I get to unzip you at the end of the night."

She turned her back to him and smiled over her shoulder. "You better or I'm going to have to call housekeeping to get me out of this thing."

Bryce eased the zipper up, then trailed his fingertips over the exposed skin of her shoulders. When she turned back to give him a proper view, he let out a low whistle. "Oh, no. You won't be wanting for people looking to get you out of that dress."

It didn't make sense to blush, but she did. "Thank you."

"I mean it. Promise me I'm the one who gets to take you home at the end of the night. Well, back to your hotel at least."

"Now you're being ridiculous."

He cocked his head and looked her up and down once more. "Because you're classy and not the sort of woman who'd abandon her date halfway through the night. But only because of that."

Chelsea put a hand on his chest and kissed him lightly. "You are so good for my ego."

He kissed her back. "And being on your arm is good for mine."

She glanced at the clock next to the bed just as the room phone rang. She snagged it. "Hello."

"Ms. Boudreaux. Your car is here."

"Thank you." She hung up and turned to Bryce. "Ready?"

He'd already snagged the glittery black clutch she'd spent way too much money on. He held it out to her. "At your service."

❖

Chelsea's heel bounced, which in turn made her entire leg vibrate. Bryce reached across the wide leather bench seat and set a hand on her thigh. "Nervous?"

She looked at her leg, then at him. "Sorry."

He gave her knee a squeeze. "No need to apologize. This is an adventure for me, but it's a public appearance for you. That's a big deal."

She took a deep breath and blew it out slowly, making him wonder if she was counting to ten. "You're right. It is a big deal. I've been to things like this dozens of times, but no one has ever known who I am."

"And now they will." He wanted to tell her he was proud but wasn't sure he'd earned that right, at least not yet.

"I'm pretty sure most won't." Chelsea lifted both hands. "And I'm totally okay with that."

"But some will. You'll have your picture taken." When she wrinkled her nose, he continued, "Because even if you're not famous yet, you'll probably be the most beautiful woman there."

She grabbed his hand and held on. "You're a liar but thank you."

"Well, I'll think you're the most beautiful woman there."

She smirked then, which he took as a win. "You don't have to sweet-talk me. We're sharing a room, so you already know I'm going home with you at the end of the night."

He studied her, still in wonder that a woman could be as gorgeous as Chelsea was—and as confident—and be so squirrelly when it came to compliments. "Is that why you think I tell you you're beautiful?"

Her playful shrug wasn't a dismissal exactly but made it clear she'd rather be talking about anything else. Since she was already nervous, he made a mental note rather than pressing it as they pulled into the queue of cars snaking up the drive to the Riverwalk. When they finally reached the front of the line, a young guy in a tuxedo opened the door and held out a hand. Chelsea took it and elegantly stepped from the car. Bryce scooted across the seat and extricated himself, thinking it was one thing to get picked up in a Town Car and a whole extra level of weird to get dropped off.

Chelsea thanked the guy before turning back to Bryce. He could tell the nerves hadn't gone entirely, but her eyes shone with pure delight. "Will you do the red carpet with me?"

"Huh?" He registered the words, their meaning, but his brain failed to compute.

Chelsea pointed. Sure enough, an actual red carpet had been set up, complete with a massive, logo-emblazoned backdrop and a line of press clicking their cameras and trying to get the attention of whoever had stopped to smile and pose.

"Oh."

"You don't have to. I just thought it would be less terrifying than doing it by myself."

Part of him found the whole thing absurd—celebrity in general, but also that the food world had its own version of it. But that part didn't stand a chance against Chelsea's playful smile and the wide, bright-eyed look that didn't quite veil legit panic. "Of course I'll do it with you. They won't care I'm a nobody?"

"You're not a nobody to me." She grabbed his hand. "Besides, most of them won't know who I am either, and it will be quick."

She wasn't lying. The whole thing couldn't have taken more than two minutes. But between the hot lights and flashing cameras, the smiling and trying to follow Chelsea's gaze at the sound of her name, he emerged at the other end more than a little dazed. "Whoa."

Chelsea blew out a breath but grinned from ear to ear. "Yeah."

He blinked, willing the spots to clear from his vision. "You liked it, didn't you?"

She shrugged. "I mean, I like what it symbolizes more, but yeah."

"I'm glad." Glad she was happy, at least. If he never had to do that again, it would be too soon.

"Thank you for being a good sport. Come on, let's get you a drink." Chelsea delivered, getting him a pint of Abita Amber from one of the bars before snagging herself a glass of champagne from a roaming waiter. They mingled, chatting with everyone from local food bloggers to a reporter from *Q*, the queer magazine. Mostly, Chelsea chatted. He smiled and nodded. A few people, like the reporter from *Q*, asked his name and what he did. His decidedly unglamorous answer got most of them to shift their attention immediately back to Chelsea.

It got Sebastian, the reporter from *Q*, going, though. His husband was a film studies professor, apparently, which gave them something in common. He asked questions about whether they were an item, how they'd met. Rather than feeling invasive, it made Bryce feel like they might be at some normal party, making small talk and getting to know new people. At least it did until Sebastian asked for a few photos and hinted they'd be included in his story about the event.

"Just online, for now." Sebastian offered them a wink. "Until I can convince my senior editor to do a feature on queer chefs."

Chelsea didn't miss a beat. "Sign me up."

"Girl, you're at the top of my list."

Sebastian went on his way and Chelsea did a happy dance. Brief. Subtle. But definitely a happy dance. Not sexy, and yet so incredibly sexy. Bryce slid an arm around her waist. "I know you're having the time of your life, but I feel like I should tell you that all I want to do is take you to our hotel and get you out of that dress."

Chelsea looked him up and down with the sort of slow appreciation that turned his already pulsing desire into more of an aching thud. "Knowing that makes all this even better."

He didn't doubt her, but he still wanted to hear it. "Promise I'll get to eventually."

"I'll do you one better." She leaned in and whispered a few of the things she wanted him to do after getting her out of the dress. When she finished, she pulled back, dropping her head and looking up at him through painted lashes. Between that and an almost demure smile, she promptly sent his libido into orbit.

"Not fair," he said.

"It will be by the time I'm done with you."

Hard to argue with that. But in the meantime, duty called. Chelsea mixed and mingled. Bryce followed her around like an obedient puppy. Not in a bad way, though. She was doing her thing and he was happy to be by her side. She came alive—witty, warm, and undeniably magnetic. Everyone she spoke with seemed smitten. Bryce didn't blame them. She had the same effect on him.

As the evening progressed, he sort of lost himself in the swirl of it all: exquisite food, elaborate cocktails, and a seemingly endless string of introductions. It started to exhaust him after a while, but Chelsea never faltered. Like she was born for it. He continued to smile and nod but found his attention settling on two undeniable truths. The first was how glad he was knowing they'd end the night together. The second was that when it came to being famous—even in this very specific circle of people—better her than him.

CHAPTER FIFTEEN

Chelsea kicked off her shoes and turned a slow circle. "I think that might have been the best night of my life."

Bryce set the key card on the dresser and shrugged out of his tuxedo jacket. "You were a rock star. If I didn't know better, I'd think you lived most of your life in the spotlight."

"I can't believe I was nervous. It was so easy. Fun, even." She practically vibrated with the energy of it still. Despite all the downplaying, people recognized her, knew who she was. Even better, they knew her cooking.

"Well, I don't think everyone would feel that way, so you're clearly a natural."

She paused her reverie long enough to study Bryce's features. He was smiling, but his eyes looked tired. "Was it too much? I'm sorry if I got swept up and missed you trying to send me signals."

He closed the distance between them and took her hand. "You were supposed to get swept up."

"But not to the point of being self-absorbed." She'd seen enough to know she never wanted to be that kind of TV personality.

"You weren't. Aren't. I had fun. A lot of fun, actually. I'm just beat and you seem to be buzzing. It's pretty damn adorable."

"Oh. I mean, I guess I am. Buzzing, that is. Wired." He didn't make it sound like criticism, though she couldn't help but wonder.

"Exactly. Which is why I said you're a natural."

She wouldn't say she craved the fame, but she didn't entirely mind it. She lifted her shoulders, let them drop. "Thanks."

"Very sexy, too. All those people vying for your attention, and I had the pleasure of knowing I was the one who got to take you home at the end of the night." He looked around the room, then made air quotes. "Home."

It didn't sound possessive. In fact, Bryce seemed to enjoy her being in demand. But the sentiment—wanting to be the one she ended the night with—sent a flutter through her. "Is that so?"

"I fully respect if you want to get some rest because you have such a full day tomorrow, but I'd be more than happy to show you."

Desire shone in his eyes now, nearly masking the fatigue. "I thought you were beat."

He slid his arms around her waist and pulled her to him. "I am. But I'd have to be in a coma to pass up the opportunity to take you to bed."

"Yeah?" The energy humming through her took on a different flavor.

"Oh, yeah."

"What did you have in mind?" It was no longer a revelation that he wanted her, but it still surprised and delighted her that he wanted her so much. So often.

He lifted one of her wrists to his lips and kissed it. "A little of this." He repeated the gesture on the other side. "And this."

"Yes, that's very nice." That sort of slow attention usually made her fidget, but with Bryce, it didn't.

"Maybe some of this." He kissed her neck below her ear. "This." He kissed the base of her throat. "And this."

They'd kissed probably a hundred times at this point, but when Bryce's mouth covered hers, her knees threatened to buckle. "How do you do that?" she asked when he finally stopped.

"Do what?"

"Kiss me until I can't see straight."

He smiled but looked genuinely confused. "Isn't that how kissing works?"

"You're telling me every time you kiss a woman, your eyes go fuzzy and your brain short-circuits?" Maybe it did. Maybe she'd been doing it wrong. Or with the wrong people.

"Okay, not every time. I should have said 'isn't that how kissing is supposed to work?'"

She thought about the kissing they'd done in the last few weeks. "I'll give you that."

"But I'd be lying if I said all I want to do is kiss you." He slid a hand up her back, catching the zipper of her dress and easing it down.

"I see."

"Do you have any idea how many people were checking you out tonight? Men, women. I'm pretty sure even the handful of gender non-conforming folks had their eyes on you."

"Stop."

He shook his head. "One day we're going to tease apart why you don't believe me."

Chelsea stiffened before she could stop herself. "It's not—"

"Shh." He pressed a finger to her lips. "I'm sorry. I didn't mean it to sound like a criticism."

It was her turn to shake her head. "Don't apologize. It's just that sometimes…Never mind. I'm glad you see me that way."

"I hope I can help you start to see yourself that way, too."

Could it be as easy as that? She didn't have the crippling body shame of some of her friends, even the thinner ones. But Bryce seemed to find her desirable—beautiful—in ways she always assumed were reserved for a select few. "I'll try."

"Good. Now, where were we?" He kissed her rather than waiting for a reply.

She answered with lips and tongue instead of words, pressing her breasts into him and willing him to toss her on the bed and do whatever the hell he wanted.

He didn't do that, but he continued to kiss her in ways that threatened to melt her brain into a sex-induced delirium. He stopped long enough to rid her of her dress. She used the opportunity to shove his shirt from his shoulders and undo his belt.

"I have my bigger cock with me, if you're into that," he said after taking off her bra, one of her breasts in each hand.

She most certainly was. "Yeah?"

"You sound surprised."

"Not surprised. I just do my best never to presume." About anything, but especially about sex.

Bryce smirked. "Same."

So many people did presume—about so many things. "I appreciate that."

"I'm glad." Bryce glanced over at his bag. "Give me one minute."

She licked her lips, anticipation already thrumming through her. "Take all the minutes you need. Well, not all."

He sauntered to the chair where he'd set his duffel and pulled out a black bag that could have passed for a Dopp kit. "Be right back."

Bryce went to the bathroom and closed the door. Chelsea used the moment alone to pull out the surprise she'd tucked into her bag: a gauzy satin and lace teddy, sheer enough to show her nipples and short enough to expose the smile lines of her butt cheeks. She'd just finished adjusting her boobs in the fabric when the door opened.

Bryce sauntered out but stopped dead in his tracks. "Damn."

Her gaze went to the silicone cock standing at attention in the leather harness. "Ditto."

He struck a pose, angling his body to give her a full view. "You like?"

"Oh, I like very much." She struck a pose of her own, arching her back in a way that sent her breasts and ass jutting prominently. "You?"

"I'm not sure 'like' is an adequate word." He came over to her and ran a hand up her thigh, sliding around to cup her ass.

Chelsea used the proximity to curl her fingers around the cock, starting a gentle push and pull that had Bryce's eyes rolling. "And that? Do you like that?"

He blinked a couple of times, like he had to force his gaze into focus. "Again, I'm not sure that word does justice to what you're doing to me."

A surge of something she couldn't name zinged through her. She'd had her share of sex. And maybe not always, but she'd felt desired. But something about the way Bryce wanted her was different—like he wanted all of her, maybe, or like he couldn't get enough. Whatever it was, it made her feel invincible. It made her feel beautiful. "I'd like to do all sorts of things to you."

Bryce's smile held a wicked mischief. "We'll get to that."

He spun them around and gave Chelsea a shove. Not forceful but firm. It sent her sprawling onto the mattress with a squeak of surprise.

"Too much?" he asked.

She grinned. "Nope."

"Good." He tucked his hands behind her knees and pulled her to the edge of the bed. "How about that?"

She'd been with very few people—okay, zero people—who had the upper body strength to toss her around like a rag doll. While the fat-positive, self-love side of her didn't care about things like that, there was a part of her deep down that thrilled at it. "Just right."

He grasped her ankles and set her feet on the bed, saving her back from an awkward overextension. "Comfortable?"

"Mm-hmm."

"You have to tell me if that changes. Otherwise, I plan to keep you here a while." He covered her sex with his palm before skimming it up and over her abdomen, her belly. Over her negligee, under it. His hand was warm and firm and left her writhing.

"Does 'desperate for you to fuck me' count as uncomfortable?"

"Depends. How desperate are you?"

He found her clit with his thumb and she let out a moan, equal parts pleasure and dear God, more please. "Pretty desperate."

"Is it wrong to say I like that?"

She shook her head.

"I really really like it." He eased a finger into her and, perhaps sensing exactly how wet and ready she was, added a second.

Her eyes closed as the rest of her absorbed the exquisite sensation of him moving inside her. "I really really like that."

He thrust inside her a few more times before moving his fingers away. Chelsea bit back the protest because she knew what came next. "Do you mind if I pull you closer?" Bryce asked.

She shook her head, flashes of scooting herself awkwardly into the right position dancing through her brain. But like before, Bryce grasped her with confidence and moved her with what appeared to be no effort at all. She couldn't help but sigh.

"Everything okay?"

She smiled. "You have no idea."

Bryce positioned the cock, sliding it lazily over her clit a few times before easing the tip in. Chelsea purred. He thrust his hips slowly forward, pushing the length of it into her. Chelsea moaned. When he hitched his forearms under her knees, both holding her in place and moving her body in perfect opposition to his, she almost came. "And that?"

She blinked her eyes open, willed her vision to focus. "You. Have. No. Idea."

He regarded her, not with arrogance exactly, but with something more than simple confidence. Maybe it was desire? Or maybe it was her own perception, knowing he had the skills to deliver and then some. Whatever it was, she wanted more. More of it, more of him. More, more, more.

He delivered on that, too, even though she hadn't technically asked for it. Not out loud, at least. And as his hips thrust more frantically, her body responded. Not chasing the orgasm, but riding it like a roller coaster—all speed and breathless thrill.

Her pussy convulsed around him, her legs squeezing his arms and torso. Wanting to pull him close, wanting to ride him hard. Wanting to drag him over the edge with her.

When Bryce tensed and groaned, Chelsea came again. Or maybe she never stopped coming. She let out a groan of her own, the mutual release multiplying her own ten times over.

Bryce released her legs, and she rolled onto her side, pulling them up enough to rest on the mattress. He removed the harness and fell into bed next to her, curling around her big spoon style. "Damn, woman."

She chuckled. "Fucking fuck, man."

He wrapped his arm tighter around her middle, bringing their bodies into full contact. "I'm glad we're in agreement."

Understatement of the century. "Yep."

❖

Bryce opened his eyes and looked around. The dark curtains he'd barely managed to pull before taking Chelsea to bed blocked most of the morning light, creating the kind of cool dimness that invited a body not to worry about the day and just stay in bed. Not that he was the type to do that. Though, if he could talk Chelsea into staying with him, exceptions could be made.

Chelsea seemed like even less the type than him, even if she skewed more night owl than morning person. Always going, always thinking about something or doing something. Usually both.

He liked that she seemed to slow down for him. He could appreciate the work hard, play hard approach to life, but even that got exhausting. He was more of a work, play, relax in equal measure sort of guy. And the older he got, the more he had the pull to add raise a family to the equation.

He and Chelsea had barely scratched the surface of those conversations, but his mind was prone to field days, and he hadn't bothered to rein it in. The mere fact that Chelsea had moved home—and bought a home—told him all he needed to know. For now, at least.

"You're thinking about fucking again, aren't you?" Chelsea asked.

He glanced down to find Chelsea regarding him with a sleepy but playful look on her face. Since admitting that seemed safer than the totality of his thoughts, he rolled with it. "Got me."

"Is it wrong that I love how much you think about sex?"

"No, because by extension, how much I think about sex isn't wrong either."

She ran a finger down his chest. "Do you like being on the bottom if you still get to be the top?"

And just like that, thoughts of work and play and picket fences evaporated like summer rain on hot asphalt. "Hmm. I might need a demonstration. You know, to be sure."

Chelsea tossed the covers aside. "It's good to make fact-based decisions."

"I say that to my students all the time."

She slung a leg over his thighs and rolled herself to a seated position straddling him. "Sound advice."

His cock, always a little hard first thing anyway, twitched to life. He settled his hands onto the swell of her hips. "I try."

"So, Mr. Cormier. Are you gathering data?" She gyrated slowly, creating an impossibly perfect combination of friction and heat between them. "We could make a chart if that would help. Or a graph."

He laughed, but it came out ragged, giving away how immediate and intense an effect she had on him. "That won't be necessary."

"No?" she asked.

"All evidence points to this being the best idea ever."

"Ever, huh?" Her head fell back and she laughed, thrusting her breasts forward.

He reached up and took one in each hand. "Though you seem to be refining and improving things by the second."

She changed her movements, shifting to a more intentional undulation that sent his cock sliding up and down her wetness, enveloping him. "Is that so?"

"Fuck. Yes."

She maintained her rhythm but leaned forward, pressing her breasts into his palms. It made him feel somehow both powerful and overpowered, in control and yet completely at her mercy. Any hope he had of holding out, of coaxing her to orgasm first, vanished in a white-hot flash. His body bucked, and he came, hard and fast.

Chelsea collapsed next to him, breathing heavy and with a satisfied smile on her perfect lips.

"Are you pleased with yourself?" he asked.

Her body didn't move, but she rolled her head to look at him. "I most certainly am."

"I hope you'll let me reciprocate. Show my appreciation."

She rolled her head the other way, in the direction of the clock on the bedside table. "I need to get up, I'm afraid."

Since he knew she did, his disappointment remained mild. "Yes, yes. Your fans await."

"I wouldn't mind some company in the shower, though." She propped herself on her elbow and gave an exaggerated eyebrow wag.

He laughed, delighted and aroused all over again. "I'd like to volunteer for the position."

She made a show of looking him up and down. "You do have some impressive credentials."

If a little voice in his head told him he was falling harder and deeper and faster than he should, he set it aside. They'd get to that. Eventually. Hopefully. For now, he had a massive hotel shower and a gorgeous woman who wanted to share it with him. He got out of bed and extended a hand. "Right this way."

Chapter Sixteen

If Chelsea's life seemed to ramp up after the Food and Wine Festival—more interviews, endless Zoom calls with Jada and the network to plan her second season—Bryce's got blissfully back to normal. Well, normal with the added bonus of dating Chelsea. It was the sort of new normal he could get behind. Low-key dinners, cozy nights, and more sex than he'd had since his early twenties. Sometimes her place, sometimes his.

Easy.

He'd started to give up hope that easy could be anything more than code for casual. More than the blips that faded and false starts and women not looking for anything serious. Easy like he and Chelsea clicked in all the ways that mattered, like they wanted all the same things. Like he'd finally found what he'd been looking and waiting for all along.

Kate would riddle him with questions if he started talking like that. Questions about what Chelsea's plans were, her intentions. But today, with Chelsea still asleep in his bed and advising season kicking off at work, he let himself simply enjoy it. It was a nice vibe to take into his eight a.m. group advising session.

Bryce offered friendly smiles and a few nods of recognition to the students who shuffled into the classroom. They settled into seats, dropping booksacks and pulling out laptops. A few would probably do homework or surf the internet during his presentation, but he'd made the commitment years ago not to police that sort of thing. One, because he hated being the heavy and two, because students would get out what they put in. Which was one of the points he would make in this presentation and every other one he did over the course of the semester.

"Good morning and welcome to the advising kickoff for first-year students intending majors in history or history with the secondary education track. If we haven't met before, I'm Bryce Cormier, an advisor in the College of Humanities and Social Sciences Student Services Office. And yes, that's a mouthful. It's a big name but a small office, full of people who want to help you succeed."

He got a decent number of chuckles for eight o'clock in the morning, which always felt like a win. He ran through his slides, handing out postcards with QR codes that would direct students to online versions of the information. Students asked about finding electives, getting into closed sections, the ability to pick up a minor or double major. Standard fare for meetings like this, but he never got bored. It didn't have quite the satisfaction of one-on-ones, but this was how he made that initial connection that would lay the foundation for more in-depth conversations about classes and curriculum and, often, life.

After wrapping up the formal presentation, he set down the clicker and perched on the old wooden table at the front of the room. "Don't forget that if you want to meet with a faculty advisor, you need to bring a copy of your degree audit. They literally won't talk to you without it."

"Is that because they're too old and crusty to use the system themselves?" Cade, a self-identified cutup, asked.

"Actually, they don't have access. It's part of protecting the privacy of your records." Several students nodded and Cade looked moderately cowed. Bryce shrugged. "That's the official answer at least."

"I feel you, bro," Cade said.

The juxtaposition of those words had Bryce biting back a chuckle of his own. "Any more questions?"

Azrah, who Bryce had already met with twice, put up her hand. When he gave her a nod, she scrunched up her face, like maybe she had second thoughts about whatever was on her mind. "This is weird, but..."

She didn't continue, so he tried an extra encouraging smile. "We've already established there are no dumb questions. As for weird ones, they're my favorite. I've been known to offer prizes to students who ask me something I haven't been asked before."

All eyes turned to Azrah. She looked around the room and bit her lip before returning her gaze to Bryce. "Were you on a cooking show this weekend?"

He lifted a hand, equal parts concession, embarrassment, and pride. "I was."

A chorus of whats and whoas filled the room.

He didn't make a habit of talking about his personal life, but since it was already out there, might as well give some context. "Chelsea Boudreaux is my girlfriend and asked me to be a guest on one of her episodes."

"That's sick, bro," Cade said.

Most of the room agreed. Someone asked the name of the show and more than a few scribbled it down or typed it into their phone. One asked if it was on YouTube. Given that most of the people on campus with any sort of celebrity were attached to the football team, he enjoyed breaking the mold. "Don't worry, I won't let the fame go to my head. I think we're good here, so you're free to go. I'll hang back for a bit and y'all know where to find me otherwise."

The room emptied. One student, Naveen, lingered to ask about keeping teacher certification but switching to political science. Azrah hovered until Bryce answered the basics and referred Naveen to someone in the department for a more thorough conversation. When he left, Azrah picked up her bag and looked Bryce's way. "I hope it's okay that I asked about you being on TV. I didn't mean to, like, out you or anything."

He smiled at the choice of phrase. "I'm pretty out about most things."

She nodded and seemed to relax slightly. "Was it cool? Being on the show?"

Something told him her interest went beyond general curiosity. "It was. More intense than I expected. All the lights and cameras. And we had to do everything twice so they could get the different kinds of footage they needed."

Azrah continued to nod, her expression taking on an air of wonder. "I always wanted to work on a TV show. Not be on camera or anything, but behind the scenes."

His own curiosity took over. Well, curiosity honed by a decade of advising college students. "Is there a reason you're studying history instead of that?"

Azrah shrugged. "Being a teacher is noble. Practical."

"Your words or your family's?"

Her rueful smile held the maturity of someone much older. "How did you guess?"

"I have a knack for that sort of thing."

"I'm the first in my family to go to college. Teaching feels like something I can do, could be good at." She shrugged.

"It feels known, too, right? It's easier to be what you can see."

Azrah's eyes lit up. "Yes. That's exactly it."

"I respect that. I can also talk with Chelsea and see if you could come check out the next round of filming." He had a hard time imagining Chelsea would say no. Jada, too, for that matter.

"Really?"

"Absolutely. And not so you'll change your major, but so you'll be able to make an informed decision."

She bit her lip and nodded but didn't say anything.

"Send me an email and I'll see what I can do. The producer of the show is great. Indian, I think. Super nice but also a total boss."

More nodding.

He didn't want to lay it on too thick, but he did want her to get over the hump of being able to imagine it. "For what it's worth, a lot of movies and shows film in Louisiana because it's tax-friendly production-wise."

Enough clicked into place that she could imagine it. The thrill of possibility was evident on her face. He loved that look. "Thank you."

"It's the best part of my job."

She glanced at her watch. "I have to go to class."

"Go. I'll be looking for your email."

"Thank you again." She called a good-bye over her shoulder as she left.

Alone in the room, he shut down the teaching station and gathered the leftover materials. Not how he expected the meeting to end, but he had no complaints. Well, aside from the slight awkwardness of being recognized from television. Now he could empathize with what was happening to Chelsea all the time. Of course, she seemed to love it. More power to her. Like he always said to students: takes all kinds to make the world go 'round.

❖

At the sound of Bryce's truck in the driveway, Chelsea wiped her hands on a kitchen towel and hurried to beat him to the front door. She paused at the mirror in the entryway, smoothing the front of the dress she'd decided to put on for dinner and rubbing her lips together to smooth the gloss. She opened the door as he reached for the knob and greeted him with a smile. "Hi, honey. How was your day?"

Bryce looked her up and down, appreciation evident on his face. "A hell of a lot better now. What did I do to deserve this? Or do we have plans I forgot about?"

She gave a spin, making her skirt twirl, before planting a kiss on his cheek. "No plans. I was feeling domestic and decided to channel my inner fifties housewife."

"I didn't know you had an inner fifties housewife." He slid an arm around her and kissed her in earnest.

"Well, I wouldn't say you should get used to her, but she has her moments." Because who didn't love a pair of heels and a string of pearls every now and then?

"I promise to keep my appreciation high and my expectations low."

"Sweet talker." She snagged his hand and pulled him inside. "Cocktail?"

"Always. Well, not always, but most of the time. You know what I mean."

She did, and she liked that he made the distinction. "Moderation is sexy. Well, most of the time."

Bryce grabbed her waist and spun her around, pressing her against the wall. He caught her wrists in his hands and kissed her again, long and slow. "I'm glad you said most of the time."

She managed a smirk despite being weak in the knees. "How about we do some eating and drinking in moderation so we can do some other things to excess a little later?"

"Gorgeous and brilliant. I'm a lucky guy." Bryce released her wrists but kissed her a third time before stepping back.

"You don't even know what's for dinner yet." Though she loved that he seemed more invested in kissing her than whatever she'd cooked for him.

He lifted his chin. "Hey, Chelsea. What's for dinner?"

"I'm testing a new recipe. Think shrimp scampi and chargrilled oysters had a love child." She wanted the decadence of grilled oysters with the accessibility of shrimp, something that felt like a party but could come together on a weeknight.

"So much yes."

"Come on. I've got a big salad, a loaf of French bread, and a honeysuckle French 75 to go with it."

He followed her into the kitchen and sniffed the air. "If it tastes half as good as it smells, it's my new favorite dinner."

She elbowed him lightly. "You're easy."

"Damn right I am."

She poured drinks, topping off the mixture of gin, lemon juice, and honeysuckle-infused simple syrup with champagne. They clinked glasses and she took a sip, pleased with the flavor profile but dubious that it would appeal to a beer guy like Bryce. "Not too girly?"

"Not at all. I mean, I wouldn't bring it to a tailgate. But for a fancy dinner with my girlfriend? It's perfect."

It shouldn't give her a giddy flutter when he said that, but it did. "Noted."

She slid the dish of prepped shrimp under the broiler and finished the salad. Bryce leaned against the counter with his drink, shooting her suggestive looks and playful smiles. What was that about giddy flutters?

"You'll never guess what happened to me today," Bryce said.

She cracked the oven door to peek at the shrimp since they only needed a few minutes to cook through. "What?"

"Aren't you going to guess?"

She closed the door and turned to him with a smirk. "Do you want me to guess?"

"Obviously."

"Hmm." Since she seriously had no clue, she plucked something from the air. "You won fifty dollars on a scratch-off lottery ticket."

"No, but I love that you went with that as your first guess. Do you buy lottery tickets?"

She shrugged, now slightly embarrassed. "Not scratch-offs, but I subscribe to Mega Millions."

"You do?" He sounded genuinely surprised.

She went for a haughty head toss. "You can't win if you don't play, Bryce."

He nodded. "This is true."

"Besides, my mother considers playing the lottery gambling, which makes it sinful, so it's slightly satisfying even when I don't win." She'd never said that out loud, which also proved satisfying.

Bryce looked more concerned than amused. "Is she really hard on you?"

"Hey, give a girl a couple of drinks or at least a little warning before poking her squishy underside." She checked the shrimp again, this time pulling them from the oven. Butter and garlic, laced with lemon and pecorino, bubbled fragrantly. "Besides, you're supposed to be telling me what happened to you today."

He narrowed his eyes briefly, like he might be debating whether or not to let it go. "I got recognized."

"Recognized?" She pulled the bread she'd left warming on a lower rack and tipped her head in the direction of the table.

He grabbed the salad bowl and followed, then waited to sit while she circled back for water glasses and hot sauce. "From the show."

Since she couldn't read his expression, she fumbled for the right response. "Did you know them or was it a stranger? Was it fun? Weird?"

He relayed the story of his group advising meeting while they ate, how one of his students threw it out during the Q&A. "The good news is I think you picked up a few viewers, for that episode at least."

She'd never turn up her nose at new viewers, but she still couldn't get a handle on how he felt about the whole thing. "I'll be sure to send you a finder's fee."

He sopped up some of the sauce with a piece of bread. "I think this covers it."

Maybe she should take the compliment, serve dessert, and let the rest go. He didn't seem bothered, and she'd learned a long time ago that little good came from borrowing trouble. "I will happily provide you with dinner for promotional and other considerations."

"Other considerations, huh?" He lifted a brow, all suggestion.

"Absolutely. You bring a lot of value to the table. I want things to feel fair and balanced."

He took her hand, kissing the tips of her fingers. "You bring plenty to the table, too. And I'm not talking about dinner."

A lick of lust coursed up her spine. "Dessert, then? I know you have quite a sweet tooth."

"Depends on how broadly you define dessert."

She tapped a finger to her lips, taking her time about it. "Well, there's a vanilla custard tart with fruit in the fridge."

He nodded. "Mm-hmm, mm-hmm. Or?"

"Or a few cookies left over from the batch I made this weekend."

"Those were good. Or?"

She knew what he was getting at, what he wanted her to say. And it wasn't like she was shy or anything, but the brazen confidence he nudged her toward still felt a bit foreign. Not bad, just different. New. "Or you could have me naked and under you."

Bryce licked his lips. "That is probably my favorite. Any chance of some chocolate sauce or a caramel drizzle to go with that?"

The image of Bryce over her, lapping things from her skin, had her nipples tightening. "Of course. There's also a little bit of custard left from the tart."

"We wouldn't want that to go to waste."

"No." She could think of a few places she'd like to use some of those leftovers.

His gaze drifted to her cleavage. "As much as I'm enjoying that dress, I think I might enjoy getting you out of it even more. You could leave the pearls on, though."

She smirked, unable to help herself. "And the heels?"

He peeked under the table. "Maybe for a little while."

"I should take care of the dishes first." More habit than any real necessity.

"If you let them wait till morning, I'll do the dishes, and I'll bring you coffee in bed."

"Sweet talker." He was. But he was telling the truth, too. His willingness—no, desire—to spoil her still caught her off guard.

"Is that a yes?"

"I think it's a yes, a please, and a thank you all rolled into one." Even if it threatened to push her thoughts out of casual boyfriend territory and into all sorts of other places. Places that fell under the Big Feelings header.

"I love it when we're in agreement." He stood and extended a hand.

She took it and stood as well. "You say that like we're often in disagreement."

"I like that we aren't."

She did, too. That whole flash of tempers that erupted into passion was great in books, but in reality, it gave her a stomachache more than it turned her on. "Me, too."

He led them through the kitchen, stopping at the fridge and angling his head. "Don't forget my dessert."

She grabbed the dish and a spoon from the silverware drawer. "Anything else?"

"I think that's everything I need." He looked her up and down, his expression turning tender for a moment. "Thank you for dinner. And the exceptionally nice welcome home."

It made her imagine what coming home to each other every night might feel like. Silly, given how long they'd been sleeping together. How much her life still felt in flux. Besides, she didn't need every night. She might not even want it, truth be told. All she needed to do for now was sit back and enjoy the nights they did have. Or maybe more accurately, lie back and enjoy. "Thank you for being so appreciative."

"Come on." He gave her hand a gentle tug. "I've got a lot more appreciation to show."

CHAPTER SEVENTEEN

Bryce sat on the sofa with his laptop and Chelsea emerged from her office, looking more than a little dazed. "That was the most surreal conversation of my life."

Bryce searched her face for hints of surreal good or surreal bad and landed somewhere in the middle. "Big statement, given the last couple of months."

"Ha! You're not lying."

"It was Natasha, right? The senior editor of the magazine?" It had been a scheduled call, one to go over the elements Chelsea would be working on for the issue she was slated to guest edit.

She nodded eagerly. "Yep. The recipes, the interview, and a piece on finding the balance between being a professional chef and a home cook."

"That's really cool."

Chelsea beamed. "It is. Especially since that's kind of the point of my show. Elevated but accessible."

All stuff she'd told him about, so it shouldn't have taken her by surprise. "What was surreal about it?"

"Planning the photo shoot. The way she wants it to tell a story. She actually used the term 'storyboard.'" She pointed to herself. "To talk about me. Like, my story."

He tried to imagine his own life like that, taped to a white board with pictures and captions, arrows and exclamation marks. "Okay, that would feel strange."

"Right? Anyway. On that note, I have a question for you."

Bryce tried and failed to imagine what that question might be. "Shoot."

"How would you feel about being in a few of the shots?" Chelsea eyed him hopefully.

"Uh, I'd feel weird." Obviously, she was joking, but it didn't strike him as all that funny.

Chelsea frowned. "Weird as in cool or weird as in you won't do it?"

"Weird as in I didn't think you were serious." It was one thing to be on the show—where having people on the show was a thing. This was different. This was…a magazine. Famous people had their pictures in magazines. Well, famous people and models. And he was decidedly neither.

"Why wouldn't I be serious?" Chelsea's hands went to her hips.

The playfully defiant gesture had him thinking about kissing her more than anything too serious. "Because why would you want a picture of me in the feature about your cooking show?"

She looked away briefly, enough to shift his attention from kissing and back to her original question. "It technically wasn't my idea," she said.

"Whose idea was it?" Jada, maybe? She'd been the one to nudge for him to be in an episode in the first place. But she'd nudged about all the guests. Besides, what would she care about a magazine layout?

"The network thinks it would be good for my brand if the article includes stuff about my personal life and not just the show."

Chelsea smiled, but he'd bet money she was hiding something. Okay, maybe not hiding. Holding back. He didn't like it, even if he more than liked the prospect of being such a concrete and visible part of her personal life. "And that includes me?"

She blew out a breath. "Well, they want to play up the relatable angle. But also, the diversity angle."

It made sense but it didn't. "I don't follow."

"I'm more appealing to a certain demographic if I've got a steady boyfriend or husband." She shrugged. "It's dumb but true."

Again, the idea of being that—the steady boyfriend—definitely appealed. But did it appeal enough to prop up her image with the kind of people who cared about that sort of thing? "And what about the diversity bit?"

"They're still doing damage control after the whole Charlie Paul blowup. They want to play up the fact that I'm queer." Chelsea looked at her feet this time.

"And being with a trans guy does that." For some reason, the tokenism bothered him less than the must have a man bit. Maybe because any kind of positive mainstream trans visibility still felt like a win. Oh, and it wasn't inherently sexist.

"Yeah."

He scratched his temple. "But doesn't that part negate the traditional couple vibe?"

"People see what they want to see. The network is willing to take that gamble." She lifted her shoulders and let them fall, like she felt stuck in the middle and didn't know what to do about it.

If the pieces made sense, the whole still seemed contradictory. But what did he know? That he wanted to help Chelsea if he could. That he wanted to make her happy. "Do you want me to do it?"

The awkward, almost defensive energy melted away and Chelsea regarded him with the kind of flirty but shy smile that had his insides melting faster than a sno-cone on an August afternoon. "I think it could be fun."

Whatever weirdness the network's motivations gave him didn't stand a chance against that smile. "Well then, I'm your guy."

"Really?" Chelsea's eyes were hopeful, but her tone held genuine surprise.

Was it too soon to admit he'd have a hard time denying her anything? Probably. "Sure. I'm not sure it'll be fun, but I'm all about making your show as popular as possible. And if it helps a few folks feel more chill about trans people, then bonus."

Chelsea closed the distance between them and ran a finger down his chest. "I should confess I don't feel very chill about this particular trans guy."

"No?" The insides that melted a moment before threatened to ignite.

"I feel pretty warm." She licked her lips. "Hot even."

"Getting overheated can be dangerous, you know. Maybe we should get you out of some of those clothes so you can cool off." He hooked his fingers in the thin straps of her sun dress and nudged them off her shoulders.

"So considerate."

"Perhaps I can convince you to go to your bedroom, lie down under the fan." The banter was as cheesy as it was seductive, but neither of them seemed to care.

"Oh, that sounds like a good idea. Though if you're with me, I'm not sure how much cooling off I'll do."

He waved a hand dismissively. "A little overheated is okay, especially if you're lying down."

Chelsea smirked. "I see."

It might be the middle of the afternoon, but where else did they have to be? Well, aside from Kate's house in a couple of hours for dinner. But he could do a lot with a couple of hours. "Come on, I'll show you."

He took her hand and she followed, even though it was her house. The path to her bedroom had become almost as familiar as his own. The significance wasn't lost on him. Would Chelsea agree? Surely, she must, on some level. She'd asked him to be in her photo shoot. Even if the initial idea came from the network, she wouldn't go along unless she considered him a significant part of her life. A part that went beyond what they had in the bedroom. A part that wouldn't be changing any time soon.

Maybe it was strange to be thinking big relationship thoughts when Saturday afternoon sex stretched out so deliciously in front of him. He couldn't help it, though. His heart remained permanently attuned to the end game. For him, that end game included a wife and kids, big old house, big old dogs—the whole bit. And it included staying in Duchesne.

He'd begun to worry it might not happen, at least not without some major compromises. Being with Chelsea changed that. She'd left and come home, so she knew what choosing a life here meant. She appreciated it, appreciated him, in ways no other woman had. They might not be talking about that yet, but for once he didn't feel like he was the only one thinking it.

He wouldn't have guessed in a million years that a photo shoot for a magazine might be the thing that made it all feel possible. Of course, he'd never have guessed Chelsea would waltz back into his life the way she had—that she'd be who she'd become or that she'd go for the likes of him. But he liked where things were going, and he wasn't about to complain.

❖

Chelsea returned to her office after her consult with the wardrobe person and found Bryce sitting at the makeshift hair and makeup station, tissue paper tucked into the collar of his shirt. He turned to her with a scowl as Vivian dabbed foundation on his forehead with a little foam sponge. "I was not informed there'd be makeup."

She cringed. He'd tolerated it for filming the episode. He'd even been good-natured about it. Still. She shouldn't have taken that sort of thing for granted. "Is it a deal breaker?"

"You're good to go, handsome." Vivian pulled the tissue away and gave him a pat on the shoulder.

The scowl evaporated. He offered Vivian a flirty smile. "Thank you, gorgeous."

Vivian headed to the bathroom to clean her brushes, leaving them momentarily alone. Chelsea studied him. "Seriously, I wasn't thinking. It's standard practice for everyone, but I get that it might be triggering."

"Not triggering. I just dislike it and wanted to lodge my complaint."

She could handle that. She understood it, too, even if she'd started to like someone else fussing over her appearance. "Your concerns have been noted."

"Thank you. It's important to feel heard." Bryce gave a slight bow before cracking a mischievous grin. "To be fair, though, I'm calculating the sexual favors I'm going to demand in return for my pain and suffering."

Oh. That's the game they were going to play. "You say that like I've denied you something."

"You haven't." Bryce's expression turned earnest. "I hope I haven't denied you something you like."

It was hard to know what she enjoyed more—the sexual teasing or how quickly he changed tone when he thought she might be upset about something. She put a hand on his arm. "I was teasing."

His features relaxed. "Good. Me, too. I want all sorts of sexual adventures with you, but I don't want them to be a bribe or a barter or anything like that."

For all her failed attempts at relationships in the past, it struck her how easy it would be to fall for a guy like Bryce. Fall for. Build a future with. The thought had no sooner landed when another one landed hot on its heels. A guy like Bryce? Or Bryce? She'd been dancing around the edges of it, but the truth at the center seemed suddenly solid. Pretending otherwise would be straight up denial.

"I've scared you, haven't I? I promise I'm not thinking of anything too depraved," he said.

He'd given her a scare all right, but not in the way he imagined.

Not that she had any intention of letting on. At least not ten minutes before they needed to smile for the camera. "I mean, a little depraved might be okay."

"Bryce, we're ready for you in wardrobe." Natasha's voice cut into both the conversation and the decidedly kinky direction of her thoughts.

"I hope we can continue this conversation later." Bryce offered a wink before turning to go.

"We're absolutely putting a pin in it," she said to his back, letting herself take a second to appreciate the view from behind.

Vivian returned and worked her magic. Julie, the wardrobe woman, brought in the dress they'd agreed on. Chelsea slipped it over her head, adjusting her boobs before doing a little twirl.

"Definitely the right call. The color is perfect on you. And the cut?" Julie let out a whistle. "I'm straight and I wouldn't mind coming home to that."

"I never pegged myself for a fifties housewife meets pinup aesthetic, but it feels weirdly on brand." Like a slightly extra version of the look she'd concocted for Bryce a few weeks back.

"Like I say, you're just working what the good Lord gave you." Vivian did a shimmy with her own chest.

Julie grinned. "Exactly. I'll have the chef coat when you're ready to change."

"Thanks." Chelsea tipped her head toward the rack of clothes. "For pulling all this together but also for the boost to my ego."

Julie waved her off. "I love your show. And any day I get to help show off a fellow curvy girl is a good day."

The comment was playful, but it made her throat constrict. As intensely as she focused on her work, she tried not to think about herself sitting at the center. But it mattered. To her, obviously, but also to all the women and girls who grew up with an Irene for a mother. Or who'd heard over and over from family and friends and complete strangers that they'd be happier—or more successful or more desirable—if they'd just lose some weight. She'd almost drowned in that self-doubt as a kid. If she could help one person feel even the tiniest bit less of that, she'd be happy. Since saying so would make her cry, and crying would ruin her makeup, she went for a brisk nod and headed to the living room.

Bryce was already there, ostensibly studying the titles on her bookshelf. He looked her way, and his gaze lingered. "Wow."

The simple declaration set her insides aflutter more than any elaborate compliment could have. It also provided a perfect distraction from the swell of emotion. "Thanks. You don't look half bad yourself."

Bryce tugged at the hem of the suit jacket. "I'm pretty sure this outfit cost more than my weekly take-home pay."

"Is that weird?" To be fair, she also had mixed feelings about that. If by mixed she meant slightly uncomfortable but mostly giddy.

"Yes." He flashed a grin. "But since they're letting me take it home, I'll get over it."

"That's the spirit." She loved that he didn't seem to take it—or himself—too seriously. But also that he wasn't flip. Sort of like the balance she tried to strike.

"Do I get to watch your part or will that make you self-conscious?" he asked.

Like so many things lately, it struck her that he asked. That he would think about her feelings more than whatever he might prefer. "Honestly, you being here makes me less nervous."

"Aw." He hung his head briefly but then looked right into her eyes. "I'd kiss you, but I don't want to mess up my makeup."

She swatted him. "I was about to say how sweet you were being."

He lifted both hands. "Fine, fine. I don't want to mess up your makeup, either."

She closed her eyes and shook her head, set on being the mature adult of the situation. Or at least playing the part.

"Okay, okay. I'll behave. Promise," he said.

The thing was, she didn't want him to behave. She loved that he got her out of her head, got her to loosen up. That not taking things too seriously managed to rub off on her. She might not have been willing to admit she needed that a few months ago but here, now, she could. She was about to say as much, but Natasha strode up to them with purpose. Esther, the photographer, followed right behind, camera in hand.

"Are you two ready to make some magic?" Natasha asked.

Bryce offered her a wink. "She's the magic one. I'm just the lovely assistant."

Esther cackled. "Well said, honey. Well said."

Chelsea headed to the kitchen for the first round of shooting. She stood this way and that, posing with various utensils and the dishes she and the food stylist had prepped earlier in the day. In some ways, it was easier than filming an episode. Not having to walk and talk at the same time. But it also gave her the chance to be aware of the angles of her body. She trusted Esther, but something about knowing the images would be immutable had little jabs of anxiety kicking in.

Silly. That's what Photoshop was for. And it wasn't like she was trying not to be fat.

"You're doing great, darling. Just a few more, then we'll grab your beau and go outside," Esther said.

She stole a glance at Bryce. As expected, he snickered at the description. She quirked a brow and smirked. Beau indeed.

"Oh, yes. That's the money shot," Esther said.

She shifted her focus back to Esther, who pulled the camera from in front of her face and studied the small screen with a satisfied smile.

"Wait. What's the money shot?" Chelsea asked.

"That face you made at handsome over there."

She could protest but why? Bryce brought out the playful in her and playful played perfectly into her brand. At least the brand she was trying to build. The one Jada encouraged her to just embrace already and take to the bank. So instead of saying something contrary, she gave a smile of her own and shrugged. "So, we're good here?"

Esther lifted a finger. "Actually, I'd love to get a few of you in the kitchen together."

Natasha had her cut the chocolate cream pie, offer Bryce an oversized slice like she was presenting a prized possession at show-and-tell. She balked when Esther had her feed Bryce a bite, but the whole bit managed to feel cute more than creepy.

They went outside next, posing like guests at a wedding, leaning against the deck, cocktails in hand. Then Natasha sent them both in to change into what she called the tailgate look—jeans for them both, an LSU sweatshirt for Bryce, and a cream-colored boatneck sweater for Chelsea. Esther expertly arranged them in the yard, complete with cooler and a mound of pimento cheese in the shape of a football. They closed with the shots of her in a chef's coat, looking determined and clutching a giant whisk.

Natasha declared the day a success a little after six, and within a matter of minutes, the house cleared out and it was just the two of them. Bryce went to the bathroom to wash off his makeup, and she swapped the chef coat for a T-shirt before opening the fridge in search of supper she didn't have to think too hard about.

"I say we order a pizza and put our feet up," Bryce said.

God, that sounded good. "Yeah?"

"Absolutely."

"I feel like I should cook for you after forcing you to endure such a long day."

Bryce shrugged. "You cook for me all the time. Besides, if we have an easy dinner and relax, I might be able to talk you into picking up that conversation from earlier."

And that sounded even better. "The one about a little depraved being okay?" she asked.

His grin held mischief. "That's the one." He made it so damn easy.

"Well, maybe what I should have said is you get to choose how we spend our evening."

Bryce nodded slowly. "I should warn you, I have lots of ideas."

Chapter Eighteen

The two weeks following the photo shoot felt blissfully normal which, to Bryce, meant blissful. He went to work; Chelsea plugged away on recipe testing and did a few promotional appearances and interviews that didn't include him in any way. They spent most of their nights together and more than once he found himself wondering how soon was too soon to move in together. Wondered to himself, but wondered.

Chelsea did go away once, spending a couple of days in New Orleans doing a spot on one of the local morning shows. But when she got back, she promptly came to his place for the weekend. They watched the LSU/Ole Miss game Saturday, and since his parents were away, they headed to Kate and Sutton's for Sunday dinner. After helping Sutton assemble the crib and processing paint colors for the nursery with Kate, he talked Chelsea into going home with him and they passed the rest of the afternoon watching old movies and having sex. They spent the evening the same way, along with the better part of the night. Well, minus the movies.

A relaxing weekend, but the lack of sleep was no joke. When his alarm went off at six, he legit groaned.

"I know, I know. I'm coming." Chelsea's complaint was more of a mumble, slurred with sleep.

"You did your fair share of coming last night." He kissed her neck, contemplating a sick day so he could keep her in bed another few hours.

Her eyes opened then. Well, one eye. "Ha ha."

"I could try to get you to come again before I go to work." Not playing hooky, just running a little late. It wouldn't be the end of the world.

"Is that so?" Both eyes opened and Chelsea regarded him with sleepy desire—a look he'd find hard to resist even if he wanted to.

He slid a hand over her warm, naked torso. "I find you infinitely hard to resist."

Chelsea rolled to her back and opened her legs. "Well, then you should know I wake up wanting you."

"Even after last night?" He woke up wanting her, too, but he woke up horny most mornings thanks to the T.

Her smile was slow but full of promise. "Maybe especially after last night."

Bryce slipped his wandering hand between her thighs. Chelsea was hot and slick, making his already hard cock throb. He let out a low groan.

"I can't help it. You do things to me," she said.

Well, at least the feeling was mutual. He stroked her lazily. "I fucked you pretty good last night. What would feel good?"

"That."

He circled her clit slowly with the tip of his finger.

"Oh, and that."

If the responsible part of his brain urged him to hurry, the rest knew well enough to keep quiet. He took his time, even as Chelsea gripped his shoulder and started to thrust against his hand. Despite his leisurely pace, she came fast, holding on to him and biting his shoulder lightly.

When she sagged back into the pillows, he covered her face and neck with kisses, making her laugh.

"That was hot," she said.

He rolled, bracing himself over her. "I think it bumps coffee as the best part of waking up."

"Only if coffee gets to be a close second," she said.

"I approve this ranking." And didn't want to think about work even making the list.

Chelsea slid a hand between them and stroked his cock. "Do you approve this?"

"Oh. Yeah. Absolutely."

She continued to work him. The combination of her hand and moving on top of her worked him into a frenzy in under a minute. He let the orgasm tumble through him and collapsed next to her. "Fuck, that was good."

"You're easy." Chelsea poked him lightly in the ribs.

"Yep." He sighed. "I'm also going to be late for work."

She sighed back. "Go, go. Thanks for the quickie."

He kissed her before getting out of bed. "Thank you. I'll be in an exceptionally good mood for a Monday."

Chelsea smiled. "I'll make you dinner tonight."

"I'll let you." Seriously, could life get much better than this? "Requests?"

"Surprise me." He headed for the bathroom, already thinking about being back in bed with her and called over his shoulder, "Something light. I'm more interested in what I get to do with you after dinner."

Chelsea groaned but laughed. He took the sound of her laughter and the buzz from having an orgasm into the shower. The feeling stayed with him on his drive to campus and even through the sprint from the parking lot to his office. It only dissipated as he darted up the stairs of his building and remembered it was a staff meeting week and he was barely going to make it.

He dashed into the conference room with less than a minute to spare, sliding into his usual seat and slipping his messenger bag over his head. He hated being late. Morning nookie notwithstanding.

Amy let out a suggestive whistle. "Well, if it isn't our resident heartthrob deciding to join us after all."

Bryce's gaze darted to her before taking in the rest of the room. Everyone else was already seated, so she had to mean him. But that logic didn't make the rest of it compute. "Are you talking to me?"

"Obviously." She pulled the magazine from the padfolio she always brought to meetings.

He'd known the issue was set to drop. Chelsea had been both nervous and giddy about it for days. But he'd also sort of blocked it out. Or, rather, blocked out that he'd be in it and people he knew would see it. "Oh. Right."

"You didn't think you could go all glamorous and glossy without us finding out, did you?" Amy asked.

Was it weird that he had? Or that, at the very least, imagined it wouldn't warrant mention. Especially in a staff meeting. "Maybe."

"Wait." Ping reached for the magazine. "Bryce is in there?"

Amy pushed it toward him. "Oh, yeah. Total stud vibes. They're billing him as the down home, hometown guy hooking up with rising cooking show star. But oh wait, he's trans and isn't that cool."

Bryce pinched the bridge of his nose, not because Amy was off the mark but because she was spot-on. "Could we not?"

"Not what?" Amy blinked a few times, faking innocence. "Talk about it incessantly until Suzanne gets here then accidentally keep talking about it when she does so literally everyone in the office will know?"

Suzanne picked that exact moment to walk in. "What will literally everyone in the office know?"

"Nothing," he said, which in no way covered Amy's reply of, "Bryce did a photo shoot with his girlfriend who has her own cooking show and we were admiring how photogenic he is."

He expected Suzanne to sniff her disapproval and start the meeting. Instead, she held out her hand. Ping looked from Suzanne to Bryce to Amy and back to Bryce before handing it over. She studied the pages thoroughly before flipping forward and back, as though looking to see if there were more where that came from. She tutted a couple of times and slapped the magazine shut before turning her attention to Bryce. "Very photogenic indeed. But I wouldn't suggest quitting your day job. Now, who's got the first agenda item?"

Ping cringed and Amy let out a snort. Despite a sudden desire to melt into an unrecognizable puddle under the table, Bryce cleared his throat. "We need to arrange coverage for registration drop-in hours."

"Excellent." Suzanne gave a brisk nod. "How many days did we decide on again?"

The rest of the meeting passed without incident, and by the time it was done, Bryce's embarrassment had faded to good humor about the absurdity of it all. The good humor gave way to genuine happiness when an email popped into his inbox just after lunch from a college friend he hadn't heard from in years and again when one of his students said his cousin who was trans asked him if he knew Bryce and he got to say he did.

He didn't love the attention and had absolutely no illusion about quitting his day job. But maybe a little bit of celebrity wasn't so bad after all.

❖

Chelsea tucked the copy of *Food TV* magazine into her purse, still on the fence about sharing it. Would being on the cover impress Irene?

Or would the contents—recipes but also the photos and the interview where she talked about learning to love her body and finding her queer identity—send her mother over the edge? She'd have to gauge Irene's mood and play it by ear. It wouldn't be the first time.

She rang the bell, thinking suddenly how strange it was to do that. She still knocked at Bryce's but didn't wait for him to answer. Just like Bryce did at her place, or Kate's. One more way spending time with Bryce, with his family, made her see things differently. Made her long for things she'd convinced herself didn't really matter.

Irene opened the door, a semblance of a smile on her face. "Chelsea."

"You seem surprised to see me. We are having lunch today, aren't we?"

Irene waved her inside. "Of course we are. I had a sense you were going to cancel is all."

She'd done that a couple of times, times when her nerves were frayed, or she'd had a particularly exhausting day. Mostly so she wouldn't wind up saying something she'd regret when her defenses were down. She tried really hard not to make a habit of it, though. Because Irene wouldn't let her hear the end of it. But also because being in Duchesne was about holding her head high, not hiding with her tail tucked. "Nope. Not canceling."

"Well, I'm glad."

Despite Irene's assertions about expecting Chelsea to cancel, the dining room table was set for two, a beautifully arranged platter of salad and a pitcher of iced tea waiting. "That looks lovely."

"I made your vinaigrette. The one with lemon and tarragon."

The one that hadn't been published anywhere but the magazine yet. So much for being on the fence. "I thought it might be one you'd like."

Irene gestured to one of the chairs, as though Chelsea hadn't been assigned the seat her entire life. "Let me get the shrimp from the refrigerator."

Chelsea sat and did what she'd come to think of as her seven-second meditation: eyes closed, breathe in for three, hold, then out for three. She opened them just as Irene returned, bowl of chilled shrimp in hand. Sure enough, a copy of the magazine sat to her left, like Irene wanted Chelsea to know she'd bought and read it. "Did you dress the shrimp, too? It goes really well with seafood."

"You're certainly welcome to." Irene indicated the gravy boat that saw more action with low-fat salad dressings than anything else.

Chelsea helped herself to salad, then shrimp, before drizzling the whole lot. "One day, I'm going to win you over to the world of tossing."

Irene's nose wrinkled. "Serving it on the side allows people to regulate how much dressing they have." Regulate being the operative word.

"Like I said, one day."

Irene gave a terse shake of her head that basically said when pigs fly. "I doubt that."

She did, too, but she couldn't resist that mix of antagonism and optimism that came with trying to get Irene to bend on something. Anything. "Have you had a good week?"

"It's been busy. A Catholic Daughters meeting on Tuesday and a dental cleaning on Friday. I had to get gas."

Oh, to live a life where getting gas counted as an accomplishment. Chelsea went for a smile rather than an eye roll and poured herself a glass of tea.

"I've gotten several phone calls from people seeing your face staring back at them from the display at the grocery store checkout."

She braced herself for the inevitable critique. "Have you?"

"Six so far. As many as when your show first aired."

Like then, it was hard to tell if Irene considered it a point of pride or a nuisance. "I hope it's been more good than bad."

Irene lifted her chin, indicating the magazine cover. "It's a flattering photo."

Technically a compliment, even if it felt like a lead-in to tearing the rest apart. "Thank you."

"I'm not sure what made you decide to air so much of your personal business." Irene shuddered. A legit shudder. Like Chelsea had written some tawdry sexual tell-all or, worse, directly criticized Irene's parenting.

"People like connecting with the personalities they see on TV or follow online. It's standard practice these days." Even as Chelsea defended it, she said a silent prayer of thanks that her mother hadn't made the leap to social media.

Irene sniffed.

"I actually shared less than a lot of people do," Chelsea said.

A dismissive tip of her head reflected Irene's sentiments on the matter. "You were very free with your opinions."

Gee, I wonder where I learned to do that? "People value authenticity."

"That's all well and good. But really, Chelsea. Such personal and private things."

Irene wouldn't know authentic if it bit her in the ass. No, that wasn't fair. She was authentically rigid and judgmental and holier than thou. "Those things are part of who I am. And part of my brand."

Another sniff.

"I know you don't understand or approve, but they're my beliefs." She raised her chin, resisting a fight but refusing to cow. "About my life."

"It would appear you've made quite a life for yourself in the few months you've been home."

For as much as Irene lacked subtlety in most things, Chelsea scrambled to suss the meaning of this particular dig. "I've tried."

"Susan Morin said she knew Bryce from him volunteering as an umpire in her granddaughter's softball league and that he's a very nice—" Irene cleared her throat. "Person."

Ah. There it was. "He's a great guy."

Irene straightened her shoulders and Chelsea braced herself for a diatribe. "You should bring him for dinner sometime."

Her eyes darted around the room, as though she might see the trap she was invariably walking into. "Here?"

"Yes, here." The impatience in Irene's voice did more to convince Chelsea of her sincerity than her forced half smile.

"Why?"

Irene laced her fingers together, clearly displeased with being questioned. "Because if you're seeing someone seriously enough to be photographed with him in a national publication, you should bring him home to meet your mother."

Chelsea's mind raced, trying to piece together whatever agenda Irene had cooked up. Did she want to undermine her relationship with Bryce? Or was Bryce beloved enough by her fellow biddies that Irene considered him suitable? Maybe he simply looked the part of who Irene thought Chelsea should be with more than the butch, androgynous, enby, and other non-conforming people she'd dated through the years. "Will you be nice to him?"

"Chelsea Margaret, I will not dignify that with a response."

Irene might not deign to answer, but the question's very existence would put her on alert. She had an image to uphold, after all, and that image required the worst of her nitpicking to happen behind closed doors. Oddly enough, that gave Chelsea the assurance she needed. "I'll ask him."

Irene gave a curt nod, effectively closing the matter. Chelsea happily navigated the conversation to safe topics—Irene's roses and the new curtains she'd ordered for the kitchen. Irene asked for the recipe for the pie Chelsea made in the episode that aired over the weekend, and Chelsea promised to email it. Then she suggested Chelsea make her grandmother's fig and strawberry preserves on the show sometime.

Chelsea got a flash of having her mother on as a guest to make it with her. Sentimentality warred with anxiety and she quickly set the idea aside. A quandary for another day.

When lunch ended, she went home to do some chores around the house. With filming for the second season only a few weeks away, she should also work on a couple of scripts and maybe do some recipe testing. What she really wanted to do, though, was tempt Bryce over for an evening of football, couch cuddles, and sex.

He did her one better, with an invitation to his place for grilled wings and the game on his much larger TV. She changed into comfy clothes and cut up some veggies to balance the wings and headed over.

"How was lunch?" Bryce asked after requisite hello kisses and pulling her to the sofa. His tone was playful, but Chelsea could see concern in his eyes.

"It was good." More good than bad, at least. When it came to Irene, she counted that as a win.

"Is that all I'm going to get?" He seemed genuinely disappointed.

"It's all relative with my mother. She can't help but be critical, but she'd seen the magazine and managed to say a few nice things." And the compliments about her appearance didn't even qualify as backhanded.

Bryce frowned.

"I know. You want her to be better, kinder. She just doesn't work that way. I've developed good boundaries and mostly keep her and her opinions at arm's length," she said.

He shook his head. "You deserve better than that."

She did. Everyone did. But she also could have gotten a lot worse. Plenty of people did. "I know. But I gave up on having a close, healthy relationship. Now I'm in it to prove I turned out happy and successful in spite of her."

"Yeah." Bryce's shoulders dropped, like the idea made him sad, but he knew better than to argue.

"She wanted to know why I hadn't brought you over to meet her yet."

"For real?" he asked.

Chelsea smiled at the memory of Irene's stilted invitation. "You have quite the reputation. The church biddies love you."

He sat up and straightened his shoulders. "I do have a way with the biddies."

"So, is that a yes?"

"Of course it's a yes." He looked her up and down. "Does this mean I'm officially your boyfriend?"

They hadn't discussed it, despite a joke here and there. She'd started to think of them that way, though, started to hope the feeling was mutual. "You tell me. I've spent whole days with your family already."

He grinned, pure mischief. "Hey, Chelsea?"

"Yes?"

"Wanna be my girlfriend?"

They should probably get into the specifics of what that meant. Like, were they exclusive? Did they consult with each other before making big decisions? But in that moment, she felt a little bit like the loner teenager—the one who nursed crushes and admired the cool kids from afar—getting invited to prom by the most popular person in school. And all she wanted to do was revel in it. "Do I get to wear your letterman jacket?"

"I'll do you one better." He got up and disappeared into his bedroom.

When he returned a minute later with what she knew to be his favorite LSU hoodie, she giggled. If she was going to feel like a giddy teenager, she might as well act the part. She took it from him and pulled it over her head, not even caring what it did to her hair. She spread her arms and stuck out her chest. "What do you think?"

He lunged at her, sending them both sideways on the sofa and leaving her deliciously under him. He kissed her with a thoroughness that would have made high school her blush. Even the high school her who hid romance novels under her mattress so Irene wouldn't know she read them. When the kiss finally ended, she opened her eyes and found Bryce grinning at her.

"You look great. And you're definitely my girlfriend," he said.

She let out a happy sigh. Yes. Yes, she was.

CHAPTER NINETEEN

B ryce climbed into the driver's seat and started the engine.
      "You're sure you're up for this?" Chelsea fastened her seat belt but eyed him warily.

"Hey, you said it first. The biddies love me."

Chelsea took a deep breath and huffed it out. "Yeah, but Irene isn't a biddy. She's a…hurricane."

He reached across the console and squeezed her hand. "I'm fine. Also, easy on the hurricane humor. We're still a little squirrelly after Ida."

Chelsea winced. "Right."

"It's okay. You're out of practice."

A fact she one hundred percent didn't mind. "You know, it's funny. I'd just moved to New York when actual Hurricane Irene tore up the East Coast. I'm not going to lie. It felt a little personal."

Bryce chuckled, but his insides churned. He and Chelsea hadn't been together that long, but he was already protective of her. And short of the asshole that had been her former boss, he got the sinking feeling her mother was the biggest negative influence in Chelsea's life. He had every intention of being on his best behavior, but it would be hard to just sit there if she started in on Chelsea. "Is she the real reason you went away for college?"

"Yes and no. I definitely wanted to stretch my wings and I knew I'd never be able to do that at home."

He didn't begrudge anyone who wanted to get out, go somewhere new. But doing it to escape feeling trapped? By one's own family? He saw it more often than he cared to admit in the students he worked with, but it still gave him a pang of sadness. "I'm sorry."

She smiled brightly, though it didn't quite reach her eyes. "Don't be. It was as much about school itself. For as rich as Louisiana's culinary traditions are, the culinary programs are kind of limited."

"Huh." He'd never given it much thought.

"I wanted to stretch those wings, too. Learn from chefs from all over the world, learn techniques and styles beyond anything I'd ever seen before."

"And that's what you got?"

She nodded, the enthusiasm radiating from all her features now. "It is. Going to a top-notch culinary school changed my life. I wouldn't be where I am now without it."

He tried to imagine feeling so passionately about something. He'd say he felt that about his family, about life as a whole, but not about one particular aspect of it. Certainly not his job, even though he loved what he did. "That's awesome."

"I know it probably sounds weird. Or ironic, I guess. All that to move home and get on television cooking the very food I wanted to escape."

"Do you feel that way, or do you wonder if other people do?" he asked.

He hadn't meant it as a probing question, but Chelsea's expression turned serious. "I'm not sure."

"For what it's worth, I think sometimes you have to go away from something to realize how much it means to you."

"Did you do that?" she asked.

To be fair, he hadn't. "More observation than lived experience, I guess."

"Well, that sounds nicer than doing it to prove a point."

"Is that what you're doing?"

She didn't answer and they were seconds away from the house she'd told him belonged to her mother. He pulled into the driveway, prepared to hold the question for another day. But then she looked him right in the eyes.

"Yes. Not exclusively, but yes," she said.

He nodded slowly, trying to reconcile his desire to be supportive with his own experience of navigating family. Or maybe more accurately, trying to decipher how to be what Chelsea needed despite having a vastly different—and unyieldingly supportive—family of his own.

"You think that's harsh," Chelsea said, a shadow of disappointment in her eyes.

"Not at all. That turn the other cheek nonsense is toxic. I want to know what you need from me."

Her expression turned quizzical. "What do you mean?"

He cut the engine. "Like, do you want me to be unflappably polite or do you want me to be Team Chelsea even if it ruffles her feathers? Because my instinct is the latter, but I will totally respect if your priority is having things go as smoothly as possible."

She chuckled. "I'm not sure I've heard it put so succinctly before."

"I'm not trying to oversimplify."

She put a hand on his. "You're not."

"So?"

"So, let's go with charming and polite. It'll make for a more pleasant meal. Besides, knowing you want to sweep in and be my knight in shining armor is nice." Chelsea punctuated the last bit with a wink.

"You got it. That said, if she says one negative thing about your body, I will have to insist you're gorgeous." He had no illusions about where her body image issues came from.

For the first time since they'd left her house, Chelsea looked relaxed. "Deal."

Irene's house reminded him of his great-aunt Mildred's: dated but pristine. Irene's manners were much the same—irrefutably polite, if a bit stiff. Bryce opted for the full charm offensive rather than a more subtle approach. Chelsea's passing comment about Irene's tendency to be all about appearances rang true. Perhaps not his preferred choice of company, but a type he understood and could manage well enough.

If Irene's titters—and the glances Chelsea shot him throughout the meal—were anything to go on, his tactics worked. Chelsea confirmed as much at the kitchen sink after he cajoled Irene into letting the two of them clear the table and handle the dishes before coffee and dessert.

"She loves you. Seriously loves you." Chelsea shook her head. "You must think I've been unnecessarily harsh about her."

"Oh, no." He slid plates into the dishwasher. "I have no doubt she's on her best behavior for company."

Chelsea rinsed a glass before handing it to him. "Thank you. It's nice that you get it."

As much as he'd wanted things to go well, he almost wanted Irene to slip so he could understand the particular flavor of criticism she used on Chelsea, if only so he could more effectively counter it when it was just the two of them. But it was hard to complain about the niceties she heaped on, ones she extended to Chelsea—in the moment at least.

"I understand you have a niece," Irene said as she cut slices of pineapple upside-down cake.

"I do. Her name is Harper."

"Your sister had her very young."

It was more statement than question, and Bryce felt himself tense. He had nothing on Chelsea, though. If eye daggers could do physical harm, poor Irene would be toast. "She did."

Whether Irene sensed she was on the verge of overstepping or simply didn't realize she'd strayed into dicey territory, Bryce couldn't say. But she gave a little chuckle. "I see her when I go to Cormier's sometimes. She's a precocious one."

Bryce mirrored the laugh and sensed Chelsea relax next to him. "That she is. I think she'll be running the place before she hits high school at the rate she's going. Though software engineering has her attention these days."

"Smart as a whip." Irene angled her head. "And you? Would you like children someday?"

He got that sort of needling often enough from the biddies, but poor Chelsea choked on her cake and coughed until she'd lost her breath. "Definitely someday," he said.

Chelsea continued to look mortified, but Irene beamed. "It's always nice to hear when young people are thinking about family. And staying local."

"I'm a Duchesne boy through and through. I can't imagine living anywhere else." He realized the implication of his words and shot Chelsea an apologetic half-smile. "Though I have complete respect for those whose dreams take them elsewhere."

Chelsea sent him a you didn't have to say that look in return. Irene regarded Chelsea with what he could only describe as affection, then added, "And those who blaze their trails before deciding to come back home."

Since he didn't know if Chelsea's leaving remained a bone of contention—or the sentiments tied to her return—he decided to change the subject. "Speaking of reasons to love Duchesne, I hear you've cultivated quite an impressive rose garden."

That got Irene going, so much so he was able to do an unspoken check-in with Chelsea. She shook her head with something resembling wonder. He managed to sneak her a wink while Irene refilled her coffee cup. And since he seemed to be on a roll, he happily accepted a top off of his own cup and a second slice of cake.

❖

"I'm telling you, she was putty in his hands. Fawned all over him." Chelsea shook her head and laughed. Well, fawned by Irene standards.

Jada, who appeared on Chelsea's computer screen from her couch in New York, sipped her coffee and shrugged. "Who'd have thought?"

"Not this chick." Chelsea sipped her own coffee. A week later and she still wasn't over it.

"I guess don't look a gift horse in the mouth?"

She frowned. "That's such a terrible saying. I can't help but think of a poor horse with crooked teeth being made to feel bad about himself."

Jada dropped her shoulders and angled her head. Funny how easily exasperation came through a computer screen. "Don't change the subject."

"I'm not, I'm not." Chelsea waved a hand. "I swear the fact that I've managed to snare him has given me more credibility in her book than getting my own show."

Jada gave a disapproving head shake. "Mothers are the worst."

She thought about Bryce's mom. And Kate, for that matter. "Not all."

"Okay, not all. Still. Has she started pestering you about getting a ring?" Jada asked.

Chelsea laughed. "Not yet. Though I imagine it's only a matter of time."

"And she knows he's trans?"

"Yes. I mean, technically. I think she can conveniently forget that part because he passes. And he's charming and has a good job and comes from a good family." Things she'd never made a point of prioritizing in a relationship but topped Irene's lengthy list of traits in a suitable partner. Husband. Because Irene wouldn't deign to use such a modern word as *partner*.

"And let's not forget the biddies love him." Jada jabbed a finger skyward to emphasize her point.

"The biddies love him." She'd told Jada about the reference, and it had become a running joke. "And Irene is apparently the biggest biddy of them all."

Jada let out a happy sigh. "I'm glad it went well. I know you were stressing."

"It did." Chelsea ran through the evening in her mind. "Except, perhaps, when Irene asked him with absolutely zero subtlety if he wanted kids."

"She didn't."

"Oh, she did." Chelsea lifted a hand. "Though it came hot on the heels of asking about Harper and noting that Kate had her young. I should probably be grateful she went there instead of on a tirade about teenage pregnancy."

Jada grimaced. "Oof. Yeah. What did Bryce do?"

"Said he did someday and gracefully changed the subject. After ensuring her he was a Duchesne guy for life but also defending those of us who followed our dreams elsewhere." She couldn't have scripted a better answer herself.

"Damn. Dude has skills."

She laughed again. "Tell me about it."

Jada shrugged. "It's kind of hot."

She never would have thought so, and might have gone so far as to argue the opposite, but it was nice to be with someone Irene liked. Someone who wasn't like Irene, but understood how the Irenes of the world operated. Someone who could handle them—her—so effectively. She wouldn't go so far as to say the evening had been relaxing, but she hadn't been a ball of nerves by the time they left. Which made getting busy when they got back to her place not feel like a stretch, so maybe it was hot in a roundabout way.

"Are you thinking about how many kids the two of you might have?"

Chelsea groaned. "I'm not going to dignify that with a response."

"I'm just saying, it's good to talk about these things so you can make sure you're on the same page."

"No. Hard no. Can we talk about work now?"

Jada let out a beleaguered sigh. "If you insist."

"I insist."

"Okay. Did you ask Bryce to go to New York with you?"

Since the New York trip was technically a work thing, Jada had technically done as she'd asked. And since she had asked Bryce and he'd said yes, she didn't mind talking about it. "Do you know he's never been?"

"I'm not surprised. Super far but also big city. That doesn't seem up his alley."

"Yeah." She'd been surprised but not. And after mulling it over, the bigger surprise turned out to be realizing how much she didn't miss the frenetic energy that came with living there.

"So, did he say yes or no?" Jada asked.

"He said yes." She'd asked him after the dinner with Irene. They were doing the post-sex snuggle thing and she'd blurted it out because she'd been so wrapped up in Irene stress, she'd forgotten about it. And then remembered and panicked that she wouldn't be giving him enough notice to get time off from work. But not only had he agreed with enthusiasm, they'd stayed up half the night talking about her time there and all the ideas he had of what it would be like from movies and TV shows.

"Oh, yay." Jada set down her mug and clapped. "But you went all doe-eyed there. What's that about?"

She relayed the story and Jada went doe-eyed herself. "You two are freaking adorable. You know that, right?"

Chelsea didn't consider herself one to gloat, but it was hard not to, at least a little. "Yeah."

Jada let out a happy hum. "I'm not sure how you'll sort out the logistics and stuff, but I'm going to say it anyway. You're going to make really great babies together."

"Oh, my God. Stop."

"Just saying."

Just saying, her ass. "No more talk of meddling mothers or hypothetical babies. We're here to discuss work. Remember?"

Jada huffed. "Fine."

"Thank you."

Jada switched into screen sharing mode and pulled up their running outline for season two. "So, have you decided to have Irene in an episode?"

Chelsea narrowed her eyes even though Jada could no longer see her face. "You're a sneaky bitch."

"Yep," Jada said cheerfully. "I was also thinking about Kate saying she would be on if it meant a lot to you. What if you threw her a baby shower?"

It was both a fantastic idea and a way of keeping both Irene and babies front and center. "You're a genius. An evil genius, but a genius."

Jada cackled and didn't even pretend to be offended. "You love me."

"Yeah, yeah. Let me talk to Kate. As long as she's really willing, we should get her scheduled. The last thing we need is a lady going into labor in the middle of shooting."

Jada added a row near the top of the document. She put "Baby Shower" in the title column and then tabbed over to the timing one. There, she went for all caps: BEFORE THE PREGNANT LADY POPS. Ridiculous, but Chelsea laughed anyway. She loved the idea of a baby shower episode. Questions about her future with Bryce—or their compatibility on the kid front—notwithstanding.

CHAPTER TWENTY

The flights might have left Bryce queasy and exhausted, but room service and an early night at their hotel in Brooklyn did wonders. Which was a good thing since they pretty much only had one day to explore the city and Chelsea had a legit list of things she insisted he needed to see. After a quick cup of coffee and the best bagel of his life, they took the Q train into Manhattan and Chelsea instructed him to brace himself.

He laughed, but the second he and Chelsea set foot on the sidewalk in Times Square, an almost otherworldly energy seemed to pump through him. He'd sort of expected New Orleans on steroids, but New York City was another creature entirely.

"I told you." Chelsea laughed and took his hand, guiding him through the throngs.

As they walked, he struggled to pull his gaze from the towering buildings. "I'm sorry. I know I look like a tourist, but I can't help it."

Chelsea squeezed his arm. "Don't apologize. You're allowed to be a tourist in a city you've never visited."

"It's the scale of it all. I thought I was prepared." He looked at her. "I wasn't prepared."

She laughed. "Gawk away. I can't wait to take you to the Empire State Building later."

"I'm really glad you didn't think that was too dorky."

"It's not. Besides, even if it was, your first time in New York gets you a free pass."

He'd yet to wrap his head around that, even though they'd discussed it, planned the trip, and flown some fifteen hundred miles. Even though he stood on the sidewalk in the middle of Manhattan, surrounded by people and noise and buildings so tall they legit boggled his mind. "Thank you for inviting me to tag along."

Chelsea grinned. "I still can't believe you've never been."

"You say that, but you totally can. You know how it is. North of I-10 is considered Yankee territory." He was kidding and Chelsea laughed, but there was a kernel of truth in it. Travel wasn't a big part of his life—not growing up and not as an adult. He'd been to a few advising conferences and done the requisite beach vacations in Gulf Shores or Pensacola, but he'd never done places like New York or LA, had never left the country. He believed in new experiences and all that, it just didn't hit the top of his list of ways to spend time and money.

She bumped his hip with hers. "Well, I'm glad you let me talk you into venturing north of I-10."

They spent the afternoon wandering—Central Park, Greenwich Village. She even bought him a drink at Stonewall, which turned out to be even cooler than the Empire State Building. Chelsea navigated the maze of streets and subway with ease. Not just knowing what line to take, but which of the entrances and exits would get them where they wanted to go. He had a hard time imagining her living here, doing the city grind every single day. It made him realize how little of her life she'd shared, all the things she'd done in the years she'd been gone.

They decided on sushi for dinner, and Chelsea delightedly steered them to her favorite place. Settled at the sushi bar with glasses of sake, those questions continued to swirl. "Do you miss it?" he asked.

"Miss what?" Their seaweed salad arrived, and Chelsea dug in.

"This. The city. Living here."

"God, no." She took a bite, closed her eyes, and smiled. "Mmm."

He helped himself, suddenly aware of his rather amateur chopstick skills. "You seem so happy to be back."

"I miss parts of it." One of the rolls they'd ordered to share came over the top of the bar. Chelsea took it, gesturing to it as she set it down. "Things like the food."

He laughed. "Okay, even I find Duchesne's options limited."

She tipped her head back and forth. "I miss the diversity of people, the way all the boroughs and neighborhoods have a different feel. So many towns in Louisiana feel the same."

"But you never considered living in New Orleans."

Chelsea smeared one of the pieces with wasabi before dipping it in soy sauce and popping it in her mouth. She took her time chewing, making Bryce wonder if she didn't want to answer. "I considered it," she said finally.

"But?"

"But when I first finished culinary school, I didn't want to be that close to Duchesne. Then I got the job at Food TV and they don't film any shows there."

A perfectly logical answer, but it left him wanting more. Like so many things with Chelsea, it seemed.

"What about you?" Chelsea asked.

"What about me?"

"Did you really never consider living anywhere else?"

He mirrored Chelsea's move, giving himself a moment to settle on an answer. "I considered it."

"But?"

"But it's home. Home means a lot to me. I'm lucky, though. My parents have been my biggest champions, and for all that Duchesne is a tiny town where everyone knows everyone else's business, it's been really welcoming for me. Supportive. I don't take that for granted," he said.

Chelsea smiled but her eyes made her seem a million miles away. "I'm sorry it wasn't that for you."

She blinked a few times, bringing her focus back to him. "But if it had been, I wouldn't be where I am now."

"I guess that's true." He liked to imagine Chelsea as she was in Duchesne all along, but it wouldn't have been like that.

She bumped her shoulder to his. "I kind of like where I am now."

For as much as he loved being home, he couldn't fault his current situation. Present company in particular. He leaned in and kissed her lightly. "I do, too."

❖

Chelsea finished the requisite thank-yous with the show's host and producer and managed to keep her cool while signing a handful of autographs. Since Bryce had been shooed out with the rest of the audience, she took the elevator down and found him waiting in the building's posh lobby, easy smile and appreciative gaze already in place. God, she could get used to that.

"What did you think?" she asked.

"You were amazing," he said at the exact same time.

She laughed. "Be honest. I've never done anything with a studio audience before and it was kind of freaky."

"You're a natural. Like, I know I've used that word before, but it's true. It's almost as if doing it in front of people gives you even more energy."

She'd felt that way but had no idea if it translated. "I'm not sure I'd want to do my show like that, but it was really cool."

"Well, you sounded great, you looked even better, and I'm pretty sure you made a couple hundred new fans." Bryce put an arm around her and pulled her close. "I'm glad I locked you in as my girlfriend before you got super famous and realized you could get anyone you want."

"Stop." Even as she dropped her shoulders in exasperation, her pulse fluttered with delight. About the girlfriend part more than the famous part.

"I will not."

The answer—instant and playfully defiant—made her laugh. "Okay, don't. But let's get out of here. I want to do a little shopping before our dinner reservations."

Bryce gave a dramatic bow. "Your wish is my command."

They'd barely taken two steps when her phone rang. She pulled it from her purse and glanced at the screen. "It's my agent."

He laughed. "I still can't believe you have an agent."

She couldn't, either. She'd actually thought the initial email from Kane Talent was a hoax, only to find out that Sylvia Kane represented some of the biggest names in celebrity chefdom. She wiggled her brows at Bryce before swiping a finger across the screen. "Hello."

"Chelsea. Sylvia. How was the show?"

She appreciated that Sylvia didn't mince words. Also, that Sylvia considered her important enough to check on after a guest spot. "I'm great. Just finished taping. I think it went really well."

"Fantastic. You're in New York for another day, right?"

"Yep. Going to drag my boyfriend on a foodie tour of Koreatown and Little Italy." Her pants wouldn't fit the following week and she didn't even care.

"Speaking of Bryce."

Sylvia knew Bryce's name? Well, he was in the magazine. And on an episode. Still. All she managed in response was a quizzical, "Uh-huh?"

It must have left her with a confused expression, too, because Bryce regarded her with concern and mouthed a, "What's wrong?"

She shook her head and tried to focus. Between Sylvia's rapid-fire cadence and the bizarro nature of the pitch, it was all she could do to keep up. When Sylvia finally stopped talking, she clearly expected an answer. Only Chelsea didn't have one.

"Is he there with you?" Sylvia asked.

"He is."

"Well, ask him. I'll hold."

For some reason, the thought of having that conversation with even the hint of an audience made her panic. "Can I call you back? Ten minutes tops."

"You got it, girlie," Sylvia said, and the line went silent.

"What was that about?" Bryce took her hand. "Is everything okay? And am I the he you were talking about?"

Chelsea nodded, more than a little dazed. "We just got asked to be guests on *Wake Up.* Tomorrow morning."

"Tomorrow?" Bryce's eyes went wide. "Wait. We?"

She nodded again. *Wake Up* was the morning show on the left-leaning cable news network. Some news and plenty of feel-good stories—not fluff, but the sort of fare folks could stomach before the first cup of coffee. She'd watched it a few times, mostly from hotel rooms. Friendly to queer and other progressive issues, for sure, but not so much known for cooking segments.

"I don't understand."

"They're doing a series on being trans in America. The producer of the segment read the magazine article and then watched our episode and decided we were perfect for it. He reached out to Sylvia, Sylvia told him we were in the city, and he offered to fit us in tomorrow so we don't have to fly back again." Even though she was the one doing the explaining, she had a hard time believing it.

"You and me. On national television. Tomorrow." Bryce ticked off the details with his fingers like they were items on a grocery list.

"Yes." It didn't sound any more believable coming from him.

"I…"

When he didn't continue after several seconds, she said, "I know."

"And you have to call your agent back in ten minutes with your answer?"

"Yes." Though, she already knew hers. It was Bryce's that hung in the balance.

"Chelsea, I don't know."

She tried to keep the disappointment from her face but didn't need a mirror to know she failed spectacularly. "You can say no."

"I don't want to say no. I just..."

"Want to say no." Disappointment or not, she wasn't really surprised.

"No. Yes. I'm saying yes." Bryce gave the sort of decisive nod that came with resolve more than genuine agreement.

"Let's talk about it."

Bryce folded his arms. It was strange to see such a display of stubbornness from him. "You have to call Sylvia back."

"She can wait." Even if the thought of making her new agent wait filled Chelsea with even more unease than this conversation.

He shook his head, stance unchanged. "She can't. Not really. I'm guessing she has to confirm with the show if it's literally about us being there tomorrow morning."

He was right. They needed to decide and decide fast. Well, Bryce needed to decide. Because he was the one they really wanted. She tried not to let that sting. "I don't want you to feel pressured."

"I don't." He sucked in a breath and blew it out in a way that screamed he absolutely did.

"Bryce." She grabbed his hand.

"It's a once-in-a-lifetime opportunity. We have to say yes."

It was hard to know if he meant once in a lifetime for him or for her. Did it matter? She didn't want to talk him into it, only to have them both regret it later. Still. If he was genuinely game, she sure as hell didn't want to talk him out of it. "We don't have to."

He nodded with vigor. "Okay, we don't. But it would be amazing exposure for you. And it would be cool to be part of that series."

Chelsea allowed herself to mirror the gesture. "It would."

"Call her. I'm in." Bryce smiled and she was pretty sure he meant it.

"You're sure? Like, really really sure?"

He took another deep breath but cracked a legit grin. "All the reallys."

Chelsea let excitement take root. It zinged through her like a mixture of adrenaline and too much caffeine. She unlocked her phone to call Sylvia back, fingers trembling. Two minutes later, she had basic details, the promise of an email with thorough instructions, and a five a.m. call time. "Holy crap."

Bryce laughed. "Pretty much."

"Do you want to cancel dinner? Try to get some rest?" She couldn't fathom sleep, but letting him pick what they did with their evening felt like the least she could do.

"Honestly, I'd just as soon go out. Not a late night, but dinner at least."

"Yeah?" She was all in on celebrating but imagined he might have a case of nerves.

"Anything to take my mind off of being on live national television in"—he looked at his watch—"twelve hours."

Her stomach flipped. Okay, so maybe she had some nerves, too. "Well, when you put it that way."

CHAPTER TWENTY-ONE

B ryce dropped his bag and let out a contented sigh. He liked going away, but he loved coming home. A sentiment brought into particularly sharp relief after the frenetic energy that seemed to pulse through the streets of Manhattan.

Oh, and the intensity of going on TV. Live. As the main focus instead of the add-on.

To be fair, the segment had lasted ten minutes, tops. The host had spent at least a few of those talking with Chelsea about her show. And while he'd snuck in a dig about the Charlie Paul debacle, he'd only had kind words for Bryce. Not softball questions, exactly, but ones meant to promote inclusion. To drive home Bryce was just a regular guy navigating the same sorts of ups and downs as anyone else. Well, save a couple of extra challenges.

Really, the interview itself had been fine. Cool, even. Getting to talk about trans stuff without feeling like a curiosity. The genuine warmth of everyone he met, from the host to the hair and makeup guy. It was the getting recognized—by their Uber driver, several times at the airport, and by one of the flight attendants—that left him drained. He'd been worried about trolls, but other than a couple of gross DM requests in his social media accounts, it had all been positive. But it was still way more attention than he was used to and, he was starting to realize, way more than he wanted.

He sighed again, slightly less contented than before.

Chelsea parked her suitcase next to his duffel and regarded him with concern. "What's wrong?"

He sucked in another deep breath, basking in the quiet and the air that smelled like not much of anything. It was fine. More, it was done. No point in making Chelsea feel bad. "Not a thing in the world."

She narrowed her eyes. "You're heaving great sighs."

He chuckled at the phrase, then pulled his brain back into glad to be home territory. "Some of us sigh when we're happy."

She added pursed lips to the suspicious stare. "You don't seem happy."

He wrapped his arms around her waist, lifting her off the ground as he kissed her. "We had a fantastic trip. And now we're home."

Chelsea nodded but seemed unconvinced.

"Okay, I'm mostly excited about being home." He kissed her again. "With you, of course."

"Oh." Her nod became one of understanding. "You don't like to travel."

"I do like it. I just like the coming home part best." He tapped a finger between her breasts. "You don't feel the same."

"It's not that I don't. It's just…"

When she didn't continue, and looked away rather than at him, he took her hand. "Just what?"

"I've never had a home I was attached to enough that it was more appealing than traveling somewhere else."

The idea gave him a pang of sadness, for the Chelsea he knew now, but also for the teenager who wanted nothing more than to get out. "I'm sorry."

She rolled her eyes and laughed. "I mean, I can appreciate my own bed. My own kitchen."

It wasn't the same thing, but it was clear Chelsea had no desire to dissect it. "I feel you."

She made a show of looking him up and down. "If I went away by myself, I'd be happy to come home to you."

Exhaustion faded and desire took over. Sexual, but also the idea of Chelsea coming home to him, always. Not something to talk about tonight, but soon. "Would you?"

"Especially if I could talk you into taking me straight to bed."

Arousal hopped in the front seat, leaving feelings to occupy themselves for the night. "Could I talk you into a shower with me first?"

"Mmm. Absolutely."

He led the way to the bathroom, where they peeled off each other's clothes before stepping under the hot spray. They scrubbed away the day of travel, a serviceable exercise more than a sensual one. In bed, clean sheets and the smell of his preferred fabric softener enveloped him, along with the lush curves of Chelsea's body. He kissed her everywhere, focusing on the places her skin was softest: the undersides of her breasts and the insides of her thighs.

"You are perfection," he said.

She lifted her head and looked into his eyes. "You're biased."

He moved up the bed to capture her lips in a kiss. "Damn right I am."

Chelsea sighed under his touch, then purred. He worshiped her with his fingers and mouth, taking his time. Although Chelsea usually started to squirm at his attentions—all restless energy and pent-up wanting—even she seemed to slow. The unhurried pace felt like a flag they planted together, an unspoken alignment with life here, rather than the city that never slept.

Her legs opened for him, and he slipped inside. She was warm and wet, welcoming him in. Welcoming him home. He braced himself over her, moved with her. Her fingers slid deliciously over his cock, around it. They moved together, breath heavy but no words.

When she came, it felt like a gift, like she was giving herself to him in ways she hadn't before. When his own orgasm swelled, it was like surrender and victory rolled into one. Like everything he'd ever wanted had coalesced into this single, perfect woman.

After, Chelsea lay curled against him fast asleep. His body slowed, but his mind revved. Trying to reconcile the public-facing persona that seemed as authentically Chelsea as the one who'd given herself so fully to him tonight. On some levels, the two felt at odds, especially when that public persona pulled him along for the ride. Yet, he didn't doubt that at least part of Chelsea's heart rested with him, with the life they'd started to build together out of the spotlight.

Could the two exist together? Clearly, they could. Was he in love with both? He must be, because he'd fallen for the whole of Chelsea, not just bits and pieces.

He let the certainty of that soothe his swirling thoughts. It would be fine. This was his life. More importantly, it was the life Chelsea had chosen, the one she continued to choose in spite of everything else. The rest was just noise.

❖

Since Bryce had to go to work, Chelsea got up with him, sending him off with a travel mug full of coffee and a kiss. Like so many things these days, it left her feeling strangely domestic. National TV one day, housewife the next. Both managed to feel on brand, which made her realize that the brand she'd created was truer to herself than several of the versions she'd embodied the last few years. So, why the hell not?

But instead of puttering around Bryce's for the day, she headed home to unpack and tackle her own laundry and chores. Not that she would have minded Bryce's boxers in with her cottons. They just weren't at that stage yet. Though, the more she thought about it, the more it felt like a formality. They were practically living together, and she couldn't imagine not having him as part of her daily life. Assuming, of course, that life still got to include her share of cooking for the masses and jetting off to New York.

She stuffed the first load in the washer and returned to the kitchen, pouring herself a cup of coffee before settling in at the table with her laptop. She and Jada had most of the episodes for her second season squared away, including the baby shower episode they'd film first. Only one slot remained.

Jada had taken to calling it the "Come On, Irene" episode, which of course she felt compelled to sing every time she mentioned it, even after Chelsea pointed out that the woman in the song was named Eileen. Chelsea remained on the fence about broaching it, much less making it a reality. Meanwhile, Jada insisted it would be the ultimate power move, bringing Irene into a world where Chelsea called all the shots.

The thing was, having the upper hand had started to lose its appeal. Coming home to Duchesne had been about coming out on top, but making friends and building a life had blurred the edges of all that. Made it feel less important. All she really wanted was to get along, enough that Irene's proximity didn't interfere with everything she cared about. Having Irene on the show might solidify that. Or it could blow it all to hell.

Certain the answer wouldn't come from a morning of stewing, she toggled to the recipes and script for the baby shower. Kate had approved the menu, so all that remained was a final test of the salted caramel cake—that would not be decorated to look like a baby bump or a baby's butt, thank you very much—and the cream cheese and pepper jelly dip. She could do both today and see if Bryce wanted to come for dinner and help with taste testing.

She got to work, texting Jada pictures as she went. Jada, in true Jada fashion, teased her about the sexual powers of salted caramel. That, in turn, left her thinking about Bryce licking vanilla custard from her nipples and left her attempting to frost a cake when she'd rather be frosting Bryce. She texted as much to Jada and not ten seconds later, her phone rang.

"Don't you know it's rude to interrupt a girl when she's having sexy daydreams about her boyfriend?" Chelsea asked.

"I'd be happy to call back in an hour. Would that give you enough time to wrap up?"

The answer she might have expected. Sylvia's Staten Island accent? Not so much. "Oh, my God. Sylvia. I'm sorry. I was expecting someone else." She'd swear on her life Jada's info had flashed on the screen.

"No need to apologize, girlie," Sylvia said. "That boyfriend of yours is pretty daydream worthy."

Chelsea dropped the hand she'd slapped over her eyes. Might as well play along. "He is, but that's probably not why you called."

"But I am calling you about another dish. The dish, if you will."

"Huh?" Sylvia had opinions about a lot of things. Cooking wasn't one of them.

"*The Dish.* The show. They want you."

One kind of confusion gave way to another. "They do?"

"Guest chef for a week. You know they do that rotating thing since Manuela's departure."

She did. Since Manuela had left Food TV to focus on running her restaurants, pretty much everyone who was anyone in the food world had been a guest host. Okay, not everyone. But all the ones who had a media presence had. Big names. Really big names. "No shit."

Even as she cringed at her unfiltered response, Sylvia laughed. "Why are you still surprised? Your star is on the rise, girlie."

Sylvia said it so matter-of-factly, Chelsea took the words at face value. And maybe did a happy dance in her chair. "Right."

"Can you get to Charlotte next week? They had someone fall through and are looking to fill from the Food TV ranks. You'd fly out Monday and they film Tuesday through Thursday for the following week."

It could have deflated her, knowing she'd be a stand-in. But it meant going and coming home the week before they were due to start filming again. Which would crunch her prep time but couldn't have worked out better. "Absolutely."

"Good. I already told them yes." Sylvia waited a beat. "Kidding. Soft yes. I won't commit you to anything without running it by you first."

"I appreciate that. And this. Everything, really. I don't know what I'd do without you." Funny how quickly a girl could go from wondering if she was important enough to have an agent to feeling like her agent was indispensable.

"Have less fun but be less busy. I gotta run, girlie, but someone will be in touch with your travel details and to discuss run of show."

Chelsea barely got a thank you in before the line went silent. She set her phone down and did another happy dance. Because *The Dish* had viewership probably ten times that of her show. Because one of the recurring hosts had been her idol since culinary school. And because this invite had to do with her show and her cooking alone. As much fun as it had been to do the interview with Bryce, the whole thing left her feeling a bit like a prop.

She might be loath to admit it, but she could use that shot of personal edification. And if Bryce's reaction to coming home was anything to go on, he'd be thrilled that it had nothing to do with him. So really, win-win. All the wins. She couldn't wait to tell Jada. And Bryce. Even Irene. It was all coming together—everything she ever wanted.

Chapter Twenty-Two

With Chelsea off to Charlotte for the week, Bryce was left to his own devices. Strange to think of it that way, given that he technically had friends and family and a life apart from the time they spent together. But the last few weeks in particular felt like they practically lived together, checking in even if one or both of them had busy days or after-work plans. They hadn't spent a single night apart.

He hesitated to admit how easy it was to get used to, how much he liked it. But the truth was it felt like all the pieces of the puzzle finally falling into place. Like his unflappable optimism that he'd find it had been worthwhile. Chelsea might not be ready for forever language, but he'd be lying if he said the word didn't already hover in the back of his mind. It's what he wanted. What he'd always wanted.

Kate, being Kate, had asked him pointedly if he wanted it with Chelsea. As opposed to simply projecting all those wants onto her. A fair question after dating only a few months. But being with Chelsea had given him glimpses of a life that felt at once more real and more like the life of his dreams than any other relationship he'd had. He couldn't help it if that had him thinking a few—or a few hundred—steps ahead.

Bryce pulled into the parking lot of the Shur-fine and chuckled. Daydreaming about marriage while buying some cliché bachelor dinner.

The store was bumping, at least by Duchesne standards. Apparently, he wasn't the only one with a last-minute, on the way home dinner agenda. He grabbed a basket, but quickly swapped it out for a cart. Might as well stock the fridge while he was here.

He'd barely made it twenty feet into the produce department when he heard his name. He turned and found himself face-to-face with Ivy

Carmichael, his insurance agent. Chatty, but sweet. He could do worse. "Hey, Ivy."

"We saw you on *First You Make a Roux*. And in the photo spread in the magazine, of course. You've gone and gotten famous on us." She gave his forearm a pinch.

"I wouldn't go that far, but it was fun. Have you had a chance to meet Chelsea yet?"

"Not yet, but I'm dying to. Her mama is a client of mine." Ivy leaned in and lowered her voice. "Not the nicest lady, if I'm being totally honest. A little holier than thou, if you know what I mean."

He did, though admitting as much felt like betraying Chelsea somehow. So he did what he often did when chatting with some of Duchesne's more gossipy residents. He smiled and nodded.

"Well, Chelsea seems to have fallen far from that tree, thank heavens. At least from what I've seen. And read, of course. And heard." Ivy leaned in again. "I've also heard the two of you are getting along quite nicely."

Ivy's sly smile implied far more than the phrases "getting along" and "quite nicely," but he had no interest in feeding the busybody brigade, even if he enjoyed the privileges of being on its good side. "It's been great to reconnect with her since she moved back," he said.

That got him an elbow to the ribs. "Is that what the kids are calling it these days?"

"Ms. Carmichael, I'm sure I have no idea what you mean. Now, if you'll excuse me, I've got to get some groceries so I can go home and make myself supper."

"Oh, that's right. Chelsea is off for that guest spot on *The Dish*. Marie down at the salon told me she stopped in for some highlights before she flew out today and would be gone the whole week." Ivy lifted her chin. "I'm sure you won't go hungry in the meantime. Your mama raised you right."

He glommed onto that last bit more than the level of detail she seemed to know about Chelsea's life and, by extension, his. "Just don't tell her what's in my cart if you happen to see me again at the checkout."

Ivy chortled.

Bryce winked and went on his way, suddenly anxious to be home. He made it to the registers otherwise unscathed, only to have the cashier—who couldn't be a day over sixteen—spend the entire time it took to ring him out telling him how she'd seen him on TV and how awesome it was. The interview, not the episode, she meant. But after the interview, she'd gone and watched the episode even though cooking shows weren't really her thing. And it was good, but not as good as the interview because to have somebody from Duchesne of all places on TV talking about trans stuff and gender identity was literally the coolest thing ever.

By the time he got home, he felt like every drop of extroversion had been wrung out of him. It didn't really make sense. He talked to more people, more complete strangers even, at an average admissions event or orientation session than he did between work and the grocery store combined. He talked to people for a living, and he loved it.

Only, in those instances, he wasn't talking about himself. Not beyond enough personal details here and there to be interesting and engaging and real. This whole thing with Chelsea made it feel like he was in the spotlight. Not like Chelsea, thank God. But more than he bargained for. And more, he was beginning to realize, than he wanted.

Hopefully, he'd done his share of public appearances and could go back to flying under the radar. Happily being her plus-one but otherwise unknown outside of work and his circle of family and friends, even if that circle included the better part of the population of Duchesne.

❖

Chelsea walked onto the set and tried not to look completely awestruck. It made the setup in her kitchen look like child's play. Hell, it made Charlie's sound stage look like amateur hour. This was the big time, at least as far as shows on Food TV went—at least a hundred feet wide and she counted six cameras. And she was about to become part of it.

"Chelsea."

She turned to find Simone Bertold beaming at her. Forget awestruck. It took considerable effort not to ogle. "Ms. Bertold. It's such an honor to meet you."

"Darling. Likewise. I'm delighted you're here." Simone grabbed her by the shoulders and lightly kissed each cheek, making Chelsea feel more like she was in Paris than Charlotte.

"I'm pretty sure I'm even more delighted to be here."

"We needed some fresh blood and I think you're going to be just the thing. Have you poked around yet?"

Chelsea shook her head. "I only arrived a few minutes ago."

Simone hooked Chelsea's arm in hers. "Come with me, then. I'll give you the grand tour." The tour included dressing rooms, a green room, the risers where the studio audience sat, and the set itself. "That will be your spot."

Chelsea went to the stool behind the counter. Her brain ticked off the notable chefs and celebrity guests who'd sat in that very spot, but it started to make her dizzy, so she stopped and settled for a simple, "Wow."

Simone wagged a finger. "Don't be intimidated. You're as talented as any of them, and you have a personality. Puts you ahead of the pack as far as I'm concerned."

It was impossible not to relax at Simone's matter-of-fact declaration. "Thank you."

"Last week we had Mr. Fifty Shades of Fusion." Simone rolled her eyes.

Chelsea wasn't a fan either, though it had more to do with his arrogance than his cooking. "Are you saying it's a low bar?"

Simone threw her head back and laughed. "You're a quick one. I can't wait to see you keep us on our toes."

"Well, Nigel and Yan at least." She had no intention of keeping anyone, including the other hosts, on their toes, but it was nice that Simone thought she could.

"That's the spirit." Simone glanced at her watch. "I'm off to get shellacked for the cameras. I'll see you at the run-through."

After her own stop at hair and makeup, and another at wardrobe, Chelsea made her way back to the set. Nigel and Yan were already there. The awe factor didn't kick in quite as hard as it had with Simone, but she still appreciated the warm welcomes and low-key small talk while the crew milled around setting the kitchen for the first segment. Simone appeared and the producer swooped in with tweaks to the script. Chelsea nodded, suddenly grateful cue cards were standard fare for tapings of *The Dish*.

They did an abbreviated run of show while the audience was seated. Chelsea double-checked the mise en place for her segment, taking a minute to fiddle with the burners of the stove and peek in the oven at the presentation dish that had been prepped ahead of time.

"Everything to your standards?" Barb, the producer, peered around her.

Chelsea jumped, then laughed and brushed off Barb's apology. "I'm great. Just getting my bearings since we're in the land of single takes."

Barb laughed at the assessment. "Yes, but we have multiple cameras, and edits can cover all manner of sins."

"Right." And she'd been assured do-overs were allowed in true disaster situations. They acted like it was a live show, but it wasn't literally.

"Besides, the audience loves a little flub now and again. Makes y'all seem more human." Barb gave her arm a friendly squeeze. "You got this."

Since they'd seemed to cross the line into friendly territory, she leaned in. "Is everyone always this friendly, or are people still overcompensating for the Charlie debacle?"

"You probably deserve the overcompensating, but this is how we do business. I'm sorry if that's out of the ordinary for you."

Chelsea shook her head, not wanting to give the wrong impression. "My crew is amazing. We're like family already. I thought this might feel a little more...show biz."

Barb tipped her head. "Nigel will do jazz hands if you ask real nice."

The snort of laughter escaped before she could stop it. She pressed her lips together. "Good to know."

Barb grinned. "All right, then. I think it's show time."

The taping passed in a blur. Cooking and talking. Eating and laughing. Had it not been for the studio audience, she might have convinced herself she was at a party with new friends. Okay, maybe not that casual, but close.

When they wrapped the episode, the three regular hosts offered kudos and quips about doing it all again. And they did. Wardrobe change, kitchen reset, and they were off to the races. The second episode flew by just as quick, but by the time it was done, she felt as though she'd run a marathon. Simone assured her it was normal, and that she'd get used to it.

She mulled over the idea of getting used to it—any of it—on the ride to her hotel, grateful the gig came with car service to and from. She texted Bryce and Jada, then allowed her eyes to drift closed. Just for a moment. To rest, sure. But mostly to bask.

Back at the hotel, Chelsea let herself into her room and it was all she could do not to immediately drop onto the perfectly made king-size bed. She managed to set down her bag and kick off her shoes first, fishing out her phone and flopping unceremoniously on her back. She'd texted Bryce on the way to the hotel, but he didn't answer right away.

Seeing no fewer than six notifications from him on her lock screen made her smile.

I'm glad it went well.

I'm so proud of you.

(Assuming you're cool with me saying that)

I can't wait to hear everything.

Also, I miss you.

And your body.

Despite the exhaustion, Chelsea couldn't keep the cheesy grin from spreading. She held the phone over her head and typed a slew of rapid-fire replies, feeling more like a lovestruck teenager than a professional chef doing a TV appearance.

Better than I could have dreamed.

Can we talk tonight?

I miss you, too.

And your body.

Since he'd be at work for another hour, then driving home, Chelsea hauled herself off the bed and padded to the bathroom. The fluorescent lights made her makeup look garish and heavy-handed. Since she no longer had to worry about smudges, she gave her eyes a good rub while the shower water warmed.

The walk-in shower, complete with rain head, made her think about the one at Bryce's place. Which of course made her think of all the showers they'd shared there in the last few months. Which, in turn, made her miss him more. Chelsea worked the high-end hotel shampoo into her hair and sighed. She liked having someone to miss and knowing Bryce missed her back, even if the missing part sucked.

Missed her back but didn't try to hold her back. She'd been nervous he'd freak out, question whether the week in Charlotte would turn into a month that would turn into forever. She'd been a little freaked out herself, though less about the opportunity and more about how attached she'd grown to being in Duchesne.

She switched to conditioner and let out a chuckle. For all that she'd picked Duchesne for her show, there was nothing squishy and sentimental about moving home. But sitting on her porch now that the weather had mellowed, toodling around town and seeing the same faces—it felt good. As did feeling like Duchesne as a whole was proud of her.

Shower done, she slipped into one of the cushy hotel robes and returned to the room. She didn't like being the kind of person who immediately grabbed her phone, but she did it anyway. Instead of messages from Bryce, though, she had one from Simone.

You won't hurt my feelings if you want room service and a night to yourself, but if you're inclined to be social, my husband and I would love you to come for dinner.

Simone Bertold was inviting her over for dinner. Simone Bertold. Was inviting her over. For dinner.

Chelsea took a deep breath and blew it out. Then she set down her phone and did yet another happy dance. She'd get to start counting them as exercise at the rate she was going.

She gave this one a little extra. Salsa steps, flailing arms, the whole bit. Over to the window, around the bed, across to the door. When she made it back to where she'd left her phone, she picked it up and repeated the deep breath. In. Out.

I'd love to.

Chapter Twenty-Three

"Uncle Bryce, do I need to take your phone away?" Harper gave him a stern look she'd one hundred percent learned from her mother.

"Sorry." Bryce tucked the phone in his pocket and picked up his fork. "How was school?"

Harper shook her head, sliding effortlessly into disapproval. "We've been talking about my day for the last twenty minutes."

"She exaggerates," Sutton said. "At least a little."

"Still. Sorry I'm so distracted."

"Is everything okay?" Sutton, God love her, looked genuinely concerned.

"He's just obsessing over what his girlfriend is up to," Kate said.

"Which is hecka rude." Harper's head shake became more of a side-to-side slide with attitude.

Bryce scrubbed a hand over his face. He was being an idiot. "It's fine. Everything is fine."

Kate's expression softened. "I thought it was. You said the show went great and Chelsea scored an invite to the grand dame of cooking's house for dinner."

He gave a decisive nod. "Exactly."

Sutton sucked in a breath that made it seem like she was debating whether to say what she wanted to say next.

"What? Go on. Spit it out." He'd never antagonize Sutton the way he did Kate, but she was family now.

Sutton's expression turned apologetic. "Are you worried that she's not having a good time, or worried that she is?"

Kate made a show of looking at everything but him. Harper stared at him unabashedly, eyes wide. Nothing like being called out after already feeling dumb. "Neither. I'm not worried at all."

Sutton nodded as though she regretted asking. "Exactly. Nothing to be worried about. Everything is going great."

"Right. So, anyway. Phone is away. Let's change the subject. How're the wedding plans?"

Sutton chuckled and Kate rolled her eyes. But he could always count on maid of honor Harper to talk about the wedding. "We went to the baker this weekend and picked out the cake. It's going to be white with raspberry and, wait for it, chocolate with cookies and cream."

"All together?" He liked the components, but all at once seemed like a lot.

"No, the bottom cake will be white with raspberry because Mom says more people like that. Whatever." It was Harper's turn to roll her eyes. "And the smaller two cakes on top will be chocolate."

"Nice." While he was in it for the change of subject, they did sound good.

Harper indicated the silhouette of a stacked cake with her hands. "Simple flowers, not all the way around but dotted here and there. It's going to be gorgeous."

Bryce smiled. "Are you sure you want to be a software engineer? You could definitely be a wedding planner."

"Could you not?" Kate said before Harper could respond.

Bryce lifted a brow.

"Not that you couldn't be." Kate looked at Harper before returning her attention to Bryce. "It's just that this wedding in particular is already bigger and more planned than some of us would like."

Harper didn't miss a beat. "It's next month, Mama. It needs to be planned."

Kate rubbed her rapidly growing belly. "It can't come soon enough if you ask me."

"Speaking of, how's the dress situation?" Bryce asked.

"It's as gorgeous as the cake is going to be," Harper said without hesitation.

"More importantly, it's going to be generously cut." Kate gave her belly a pat. "Lots of room for the two of us."

As unexpected as Kate's first-attempt pregnancy had been, she was taking the whole eight months pregnant at her wedding thing in stride. Of course, she'd capped the guest list at sixty, even with the size of their family, and held firm on doing the whole thing under a tent in their parents' backyard.

"I love that maternity bridal gowns are a thing. It feels like we've come a long way," Bryce said.

Kate smirked. "I think it's about companies working an untapped market more than any nod to being progressive."

He laughed. "That's capitalism for you."

"Speaking of capitalism," Sutton said. "You're coming to the baby shower, right?"

He couldn't decide which part to make fun of—the ungraceful segue or Sutton's seemingly genuine terror about the shower. "Of course I'll be there."

"Yeah. Okay. Good." Sutton nodded, but the look of fear didn't leave her face.

"What's got you spooked? The center of attention part or the being on TV part?"

Sutton cringed. "Yes."

"Uh-uh. None of that." Kate wagged a finger. "If anyone gets to play that card, it's going to be me."

"Y'all know if you really don't want to do it, Chelsea would deal." Though the thought of being the one to tell her gave him his own decent-sized dose of terror.

"We wouldn't do that," Sutton said.

"Even if we wanted to," Kate added.

Once again, Harper shook her head like a put-upon grownup at a table full of petulant children. "It's not that hard, y'all. Seriously."

Bryce snickered. He wouldn't have said it, but he sure as hell was going to enjoy the fact that Harper had.

"You shut up, Mr. Interviewed on National TV," Kate said.

For all that Sutton usually played the part of peacekeeper, she let out a derisive snort. "Yeah."

Bryce picked up his beer. "Maybe we should go back to talking about the wedding."

"Coward." Kate laughed as she said it, though, and launched into the saga of getting her wedding band sized since the one they'd picked out was already too small.

He hadn't gone to dinner looking for a distraction, but that was exactly what he got. By the time he slipped on his jacket and said his good nights, he'd almost forgotten how focused he'd been on wondering what Chelsea might be up to. It lasted right up until the second he got into his truck and peeked at his phone.

Nothing.

He peeked again when he pulled into his driveway. Still nothing. He changed his clothes, put on a movie, and did a quick check of his work email. With each task, he checked, as though the ringer—which he'd turned on and all the way up—might not be working.

He really was being an idiot about this. Chelsea was safe and probably having the time of her life. And despite Sutton's probing earlier, he didn't begrudge her that. It was simply that he missed her. They'd been spending so much time together, having her away felt strange. Not that he was clingy. Or insecure. Or anything like that.

Right?

At eleven, he gave up. The six a.m. alarm stopped for no one, even anxious boyfriends. He'd hear all about it tomorrow. And Chelsea would be home at the end of the week. With filming starting up again, she'd probably stay put for a few weeks. Things would settle down and go back to something resembling normal.

Well, as normal as they could be with a film crew in Chelsea's house, Kate and Sutton's wedding right around the corner, and a new niece arriving only a few weeks later. Bryce turned off the light and chuckled about being the boring one of the lot.

❖

Jada arrived the day after Chelsea got home from Charlotte. Layla and Gio and the whole production crew landed the day after. She managed to fall into bed with Bryce each night—thank God—but otherwise ate, slept, and breathed *First You Make a Roux*.

After a semi-frantic two days of scripting, staging, and grocery shopping, season two was off to the races. If by races, she meant throwing a baby shower for a super pregnant Kate and a slightly apprehensive Sutton. Which she did.

"Cut," Jada called, no more than thirty seconds into their intro spot.

Sutton groaned. "It was me again, wasn't it? I looked at the camera."

Kate raised a hand. "I would like it noted that I did not, in fact, look at the camera."

"Noted but not helping." Sutton looked from Kate to Jada. "I can say that because she's already agreed to marry me."

"Hate me 'cause you ain't me," Kate said.

Chelsea let out a snort at the Harper impersonation, which earned her "not helping" looks from both Jada and Sutton.

"Just relax," Jada said for at least the tenth time. "Pretend the cameras aren't there."

Sutton scrubbed a hand over her face. "Sorry. I don't mean to be high maintenance."

Kate squeezed Sutton's hand. "You're not high maintenance."

"You really aren't." Jada nodded with more enthusiasm than the situation called for.

"Truer words, babe." Kate gave the hand a tug. "You got this."

Chelsea took that as her cue to wade in. "And if you're really not cool, we'll deal. You can just be in the party sequence at the end."

"I'm fine. I can do it." Sutton gave the sort of full body shake Chelsea would typically attribute to a teenager. Or maybe a dog. Seeing the usually calm, cool, and collected Sutton resort to even low-level histrionics made her feel bad even as it made her laugh.

Jada, never one to squander a moment of resolve, clapped her hands together. "Fantastic. You're more than fine. You're amazing. Now, let's take it from the top."

Whether Sutton actually managed to relax, or she powered through by sheer force of will, Chelsea couldn't say. But they got through the intro and Sutton's segment without a hitch. By the time they wrapped the cooking and started setting up for the shower shots, Sutton seemed to be genuinely enjoying herself. Kate seemed to relax even more in response, and when Bryce and a few of Kate's friends showed up for the final stretch of filming, it felt like a legit party.

And then Jada wrapped production, the crew headed out for the night, and it was a legit party. Kate and Bryce's parents, Sutton's dad, and a few more aunts and cousins and friends showed up. The next thing she knew, forty people crowded into her house, eating and laughing and giving enough baby advice to make her seriously question becoming a parent herself.

Though, even as she wavered, a more persistent thought took root in her mind. Not a thought, exactly. More like a vignette. Flashes of her with a round belly. Bryce assembling a crib. Bryce in the kitchen with a baby tucked into the crook of his arm. The images were so clear, she had to go hide in the bathroom for a second to shake them off. She knew Bryce wanted that for his life. He'd said as much to Irene at dinner, and he practically radiated settle down and start a family energy. The more pressing question, vignettes aside, was did she?

Oy. *Not the time or the place, Chelsea.*

She managed to laugh at herself and chase the images away, along with the inexplicable longing they'd somehow stirred, and rejoined the party. Eventually, the crowd cleared. Kate and Sutton were effusive in their gratitude, Harper angled to be on another episode, and Jada, who'd stuck around for the shower, excused herself in a veil of vague references to some dinner plans. In the end, only Bryce remained.

"I can't thank you enough for today," he said.

"Are you kidding? Kate and Sutton were doing me the favor. Jada says this might be our best episode yet."

Bryce slapped a hand to his chest. "Better than ours? Say it isn't so."

"I think she might be using that as leverage to get you back on." Though that had as much to do with Jada's teasing about their relationship as it did the quality of guests.

"Sneaky little thing she is."

Chelsea laughed. "Don't tell me you're just now noticing."

"No, Jada strikes me as a woman who is very used to getting what she wants." Bryce lifted a hand. "Which I have mad respect for."

"Same. I always tell her I want to be her when I grow up, but she gets annoyed because it implies she's older than me."

"Well…" Bryce angled his head. "Wait. I thought you had all your episodes planned."

"There's the matter of Irene." Despite the slight thaw in their relationship, Chelsea still struggled to imagine playing the loving mother/daughter duo on screen.

Bryce frowned. "Has she not agreed?"

If she ever really wanted something from Irene, she should just send Bryce over. Irene would trip over herself trying to accommodate him. "She hasn't. Of course, I haven't asked."

"Chelsea." His tone came off more sympathetic than judgmental.

"You sound like Jada."

"I can think of worse things."

She twisted her body to hip check him. "Don't tell her that. She'd be unbearable."

"Deal." Bryce snaked his arms around her and tugged her close. "How about, if she says no, or if you decide you don't want to ask her, I'll be your backup."

Had she truly found herself in a pinch, she didn't doubt Bryce would come to her rescue. The immediate offer, though, before she even needed him, was different. It was like he really knew her, really cared about her. Like he loved her. "You're the best."

His grin turned shy. "I'm glad you think so."

"I do." In ways she hadn't even imagined she wanted or needed.

"I think you're the best, too." Bryce nodded earnestly even as his hands slid down to squeeze her butt.

"In bed, you mean?"

"I mean all the ways." He pulled their bodies close. "Just extra especially in bed."

Not unlike conversations they'd had probably a dozen times, but something brought back that longing from before. Longing for a baby of her own, for a partner to build a life with. Not things she'd wanted or prioritized before, yet not wholly unfamiliar. Like a cousin of the longing she had for family more generally, for home.

"Did all the baby talk ruin your libido for the night?" Bryce asked.

"Huh? What? No. Not at all."

He tucked a stray curl behind her ear. "You looked about a million miles away just then."

"Nah. I'm right here." No need to focus on the fantasy future part.

"Can I take you to bed now, then? I know you have another early morning tomorrow."

She did. Tomorrow and every day for the next two weeks of filming. That's where her focus needed to be. Well, there and on the sexy, amazing guy in front of her. The rest would keep for another day. Or another decade.

Chapter Twenty-Four

With half the season filmed, and with Jada breathing down her neck, Chelsea bit the bullet and invited Irene over for lunch. With the question of having Irene on the show looming—and without the buffer of Bryce's infinite good nature—she spent the better part of the morning working herself into a ball of stress. It didn't help matters when Irene breezed in a little before noon in peak nitpick mode.

"Have you considered making the decor a bit more elegant?" Irene asked, though she'd been in the kitchen several times before.

"What do you mean?" Chelsea knew exactly what she meant.

"More subtle. Mature." Irene flipped her hand back and forth. "Something more suitable for a grown woman."

"I like the decor. The network does, too. It's modern, with a touch of whimsy."

"Whimsy." Irene sniffed.

"Shall we eat?" Chelsea gestured to the table, taking grim satisfaction in the fact that she'd set it with mismatched vintage plates.

Irene settled at the table and gingerly placed a polka-dot napkin in her lap, as though afraid whimsy might be contagious. "Where's Bryce? You're still seeing him, aren't you?"

What the hell kind of question was that? "He's helping his sister with some projects for her wedding. And yes, I'm still seeing him."

Irene nodded curtly.

"What?" Chelsea asked.

"What do you mean what?"

"Why would you ask if I'm still seeing him?" Chelsea asked. It was like Irene expected things to crash and burn.

"Because you jetted off to New York, then to Charlotte, and you haven't mentioned him."

She hadn't mentioned Bryce going on the first trip with her, or the TV appearance they did together. Irene obviously hadn't seen it. "He knows I travel for work. It's not an issue."

"Ah."

Impatience flared, even though she couldn't quite identify what she was impatient about. "What?"

"Do not take that tone with me, Chelsea Margaret." Irene's jaw clenched. "And complete sentences, if you don't mind."

Chelsea cleared her throat and resisted the urge to talk back on principle. "It feels like you expect, or maybe even want, Bryce to break up with me and I don't understand why."

Irene laced her fingers together. "Because I get the sense Bryce is the settling down kind, and I'm not sure you are."

The observation—and everything it implied—landed like a fallen soufflé, heavy and sad. Chelsea sighed. "You don't think I'm good enough for him."

"It's simply an observation that you might not be suitable together in the long term."

There was that word again. "And heaven forbid I do anything unsuitable."

"Unsuitable as a couple."

"So, you're saying you don't approve?" The second the words were out of Chelsea's mouth, she regretted them. Asking the question implied she wanted the answer. That the answer carried weight. That it meant something.

"Approve of what? Of you dating Bryce Cormier?"

It was what she'd meant in the moment, though in truth, it just as easily could have been any aspect of her life. Every aspect. For all that she told herself she'd moved beyond needing gold stars and warm words from her mama, the longing for them had never left. "Yes, but it doesn't matter."

Irene let out a sniff. "I wish you weren't so flip about your life, Chelsea. It does matter. Things matter."

She scrubbed a hand over her face, disappointment and regret vying for top billing. "That's not what I meant."

Despite her ramrod posture, Irene's shoulders visibly stiffened. "Then why don't you try telling me what you mean."

She could deflect. Demur. It had been standard operating procedure for so long, it felt like second nature. But something in her chest cracked and she didn't have it in her, even if it meant breaking the peace she'd worked so hard to keep. "It means nothing I do has ever been good enough for you. Will ever be good enough for you."

Irene frowned.

"So I've had to stop living with that as my standard because otherwise I'd hate myself."

Chelsea braced herself, but instead of an onslaught, Irene countered with a look of genuine confusion. "Is that what you think?"

"I'm queer. I'm fat. Until recently, I was single. No kids." She held up her hand and ticked off each failing. "And let's not forget abandoning my faith."

"Chelsea." Irene's voice was quiet, barely above a whisper.

"It's fine. We're different people who want and believe and value different things. I've accepted that. Most days, it doesn't even bother me," Chelsea said.

"You…you think I'm disappointed in you?"

Since Irene looked more devastated than defensive, Chelsea gave her the benefit of the doubt. "Aren't you?"

"Nothing could be further from the truth," Irene said.

Was she being punked? They might have been on the cusp of a moment or a revelation or something, but all the years of biting her tongue seemed to catch up with her at once and she couldn't contain herself. "Could have fooled me."

"Oh, Chelsea. I'm so proud of you."

Despite whatever frantic attempts she may have been making to put the walls safely back in place, they didn't stand a chance against the simple declaration. She locked eyes with her mother and her own tears kicked in. "I think that's the first time you've ever said that to me."

Irene's lips pursed. "Now you're being dramatic."

Chelsea merely raised a brow.

Irene's whole demeanor changed. Like the revelation Chelsea had sensed a moment before had raced ahead so Irene could crash into it headfirst. "You think that me being hard on you means I don't love you."

Any hope she had of backing out now, of backing down, vanished like the puff of smoke from a twenty-five-cent firecracker. But even as the inevitability of that sank in, so did compassion for a woman she'd worked very hard to forgive. "I know you love me."

"But you think that love is conditional."

That implied she might actually meet some of the conditions Irene laid out in neat rows, perfectly paving a path to all that was good and proper. "I think you love me because I'm your daughter. But you don't think very highly of who I've become."

Irene looked down at her hands and sighed. "I only ever meant to encourage you, to push you to be the best version of yourself."

The thing was, even as the words stung, Chelsea believed her. "Don't you get it? Your version of that and mine aren't the same. And your version made me feel bad about myself for most of my life."

She'd kept her tone calm—kind, even—as much for her benefit as Irene's. But something in Irene seemed to crack. When she looked up, her eyes had gone glassy with tears. "I see that now, and I'm sorry."

The simplicity of the statement landed with more force than a fervent soliloquy would have. "Thank you."

They sat in awkward silence for a full minute at least before Chelsea cleared her throat and started to serve lunch. Conversation drifted to more banal topics, as though they both needed time to let things percolate. She sat on the question she'd been harboring all week, perhaps even less sure of what to do than before.

When they'd finished eating, Irene stood rather abruptly. "I should let you get on with your day."

It was hard to tell whether she meant to give Chelsea an out or wanted one for herself. Honestly, Chelsea didn't mind one way or the other.

At the door, Irene paused. "Bryce is a good catch. You should do whatever you can to hold on to him."

Chelsea gave her mama a squeeze and let out a sigh. It may have been a banner day, but some habits died hard.

When the embrace ended, Irene put a hand on each of her shoulders. "But you're a catch, too. And Bryce should be thanking his lucky stars he caught the eye of such a remarkable, talented, beautiful woman."

Under other circumstances, she might have laughed and congratulated Irene on the quick recovery. But her mama had just called her beautiful and the waterworks she'd managed to get under control returned full force. She sniffed and the resulting sound was neither dainty nor polite. "Sorry."

"I'm the one who's sorry. I never meant for you to doubt yourself." Irene hugged her again.

God, what she wouldn't give to get her mother in a chair with a really good therapist. Maybe one day. For now, she'd take the victory she hadn't been looking for, and the healing she hadn't known she needed. "I'm sorry, too, for not telling you how your words made me feel."

"None of that. I should have known better."

Since she should have—and since Chelsea had spent years with her own therapists getting to the point of accepting that—she let the statement stand. "I'm really glad we talked."

Irene nodded, though it looked like she might be on the verge of another crying jag as well. "Me, too."

"Do you want to be on my show?" Since she'd blurted out so much else today, might as well put that on the table, too.

"You want me on your show?" To Irene's credit, she seemed awed by the question.

"It's a thing, you know, to have people come on. Makes it feel more conversational."

"I watch your show, Chelsea. I know it's a thing."

What could have been a passive-aggressive statement felt strangely like a moment of vulnerability. "I thought we could do an afternoon tea, but with a Southern twist. Pimento cheese sandwiches, scones with Mawmaw's fig preserves."

"I'd be honored."

She hadn't expected a no, exactly, but something tepid at least. Reluctant. With a heavy dose of doing Chelsea a favor. Honored? Go fucking figure. "Great. I think we'll film Friday, if that's enough notice."

Irene smiled, and Chelsea would swear on a Bible there was mischief in it. "I think I can manage to clear my schedule."

"Okay. Um, I'll be in touch. There's some stuff about wardrobe that's camera friendly and we have a woman that comes in to do hair and makeup."

"I'm sure your people know what they're doing." Irene angled her head. "Just like you."

Chelsea laughed then. She couldn't help it. "Go easy on the compliments, now. I've got to recalibrate my system."

That got her a stern look, but Irene's smile returned with a brisk nod. "You give me a call. I'll see you soon."

Irene left and Chelsea slumped against the door. She most certainly would.

❖

Bryce made the mistake of checking his email on a Saturday. In addition to a slew of students scrambling to make appointments last minute, he had an effusive note from Chase, the director of the campus LGBTQ Resource Center. The result was some pacing, a whole lot of mulling, and getting to Kate's later than expected. He found her already set up at the dining room table with trays of her handmade glass beads, spools of wire, and other crafty detritus. He offered a "hey" and a "sorry," along with a one-armed hug.

"Don't worry. I'll take it out of your wages." She gestured to a spot at the end where a pile of finished Christmas ornaments waited. "You're on bagging duty."

He offered a salute and settled in, slipping each one into a small mesh bag. "These are pretty swanky wedding favors."

"I could say I wanted to do something nice, but mostly I wanted something I wouldn't dread getting as a guest myself."

"Could there be a more Kate answer?"

She shrugged.

They worked for a little while in silence. Kate hummed, her hands sure and quick. He had no doubt she could make a living with her jewelry business if she ever decided to leave the hardware store. Though, honestly, she seemed to love both, and maybe the fact that she didn't have to choose was the whole point.

"Why so glum, chum?"

Kate's choice of phrase was a throwback to their grandfather, who had a penchant for rhyming. And hair ruffling and pipe tobacco. The memory made him smile even as his mind churned. "The director of the LGBTQ Resource Center asked me if I would be the keynote speaker at the Trans Day of Remembrance event on campus."

"The nerve."

He huffed out a breath. "That's not what I meant."

Kate set down her wire cutters. "What did you mean?"

"It's a total honor, you know?"

"I do." Kate folded her arms, more curious than judgy.

"But it feels like one more public performance." He wasn't articulating it well but couldn't seem to pull together anything better. Like, being asked had everything to do with the pseudo-celebrity that had landed on him via Chelsea.

"Is it the public part that's bugging you, or the performance?"

"Neither. Both." He groaned.

Kate nodded. "The amount."

Was it? Sort of, but not quite. "It's that it's starting to feel like being Chelsea's boyfriend is my primary identity."

"Oh." Kate let the word hang.

"That makes me sound like a total ass, doesn't it? Like I can't just be supportive and happy for her success." Ugh.

"Well, success and celebrity aren't the same thing. And it's not like you get to stand next to her and smile. You've..." She paused and looked at the ceiling, twitching her lips this way and that. When her gaze returned to him, she shrugged. "You've become the trans poster boy."

He blinked in that way of being aware of the fact that he was blinking. "Uh."

Kate winced. "No? Too much?"

Given that Kate never hesitated to give him a hard time—about anything—her hesitation landed extra hard. The combination left him woozy almost. "That's it."

"To be fair, you make an excellent poster boy. But I get why you might not want to be that."

He nodded slowly. "I was afraid of trolls at first and it was so nice to get all the positive stuff instead. Well, way more positive stuff than negative, at least."

"But even good attention is attention when it comes down to it. You're not big on being the center of attention. Well, aside from the first ten years of your life, perhaps." Kate smirked.

Normally, he'd take what she dished out and give it right back. Sibling rivalry code and all. But he was too busy having an epiphany. "I don't like public attention."

"Which I totally get. Even if it's for a good cause."

It was the good cause part that tripped him up. He wanted to be out and visible with his trans identity. More, he wanted to use his circle of influence to make others more aware and open-minded and accepting. The problem was, his circle of influence had gone way beyond anything he'd ever imagined. And now he was stuck in the spotlight and didn't know how to get out. "Yeah."

"Can you just say no?"

He could. But even the thought gave him a pang of guilt. If speaking on campus—or being on television—got one conservative mom to think differently about her trans kid, or helped one trans kid feel a little less alone, was he really going to walk away from it because it made him uncomfortable? "I'm not sure I can. Or, maybe, I don't want to. Even if I kind of want to."

She raised a brow at his circular logic.

"I care about the reason I'm putting myself out there."

Kate nodded. "But don't like the actual being out there part."

"Exactly." It helped to finally have a handle on the underlying cause of his discomfort, even if it didn't solve things.

"So, what are you going to do?"

"Well, I'm going to say yes to this, because Chase is a friend as much as a colleague. And I'm not football famous on campus, but I'm out and about and visible." Saying it out loud only solidified that it was the right decision for him.

"And the rest?"

The rest. "I think I'm going to tell Chelsea I need a breather."

"Yeah."

"I don't begrudge her a moment of it for herself." Even if he missed the hell out of her when it took her jetting off to some interview or appearance.

"That sounds fair." Kate reached across the table and gave his hand a squeeze. "She can hardly find fault with that."

"Right." Because at the end of the day, it wasn't about him. She might even appreciate having less of the spotlight pulled away from her cooking and her show.

"Feel better?"

He and Kate might drive each other up a tree now and then, but he couldn't imagine anyone he'd want in his corner more. "I do."

"Good." She lifted her chin in the direction of the ornaments. "Now, back to work."

CHAPTER TWENTY-FIVE

Chelsea took a fortifying breath and clicked on the virtual meeting link. She told herself meetings with the network people didn't make her nervous but didn't manage to convince herself. At least Jada and Sylvia were on the call, too. It would make commiserating after the fact easier.

Dave kicked things off with the requisite pleasantries then handed things over to Shauna, the director of programming.

"We've taken a deep dive into your numbers." Shauna's face disappeared from the screen. In its place, a spreadsheet with a blur of figures.

"Okay." Chelsea swallowed. Shauna's face had given nothing away. Unfortunately, the numbers didn't either. At least not to her.

"The episode with Bryce has the most streams by far."

Her brain tripped slightly over Shauna's referencing her guest rather than the show title, or even the dishes she'd made. "Gumbo, you mean?"

Shauna's face returned. "I mean the episode with Bryce."

He had been charming. Funny, too. Honestly, it had been her favorite episode as well, but she considered that a biased opinion. "What are you saying?"

"We're saying we want him to feature more prominently in the show," Dave said.

Jada, who'd been quiet so far, scratched the back of her neck. "Like a cohost?"

"No, no."

Shauna's quick denial didn't stop Chelsea's stomach from twisting. "Like what, then?"

"Like an appearance at the beginning or end of most episodes.

References to him. Maybe feature him in the opening credits." Shauna made circles with her hand. "You know, like *Girl on the Farm.*"

She did know. She loved both the concept of the show and the feel. And the host's farmer husband was a staple of that, even if he wasn't on screen with her the whole time. Key word being 'husband.' "But they're married. And the whole point is that they're taking care of the family farm together."

"I promise we're not looking for nuptials." Shauna laughed. "Though I'm pretty sure it would do wonders for your ratings."

Chelsea's mouth opened, but no words came out.

"But no pressure." Jada laughed extra loud, somehow diffusing the shroud of awkward that threatened to envelop the call.

"No pressure." Shauna gave a decisive nod. "But the network does love the idea of more screen time for Bryce. Really making him part of your brand. They'd also like to extend an invitation for him to join you for a second stint on *The Dish.*"

"You want me back on *The Dish?*"

Dave lifted a finger. "Oh. Yes. I should have led with that. They're continuing with a rotating fourth host and we're going to continue cycling Food TV personalities into the slot. Your name topped the list."

A giddy wave swept over the discomfort of being put on the spot. "I'd love to."

"You don't have to bring Bryce, but we'd love it if you did," Shauna said.

"Um." The flurry of thoughts prevented her brain from settling on one.

Shauna didn't wait for her to continue. "We think leveraging the Bryce factor will boost your profile with the millennial moms in particular."

Millennial moms was code for the demographic advertisers coveted most. Chelsea swallowed. "I can ask him."

Dave jumped back in. "Please do. All expenses paid, obviously. But the network would also pay the standard guest honorarium."

It wasn't a huge sum, but the fact that they were prepared to pay Bryce what they paid her made it clear how much they wanted to hawk them as a couple. "I'll let him know that as well."

"Excellent. We love him. Not more than you, obviously, but you make an exceptionally good package deal." Shauna chortled, but then her face turned serious. "And we're all invested in keeping your ratings healthy."

Chelsea scrambled but failed to come up with a reply. Fortunately, Jada jumped in with questions about the rest of the data and timing for season three.

Chelsea tried to pay attention but struggled to focus. Mostly because Shauna had actually used the phrase "Bryce factor" and she hadn't been joking. Excitement warred with a vague unease she couldn't define but couldn't shake, either.

The conversation plowed ahead without her, which was just as well. Jada would tell her what she needed to know when they finalized the next sequence of episodes and started ironing out scripts. And she could spend her time figuring out how to handle the network's infatuation with Bryce. She zoned in long enough to finish the meeting, complete with Shauna's enthusiastic vote of confidence and Dave's promise to have the producers of *The Dish* reach out ASAP.

Shauna no sooner ended the meeting than her phone rang with a FaceTime from Jada. Since Chelsea was already at her computer, she clicked the accept button on the screen. "Hey."

"You okay?" Jada asked in lieu of a greeting.

"Yes?" Probably less convincing when phrased in the form of a question.

"Chelsea." Jada said her name slowly, rocking a disapproving mom voice. Which was funny considering Jada's opinions on becoming a mother.

"I am. A little thrown, but it's not like it's completely out of left field." Even if it had felt that way in the moment.

"It's not?"

"I mean, they're the ones who wanted Bryce in the photo shoot, in the magazine. He checks another box in their rainbow flag chart but also appeals to suburban stay-at-home moms." She might try to forget that was one of the reasons she got her own show in the first place, but it remained a reality either way.

"Does it bug you that we spent more time talking about him than you?" Jada asked.

"Eh?" It was hard to put into words. She liked Bryce on the show, with her at events. Like, it let her be in the limelight, but not the sole focus. "It's not like I want it to be all about me, either."

"And you know better than to think it's all about the food," Jada said, sounding more than a little jaded.

She laughed. "Exactly."

Jada pursed her lips. "Do you think Bryce will go for it?"

"I honestly don't know." A fact that kind of terrified her.

"I thought he had fun with us."

"He did. Or, at least, I'm pretty sure he did. This is different. I don't want him to feel like a prop." She'd had her share of that, and it was gross.

Jada sighed. "Yeah."

"And he does have a job and a life and stuff." Even if it felt like their lives were getting more entwined by the day.

"So does Mr. Farm Girl," Jada said.

"Yeah, but they're married. They live together. And he's never not the man of the farm." She remained stuck on Shauna's comment about nuptials, even if Shauna sort of took it back.

"Do you want to live with Bryce? Marry him?" Jada asked with the sort of offhanded casualness she'd use to inquire about Chelsea's preference for lunch.

"I plead the Fifth," Chelsea said after a beat.

Jada folded her arms. "You can't plead the Fifth. You're not on trial."

Chelsea smirked. "Feels like it."

"Stop."

"Uh-uh." Chelsea shook her head. "You used the M-word. That's got to be leading the witness or something."

"That's not what that means." Jada put both hands up. "But fine, fine. I should have led with the L one instead."

"You're relentless." Though she'd be lying if she hadn't started to use that word in her own head.

Jada didn't miss a beat. "You're a liar."

"Hey, I haven't denied it," she said, even though she immediately regretted it.

"So, you confirm."

Chelsea laughed. Relentless was an understatement. "Neither."

"You're such a chicken."

"Oh, my God," Chelsea said.

Jada merely started clucking. With a side of arm flapping.

"I have feelings, okay. I'm not prepared to name them or declare them, but I have them." It was surprisingly easy to say so, at least to Jada.

"Girl."

She shrugged. "Are you happy now?"

Jada mimicked the move. "Yes."

"You're a pain in my ass, but I love you." She'd loathe Charlie Paul for all eternity, but at least working for him had brought them together.

"Love me enough to have me show up a few days early?" Jada asked.

She'd invited Jada down for Thanksgiving, not wanting to bank on an invitation from Bryce. Or Irene, for that matter. Now, there was every possibility she'd have three dinners before it was all said and done. "Of course. Always. Is everything okay?"

"Just thinking I miss you." The nonchalance of Jada's answer gave her away.

"Bullshit."

"Okay, fine. I've been talking to Billy."

It took Chelsea a minute to place the name. "You mean Bryce's cousin?"

Jada's expression turned to mischief. "That's the one."

"The white, cis dude, sugarcane farmer." They'd flirted at the Fourth of July party, but she'd chalked it up to Jada's use of flirtation to pass the time.

"He's actually really cool. Thoughtful. Well read."

"I'm not judging. Just surprised." Really, really surprised. Though, if she looked at her own life over the last year, stranger things had happened.

"You should get to know him. Maybe we could do a double date."

"Yeah. Okay. Sure." She made a mental note to pick Bryce's brain and find out if Jada's assessment was accurate.

"Hey, if you can fall for a good ol' boy, I can, too."

She could think of about a thousand reasons why their situations were different, but did it matter? "I can't wait to see you and hear all about it."

"And I can't wait to hear how Bryce reacts to the prospect of being Mr. First You Make a Roux."

Chelsea groaned but laughed. "Bye, Jada."

"Bye, hot stuff. I'll book a flight and send you the details."

They hung up, but Chelsea stayed at her desk. She picked up her phone to text Bryce but set it down. Better a conversation to have in person, and he was already coming over for supper. That gave her a couple of hours to figure out how to pitch the idea. Preferably one that didn't include the words Mr. First You Make a Roux.

❖

Bryce did his best not to cringe. "Really?"

Chelsea shrugged, looking about as uncomfortable as he felt. "People who watch the show love you. And they think we have good chemistry."

That got him to smile. "Well, they're not wrong."

"It's a proven formula. Another show has the husband popping in regularly. They banter. It's cute and homey." Chelsea's delivery was a little too perky to feel genuine.

"That one with the girl on her family's farm, right?" A big part of him loved what that sort of move implied. What it said about their relationship, their future. But he couldn't shake the sense the push was coming from the network, not Chelsea.

"Yes, that's the one." Chelsea nodded with enthusiasm. "It's great, right? The way they play off each other?"

"Sure." He didn't disagree. And he obviously wanted to do anything he could to help Chelsea's show be as successful as possible. But the limelight was already starting to wear on him. The idea of ignoring his plan to be less a part of Chelsea's public persona had a knot of dread forming in his stomach.

"You don't want to do it." Disappointment shone on her face.

"It's not that I don't. I have a few reservations."

Chelsea raised a brow. "You can say you don't want to."

"I love doing the show with you. It's fun and I like being part of it with you. And Jada is great." Could he sound any less convincing?

"But?"

He sucked in a breath, blew it out. "But it's all the other stuff."

Chelsea looked genuinely confused. "What other stuff?"

The fact that she didn't even register what all the other stuff was spoke volumes. "The celebrity. Being recognized, doing public appearances. And the photo shoots." He shuddered at the memory. "It makes me feel like the all-American trans guy. The poster boy."

"Oh." She let the word drag. "But I thought you liked helping promote awareness and acceptance. Did I misunderstand that?"

"You didn't. And I liked it more in theory, I think, than practice. It felt good to be a part of that, but the level of attention is more than I bargained for."

Chelsea nodded but looked down at her lap. "I get it."

"Are they saying you have to do it?" He wished he had a better idea of how all this worked.

"It was a suggestion." Chelsea sighed. "A strong suggestion. They think you'd be a good addition to my brand."

Bryce balked.

Chelsea cringed. "I know. That part is weird. And a little icky. But my brand is basically me and you're a part of that. I mean, I want you to be part of that."

How could they be so close to on the same page while being so decidedly not? "You know I support you, right? Want to help?"

"I do." She looked up and nodded again, blinking in a way that made him think she might be holding back tears.

"Are you being honest with me?"

She rolled her eyes but laughed. "Yes. But I hadn't gotten to the part where they want me to do another stint on *The Dish* and want you to come along."

"Come along?" He could think of little he wanted to do less. Well, again, not the actual doing. Just the side effects of that many more people knowing who he was and wanting to tell him about it.

Chelsea pouted. "I know. You really, really don't want to do that."

"It's not—"

"It's okay, Bryce. It isn't your show. Or your career. Or your life."

She might have been trying to help, but each assertion felt like a knife to the gut. Because it was Chelsea's show. Chelsea's career. Chelsea's life. And he was almost as deeply invested in hers as he was his own. "I care about those things."

She sniffed and swiped at her eyes. "And I care about you. I'm not going to ask you to do something that makes you miserable."

Miserable was such a heavy word. Heavy enough to send him backpedaling. "I'm not miserable."

"I don't want you anything close to miserable."

"Could we compromise? Like, I'm happy to pop in on your show, but I really don't want to do other shows or TV appearances or things like that." It wouldn't be that much of a leap. Truth be told, he had to make a point of keeping away when Chelsea was filming. It would be nice to have excuses to stop by after work, hang out with Jada and the crew.

"Are you saying that to be nice?"

He gave it a second, did a gut check. Because if they weren't honest with each other, what was the point? "I'm not. I love the show.

I'm comfortable with the crew, and obviously I love being at your house. And with you."

She searched his face, like she was trying to suss out his real feelings. Ones he might be holding close.

"I mean it." The fact that she was pressing made him feel like she wanted a real answer. Cared about getting one. "Besides, I doubt doing that will land me in any more magazine spreads."

She laughed. "You were really scarred by that, weren't you?"

"Not...scarred."

"Scarred," Chelsea said even more decisively.

"Okay, maybe a little. But it was the number of people who felt the need to show it to me and have a conversation about it more than the photo shoot itself." So. Many. People. And with that weird assumption of intimacy he'd heard celebrities gripe about but never understood before.

Chelsea nodded. "That's fair."

"Do you think that will fly? I know you feel like you're at the whim of the network. I don't want to put you in a bad position." Because he didn't want that for her, but also because he didn't want to think about what Chelsea would do—where she might go—if her show didn't stay on the air.

"I mean, we're contracted for the third season. Shooting starts right after Thanksgiving. They're not going to pull the plug on that. I'll just have to be infinitely charming on my own."

He grabbed her hand and gave it a squeeze. "Not completely on your own."

"No." She squeezed his back. "I am going to do another trip to Charlotte, though. Solo. Is that cool with you?"

As far as he was concerned, it was cool that she asked. That their relationship was at the point of checking in about things like travel. Negotiating and navigating together. He wanted that, wanted it with Chelsea. He might not have bargained for the exact details they had to navigate and negotiate, but it certainly kept things interesting.

He liked interesting, after all. And when it came to the big stuff—things like being in Duchesne, being fully and openly queer—they were on the same page. That's what really mattered.

CHAPTER TWENTY-SIX

Chelsea stepped into Barb's office, trying to reconcile being summoned with how well the week of taping had gone. "You wanted to see me?"

Barb looked up from her computer and smiled. That had to be a good sign, right? "Chelsea, come in."

Since she was technically already in, Chelsea took one of the chairs across from Barb's desk. She hadn't done that—sat across a desk from someone—since that fateful meeting with the network executives. The one where they offered her a show of her own for the low, low price of her signature on an NDA. Whatever Barb wanted could hardly be as life changing as that meeting had been, but the air practically vibrated with significance. "I've had such a great week. I can't thank you enough for having me back."

"I should be the one thanking you. Your energy has been exactly what the show needs."

"Thank you. It's been an amazing opportunity. Though, if I'm being honest, it's been a lot of fun, too." She'd worried the opposite might be true. She didn't have the flash or the catchphrases of some of her counterparts. She also didn't have the on-camera boyfriend, who the network had somehow decided was her equivalent.

"I'm glad to hear it, especially given the proposition I have for you."

Had Barb not gotten the memo? She'd broken the news to Shauna about Bryce turning down the gig on *The Dish* in an email. Was Barb going to ask if she'd come back again as part of a power couple? Did people still use the phrase power couple? "Um."

"I'd like to offer you a full-time slot on *The Dish*."

Chelsea scrambled to process the enormity of that kind of offer.

What it said about her talent as a chef, her skill as a TV personality. What that would mean—for her career but also for her own show. Oh, and there was the matter of the show taping in Charlotte. She didn't get very far before the original worry elbowed in. Maybe Barb didn't get the memo. "You know about Bryce, right? That he's flattered but not interested?"

Barb waved a hand. "Oh, that. The network is enamored with him. He's great, but you're the one I want."

Satisfaction swelled in her chest. "Now I'm the flattered one."

"Flattery has nothing to do with it. You bring what the show needs. And not to disparage your show, but it could use the cross-promotion being on *The Dish* would offer."

Okay, so if that was one of Barb's angles, her own show wasn't on the chopping block. "So, I'd keep my own show?"

"Absolutely. We film forty weeks a year. That's plenty of time to fit in two to four seasons of a standalone, based on what the network ultimately wants."

Chelsea nodded. What the network wanted. That's what it came down to. Sure, she'd draw the line at compromising her integrity or cooking crap. But otherwise, she'd signed up for this and wanted—needed—to be that. "Wow."

"I know, I know. It doesn't leave a whole lot of time for vacation. We can accommodate a week off here and there for you, and as you know, we only film three days a week."

It was all she could do not to laugh. What Barb put on the table would officially be the cushiest job she'd ever had. And it would mean working alongside Simone Bertold pretty much every day. Well, three days a week. Hence the cushy. Though, even as the magic of possibility pulsed through her, tremors of doubt cut in like overly aggressive bass notes in the club remix of an otherwise enjoyable song. "I don't know what to say."

"I'd take a yes, or perhaps a when do I start." Barb chuckled. "Kidding. It's a big decision. One you'll probably want to discuss with your agent and Shauna before signing on any dotted lines."

Chelsea nodded. "Right."

"And maybe with that boyfriend of yours." Barb offered a wink, but the smile that accompanied it seemed rueful. "It would make for one hell of a commute."

"Yeah." A doable commute, though. People managed with worse things than four-day weekends and direct flights.

"Think about it and we can talk next week. I'm sure Shauna will start nagging you before I will."

Barb's phone rang and Chelsea pounced on the chance to escape. She mouthed a thank you and hightailed it out of Barb's office. The hosts were long gone and even the crew had scattered. Chelsea wandered the empty set and tried to imagine spending most of her days there.

The money would be fantastic. Exposure for her show, for the cookbook she'd already started writing in her head. It wasn't a leap to imagine a line of cookware or sauces with her name on them. She wasn't there yet, but she could be. One day. Taking this job would be a big step closer to that.

But what about Bryce? That question sat like an elephant on her chest. Along with the prospect of spending as many nights in some efficiency apartment as her house. And those inklings she'd started to have about adopting a dog. Even a cat would be a stretch if she was gone half the week.

Ugh. How could such an amazing opportunity trigger so much ambivalence?

Because she'd started to think of Duchesne as home. Really home, not just her place of origin. Because she'd made friends and settled into small-town life way more than she'd ever dreamed. Had broken through previously impenetrable walls when it came to Irene. Because, she realized with a start, she was happy.

She couldn't do this. Whatever this was. The mulling, maybe. The soul searching. She needed to get away, to sort things out. And if nothing else, fucking celebrate what a big deal it was to be asked in the first place. Because the fat girl that nobody wanted, the one who'd spent years relegated to hustling behind the scenes, was on the cusp of having it all.

With a decisive nod, Chelsea gathered her things, ordered a car, and headed to the side door. On the way to the airport, she checked her messages. Some show notes from Jada, along with some snark over Charlie appearing on one of the conservative cable news talk shows. A few delightfully random observations from Bryce about one of his colleagues. And an uncharacteristically casual check-in from Irene, wishing her safe travels home. At this rate, she'd have to start thinking of Irene as Mama again, which she'd decidedly not done since her early twenties.

She dashed off replies to Jada and Irene first, then toggled to her text thread with Bryce. *I have exciting news.* Even as she typed the words, a knot of anxiety formed in her stomach.

I love exciting news. Tell me. Bryce punctuated the statement with a heart, which of course made the knot worse rather than better.

Chelsea typed several variations before settling on the simplest. *They've asked me to be a permanent member of The Dish.*

The telltale dots started and stopped several times, making her wonder if Bryce was changing his mind, too. Eventually, a reply appeared: *Wow.*

So, that answered that.

Then knot became more of a churn. *I want to talk to you about it, obviously. About what it would mean But it's a huge honor to be asked.*

No dots this time. Just a long pause before: *For sure.*

Despite the anxiety, a jab of defensiveness made its way through. Yes, getting an offer like this would complicate things. But it was an amazing offer and one she should be able to simply celebrate. Bryce should know that, should let her have that moment of celebration. Hell, he should be slathering on compliments and congratulations like butter on a hot biscuit.

These tepid and terse replies were a far cry from that.

Anyway. I'll tell you all about it when I get home. Made it to the airport. Flight is at six and I should be in NOLA by eight.

Chelsea waited. She fidgeted. She toggled over to look at her email.

I'll be there!

She thought that might be the end of it and let annoyance take root. Then she texted a screen shot to Jada in hopes of commiseration. But Jada was with Billy, which meant she could go hours without looking at her phone. Chelsea huffed with requisite indignation as she exited the car and made her way to the security checkpoint.

I confess I'm a little freaked out by what it means, but I'm thrilled for you. You're a rock star and deserve that and more.

The tears took her by surprise. She swiped at her eyes and locked the screen. Why did he have to go and say the exact right thing? She was perfectly prepared to be mad at him and now he'd gone and made her all squishy and emotional. In the middle of the freaking airport of all places.

She hemmed and hawed for a moment before settling on a heart emoji as her reply. They'd talk when she got home. And they'd find a way to figure it out and make it work. They had to.

❖

As much as Bryce had looked forward to Chelsea's return, and to a blissfully unscheduled weekend, the reality of two uninterrupted days together fell sadly short. Despite Chelsea's professed excitement about her offer to join *The Dish* permanently, she seemed even edgier about it than he was. And he was pretty damn edgy.

Things only got worse on Sunday, after what should have been a lazy brunch at home. The promise of afternoon sex and a nap—a rare treat—fizzled into Chelsea on her computer and Bryce distractedly watching the Saints lose to the Ravens. "Are we going to talk about it?" he asked eventually.

"Talk about what?" Chelsea's irritable tone made it clear she knew exactly what they needed to talk about.

"The job offer. Whether you're going to take it. Whether you want to take it."

Chelsea closed her laptop slowly. "I'm not sure I can say no."

Bryce bristled and told himself it had to do with the idea of anyone feeling pressured to do something they didn't want. "Why couldn't you say no?"

"Because the network wants me to say yes. And I already told them no about something else." She said it flatly, like an observation of fact.

"Are you only allowed one? Is that in your contract?"

Chelsea folded her arms. "Did you want to talk, or did you want to be snarky about my work?"

He deserved that. "I want to talk."

"Okay, fine." She lifted her chin. "Why can't you be happy for me and trust that we'll find a way to make it work?"

"I am happy for you. Especially if you tell me this is exactly what you want." He couldn't shake the feeling it wasn't, though Kate would call that transference.

"But?" Chelsea spat out the question more than she asked it.

"But I can't ignore all the questions it raises, and I have to be honest, I'm not sure I can see how we're going to make it work."

By rights, he was picking a fight. He'd probably regret it, but for now, he braced himself to have it out. Only instead of swiping back, Chelsea looked at him and the tears started. Subtle, silent, but tears nonetheless. With them, Bryce's resolve. Chelsea sniffed and he opened his mouth to say whatever it took to make her feel better. But she didn't give him the chance.

"I know. You don't want to live somewhere else." She sniffed again. "You were clear about that from the get-go."

"I—"

She lifted a hand. "I'm not asking you to move. I'm just coming to terms with the fact that you're not willing to budge on that."

Every instinct told him to say whatever it took to chase away the look of sad resignation now haunting Chelsea's features. Only he couldn't. Because as much as he loved Chelsea—more, perhaps than he'd ever loved a woman who wasn't his sister or his mother—it was the one thing he swore he'd never compromise on. Giving in now would be worse than a thousand television appearances and being recognized and swarmed anywhere he went. It would be losing one of the deepest and most essential parts of himself. "I'm sorry."

Chelsea swiped at her eyes and nodded. "Okay."

"Okay?" He clung to the prospect of agreeing on something but couldn't see where they'd agreed on anything.

"Okay, I know where you stand. I need to decide what to do with that."

Rather than weaving together, the threads of optimism snapped like the wispy filaments they were. "I don't want to lose you over this. I just don't want to lose myself in the process."

Chelsea stood and the detached look in her eyes gutted him even more than the tears. "That's all well and good, Bryce, but it doesn't leave much room for me to maneuver."

"I thought you were happy here. If that's true, how much room do you really need?"

Her eyes went dark. "That's an easy assertion for the guy who never had a reason to leave."

"You're right, I didn't. I wish I could go back in time and change that for you, though I love the person you've become, and I wouldn't want to change much about her," he said.

"You don't get to pick the parts of me that suit you. I want to make something of myself, and that's not going away so I can play housewife."

He scrubbed a hand over his face. "No one is asking you to play housewife. And last I checked, you had made something of yourself. Why are you running away from that?"

Chelsea flinched like he'd hit her. He already regretted saying as much as he had. Now, he wanted nothing more than to take it all back. Even if the truth of it hung heavy, like stale smoke lingering in the air. "I'm going to go," she said.

"Chelsea, don't. Let's talk."

"I'm not sure what there is to talk about. You made your feelings clear."

"I didn't mean to upset you."

Chelsea stood. "But you did. Though, maybe, it's my fault. You were up-front about who you were and what you wanted. It was foolish of me to think I could be that."

"You could. Can. Are. Fuck." He wanted to reach for her but stuck his hands in his pocket instead. Why was he making this worse?

"You're right that I could be, but I'm not. And like you so eloquently put it, I'm not willing to lose myself in the process." She picked up her computer and headed to the kitchen, where she set it down just long enough to yank on her shoes.

"Please don't go."

"I need some space." Chelsea sniffed. "And some time."

Knowing he needed to respect that didn't make it easier to let her leave. When she closed the door quietly behind her, his gut constricted as though she'd slammed it in a rage. It was the first time since spending that first night together that they parted ways without at least a passing moment of physical contact. The realization left him both heavy and hollow.

With Chelsea gone, the house went from quiet to almost eerily still. Bryce returned to the living room and paced for a minute. Feeling like a caged tiger, he dropped onto the sofa, only to get up a few seconds later. He went to the kitchen, then, opening the fridge door and staring at its contents until it started to beep at him.

He closed it with a growl and headed to the back door for his own shoes. A run wouldn't make things any better, but it would give him something to do and maybe clear his head. At this point, he'd take what he could get. He had to fix this, had to find a way to make it right. But for the life of him, he couldn't figure out how. At least not a how that wouldn't leave him full of resentment and regret in the long run.

CHAPTER TWENTY-SEVEN

What made me think I could pull it off? Chelsea had posed the question to Jada but had yet to get a reply. Not that she needed one. She knew the answer. She'd gotten a taste of getting everything she ever wanted and let herself believe she might. Hubris, plain and simple.

She'd been selfish, too. Or at least self-centered. Though she'd been burned enough times in relationships that she wasn't about to put someone's wants and needs before her own. Not even Bryce's. Not that he'd asked her to. Not really. No, he'd simply held firm that his life was in Duchesne and he had no intentions of changing that. Even when she'd essentially asked him to.

That was the part that stung. She'd opened the door for him to pick her, and he'd shot her down without a moment of hesitation, much less negotiation. No matter how good whatever they had was, he wasn't willing to compromise.

Of course, he hadn't said that, either. Not technically. They hadn't gotten to the part about what long distance might mean. Whether he might be able to swing remote work here and there to be in Charlotte with her. Whether having weekends together would feel like enough. She'd been too busy accusing him of being rigid.

Pot calling the kettle, for sure.

A curt knock on the door yanked Chelsea from her self-loathing. She hurried to open it, apologies and ultimatums slapping around in her brain like overworked cake batter in the bowl of her Kitchen Aid mixer. Only, when she opened it, Bryce didn't stand on the other side. Jada did.

"What happened? What did you do?" Jada breezed in without waiting for an invitation.

Chelsea closed the door and resisted letting her body slump against it. "Why do you assume it was something I did?"

Jada merely raised a brow. "Wasn't it?"

"Well, if you count being offered my dream job and wanting my boyfriend to be happy for me, fine. It's my fault." Though again, technically he had been. He just hadn't been happy about what it would mean.

Jada didn't answer right away, leaving Chelsea to stew and squirm.

"And sure, it's my fault for falling for a guy who's stubborn and set in his ways and refuses to consider anyone's hopes and dreams but his own." Even saying that felt unfair, but since she'd decided to throw a tantrum, being fair wasn't required.

Jada folded her arms then. "I thought you already had your dream job."

Of all the shots she'd teed up, that wasn't the one she expected Jada to take. "I do. But I'm trying to keep it past its first two seasons. Taking the gig on *The Dish* will help ensure that."

"Ah."

"Really? My life is coming apart at the seams and all you've got is ah?" The "ah" was shorthand, of course, but she didn't like anything it implied.

"Do you believe the show is in jeopardy or do you like being the network's new yes girl?"

"What is that supposed to mean?" She knew what Jada meant.

Jada, who knew she knew, didn't back down. "It's a simple question." Not a fair one, though. Jada, of all people, should know that.

"You know how the network is." They giveth until they decide to taketh away.

"I do," Jada said.

"So you know I'm at their mercy." Hell, their whim.

Jada did not appear swayed. "I know you're a hot enough ticket to be offered a spot on their top-rated show. I'd say that hardly puts you in danger of imminent cancellation."

"Yeah, but they wanted the package deal with Bryce, and I couldn't give them that." The fact that they wanted it stung more than Bryce's reticence about being half of that package. Which made getting the offer from Barb all the more significant.

"Do you really not believe in what you have to offer?"

Chelsea rubbed both hands over her face and then through her hair. "Loaded question much?"

Jada didn't appear cowed. "It's only as loaded as you make it."

Chelsea groaned, a more apt response than any words she could have mustered.

"I know, babe. I know." Jada, who'd flopped on the sofa, got up and gave her a hug.

"So, you're saying I should turn it down? Settle for what I have and hope the rug doesn't get pulled out from under me?" The very thought had panic flitting at the edges of her consciousness.

Jada waited what felt like an eternity before she asked, "Does what you have right now feel like settling?"

She thought about seeing her show on the air, about the crew that descended on her house and worked with her to make it happen. About her house and how much it felt like home and not just a TV set where she also happened to sleep. Irene and the reconciliation she hadn't bargained for. Kate and Harper and how they'd become the kind of friends that might as well be family. But most of all, she thought about Bryce. "No."

"And yet you'd rather give it up than—what? Risk hypothetically losing it at some point in the future?"

"When you put it that way, I sound like an idiot." Though, to be fair, she already felt like one.

"You're not an idiot. You have trouble trusting when good things happen to you." Jada slung an arm around her, and they flopped on the couch together. "I think it's pretty common with women who've been fucked over as many times as we have."

She'd given up naïveté a long time ago. But she'd never meant for jaded and closed off to take its place. And yet, that's exactly what had happened. Even as she reveled in making her own show, a part of her anticipated it crashing and burning at a moment's notice. Just like how, even as she fell for Bryce, she held a part of her heart back. Waiting for things to end badly. Expecting them to. "I really am an idiot."

"I prefer the term 'wounded.'"

Chelsea flinched. "That's way worse."

"No, it's not. It's acknowledging that sometimes bad things happen and they're out of our control."

"Ugh. Definitely worse." But even as she said it, she laughed. Because Jada was right, damn her. It might suck to admit it, but it was a hell of a lot better than lying to herself.

"Spoken like the gorgeously independent, fiercely stubborn woman you are."

Chelsea let out a harumph. "Takes one to know one."

"Do you even want to move to Charlotte?"

When Jada put it that way, it magically became a no-brainer. "No. No, I do not."

❖

Bryce set the ladder down and let it rest against his leg. He needn't have bothered; Melody opened the door before he had the chance to knock. He offered a playful salute. "Santa's elf, reporting for duty."

"Santa's elf, huh?" Melody folded her arms and leaned against the doorframe. "And here I've been, referring to you as my hero."

He shrugged. "Nothing heroic about it. I'm always happy to help a friend. Especially when she makes me supper."

"This friend will happily make supper anytime you show up with a ladder."

He'd barely set foot inside when Kayla and Ellie came running, complete with squeals of delight and big hugs. They weren't so much younger than Harper, but the difference was palpable. Perhaps because he didn't see them all that often. Harper loved him, but he didn't rate squeals anymore.

He asked about school and the switch from softball to soccer for fall, learned about the kitten who'd appeared under their carport and decided to adopt them. Melody indulged the stream-of-consciousness storytelling for a few minutes before saying, "Okay, girls. Bryce is here to help us with our Christmas decorations. Let's let him do that."

Kayla and Ellie found that equally delightful and didn't protest. As they all paraded outside, Bryce whispered, "You're wrangling me as much as them, aren't you?"

Melody's smirk was all the answer he needed.

Stringing colored lights along the house and hanging huge inflatable Christmas ornaments from the oak tree in the front yard proved a family affair, complete with four little hands wanting to help and requisite bickering. It made him wonder if Harper and her soon-to-be sibling would have moments like that or if Harper was old enough that she'd simply dote on the baby for the duration. Once the yard was deemed Santa-worthy, Melody herded them in to clean up. Supper consisted of sloppy joes and tater tots, a meal he never made for himself but vowed to start.

After, Melody sent the girls off to finish homework and start baths, leaving the two of them side-by-side on the sofa. "You put on a brave face, but I can tell you're miserable. What's going on?"

He could have lied, but Melody deserved better than that. And he could use a friendly ear besides Kate, who loved him but felt the need to give him hell in the process. "It's a long story."

"You listen to me moan and groan. Let me return the favor."

"Falling in love is a big, complicated mess."

Melody let out a small chuckle. "Oh, honey. Of course it is. Tell me everything."

He did, pausing for good night hugs with the girls and Melody's assertion that they deserved a glass of wine for all they'd been through of late. They returned to the couch, glasses in hand, and it struck him how easy it was. How comfortable. They'd lost that in the last few years, but it came back as though no time at all had passed.

Melody listened, tutted, and patted his knee. He imagined she'd have some pointed questions, but for now, it was all empathy. By the time he was done spilling his guts, he didn't have answers but managed to feel a modicum better.

He leaned so that his shoulder pressed to Melody's and the side of his head touched hers. "You're the best."

Melody gave his thigh a squeeze. "I know."

He sat for a moment, appreciating the quiet that settled between them as much as the pithy assessment. "Why don't we live happily ever after?"

"That's dark, dude. What makes you think we won't live happily ever after?"

"I meant we. Like you and me." It made perfect sense on paper. Maybe more sense than things with Chelsea, given the current state of things.

"Like, together?"

"Yeah." Even as his heart clung to Chelsea, his brain argued the logical side of the equation. He and Melody had known each other forever and now that she wasn't married, maybe they should give it a go.

Melody didn't move away, but she did take a deep breath, letting it out in whoosh. "Because you're not in love with me."

"Maybe I could be." She was smart and gorgeous and a fantastic mom. He could do a lot worse. But even as the words formed, he knew it was a dick thing to say.

"I deserve better than that."

And damn if that didn't drive home the point. "I'm sorry."

"Don't be. I'm not in love with you, either. We both deserve better than that." Her tone made it clear she hadn't taken him seriously in the first place.

Instead of apologizing again—or digging himself into a deeper hole—he sat with Melody's assertion. "Yeah."

This time Melody bumped her shoulder to his. "Chin up, stud. If I can figure it out, so can you."

He sat with that, too—everything she'd been through and her unwavering belief that something better waited for her on the other side. "I hope you find it. Love, I mean. Someone who is head over heels for you and will love you the way you deserve to be loved."

"I will." Melody smiled. "I hope you pull your head out of your ass long enough to realize you have that and not throw it away."

What was that about driving home the point? "Ouch."

Melody merely shrugged. "You don't love me because I sugarcoat things."

He didn't. "For the record, you're still nicer about telling me I'm wrong than Kate is."

"Sisterly prerogative."

He chuckled and realized it was the closest he'd come to a real laugh since Chelsea walked ever so calmly out of his kitchen. "Something like that."

"I'm serious, though. You've been living with this fantasy of finding the perfect woman, thinking that if you were nice enough and patient enough, she'd come along, and everything would fall magically into place."

He stuck out both hands. "She literally did."

That got him a rather forceful poke in the chest. "Yeah, but you also figured she'd want to settle right down and live the life you dreamed up in your head instead of one you planned together."

His shoulders fell and he didn't even try to hide his disappointment. "Are you trying to make me feel like an idiot or an asshole?"

"Neither. I'm simply pointing out that love doesn't work that way. It takes work and compromise and usually doesn't wind up looking the way you thought it would."

"Like you and Keith, you mean?" It was a low blow and he instantly regretted it. "I'm sorry."

Melody shrugged. "Don't be. Keith and I looked perfect on paper. So much so that a lot of people told me I was a fool to ask for a divorce.

But I know in my heart of hearts there's more. And it might be messy and not always easy, but it will feed my soul and make me the best version of myself, and that's what I want."

Her words landed like a kettlebell after one too many goblet squats. And yet, just like when dropping the extra weight, the burning tightness in his chest loosened and he took a deep breath for what felt like the first time in days. "You're right."

She smirked. "I know."

"I'm going to have to tell Kate she's got some competition in the tough love department."

"Or you could get your shit together so you don't need two grown-ass women pointing out the obvious."

Bryce cringed. "I know it's bad when you use two cuss words in a single sentence."

"It's past the girls' bedtime, so I take liberties. But yes. It's pretty bad."

He still struggled to imagine a future anywhere but Duchesne. But, he realized with a start, he had an even harder time imagining a future without Chelsea in it. "Okay, smartypants. I've got one more question for you."

Melody spread her arms wide. "Hit me."

"Is"—he glanced at his watch—"nine forty-five on a Tuesday too late to show up at a woman's door?"

She tipped her head back and forth before looking him right in the eye and lifting her chin. "Not if it's to grovel."

He stood. "Then, if you don't mind, I've got somewhere I need to be."

Melody stood as well. "I don't mind at all. Text me if you crash and burn."

He winced at the very real possibility.

"You got this." She gave his arm a squeeze. "If I don't hear from you, I'll assume you're too busy kissing and making up."

CHAPTER TWENTY-EIGHT

By the time Bryce stood on Chelsea's doorstep, the levity from his conversation with Melody was long gone. In its place, a gnawing dread that he'd messed things up beyond repair. That Chelsea no longer trusted him to support her without conditions. That she no longer trusted him, period.

He knocked on the door anyway, if for no other reason than the prospect of getting back in his truck and driving to his empty house felt like more than he could face. After waiting what was likely a minute or two but felt like hours, the porch light flicked on, and Chelsea's figure appeared in the frosted glass. When the door opened, he had half a mind to head for the hills. Only it was south Louisiana and there were no hills. And his heart screamed that it wasn't going down without a fight.

"Is something wrong? Is it Kate? The baby?"

"No, no. She's fine. Everyone is fine. I'm sorry to show up so late." He shifted from one foot to the other. "Unannounced."

Chelsea lifted a shoulder. "I don't mind."

Not a concession by any stretch of the imagination, but Bryce glommed onto it with all the optimism he could muster. "I was hoping we could talk."

Her eyes held suspicion, but she opened the door the rest of the way. "All right."

Inside, her living room felt almost as much like home as his own. It struck him then, as attached as he was to his own house, the feeling wasn't some immutable thing. "It has been brought to my attention that I've been an ass."

Chelsea eyed him warily. "I think that's my line."

"It's not. I was stubborn and unyielding and, by extension, unsupportive."

She chuckled then, though he couldn't fathom why. "Again, my line."

"No. It's not. You were offered a once-in-a-lifetime opportunity and I acted like a jerk because it didn't fit into my idea of what our future should be." He jabbed a finger into his chest. "Asshole. Right here."

"You're not." Chelsea shrugged. "I didn't even give you the chance to be supportive."

"Well, whether I am or I'm not, I think you should take the job."

Chelsea didn't speak. Or smile. She barely blinked. He wasn't sure what he expected, but it sure as hell wasn't that. Then it hit him.

"You should take the job and we'll figure it out. Especially if you're not planning to move to Charlotte full-time. I really don't want to be completely away from family with the baby coming and stuff, but maybe we could do some sort of split arrangement? Like, you here on the weekends and I could come up at least once a month for a few days." Bryce sucked in a breath and plowed on. "I have a couple of colleagues who do a hybrid work arrangement. I might be able to put in for something like that. At least for a few months or a year. Then we could assess and regroup, decide what's working and what's not."

Chelsea steepled her fingers, tapped the tips together. "I appreciate where you're going with all that, but there's one big problem."

His heart sank. "It's not enough, is it?"

She shook her head, the smallest hint of a smile playing at the corners of her mouth. "No."

Why was she smiling? Had she already started planning her life without him? "I want to offer more than that, but I'm not sure I can just up and move."

The smile grew. "No, I meant that's not the problem."

"Oh." Even without knowing what she meant, it had to be an improvement.

"I don't want to move to Charlotte, either."

Despite the obvious simplicity of the statement, it didn't compute. "But that's where *The Dish* is."

"And as cool as it would be to be one of the permanent hosts, that's not the job I actually want. Or the life. Or, it turns out, the location."

Hope bubbled up, however prematurely. "It's not?"

"It's not. I got so caught up in what it symbolized, I didn't stop to think if it was something I really wanted." She looked away briefly, bit her lip. "Or what it might cost me."

Guilt swooped in, effectively elbowing hope to the sidelines. "It shouldn't have to cost you anything. You should have everything you want."

"Maybe I should, but I can't be in two places at once." Chelsea smirked then, and for some reason, it made him think everything was going to turn out okay. "And it turns out I really, really want to be here."

"You do?" Could it be that simple?

"It's not all about you, Bryce."

He lifted both hands, cowed but at the same time delighted. "I would hope not."

"But I'd be lying if I said you weren't a huge part of the equation."

Even as that delight blossomed, the guilt hovered like a stubborn morning fog. "I feel like I'm backing you into a corner."

"If anyone got backed into a corner, I think it's the other way around. You didn't ask for any of this."

He lifted a shoulder. "I didn't. But I didn't say no, either."

She chuckled. "You kind of did. At least to the celebrity part. Either way, aren't you the one who said consent has to be clear and enthusiastic?"

The memory of the conversation made him smile. "That was about sex."

"Same difference, no?" Her playful tone gave him courage.

"Um, no. Not the same at all. We're talking about love now." If they were doing this, he needed to put all his cards on the table.

"Are we?"

"I'm pretty in love with you, Chelsea Boudreaux. It only feels fair to tell you."

She lifted a brow. "You're *pretty* in love with me."

He'd been going for cheeky, not qualified. "Not pretty in love. A lot in love. All the way, honestly."

"I…"

When she didn't continue, he offered a sheepish smile. "Wasn't expecting that?"

"I wasn't, but I'm glad that's where you went."

He nodded and his whole torso joined in, rocking forward and back. Equal parts relief and anticipation.

"It's mutual, by the way." She shrugged, more a sign of inevitability than defeat. "I'm in love with you, too."

Bryce went still. "You're serious."

"Quite." She tipped her head back and forth. "A lot. All the way."

Air rushed out of his lungs. "I thought you were going to break up with me."

Chelsea stuck out both hands. "I thought you were going to break up with me."

For all that, it turned out to be pretty damn easy after all. "Okay, then. Wow."

Chelsea grinned. "I know."

"Are we crazy? Wait, not a cool term. Sorry. What I mean is, are we really doing this?" Not that he wanted to give her an out, but he wanted—needed—her to be sure. And maybe he needed to hear her say it.

"I suppose it depends on what you mean by this."

"You and me. Us." He took her hand. "Whatever wild ride life throws our way."

"Right. In that case, sign me up."

❖

For maybe the first time ever, Chelsea woke up before Bryce. Woke up, got up, made coffee, got in the shower—all before his six o'clock alarm went off. She'd just poured her second cup when he came into the kitchen in boxers and a T-shirt, scratching his belly like an old man. She stopped tapping her foot and fretting long enough to kiss him good morning.

"Good morning," he said. "Did I misunderstand? Is your meeting with the network early?"

"No, no. It's at ten."

"So you're…"

"Turning into a morning person?" She lilted her voice high and tried for a big smile.

"Baby, you should have woken me up. I would have happily taken your mind off things."

Even through her stress, the suggestive tone made her laugh. "I'll keep that in mind."

He ran his hands up and down her arms, gave her shoulders a squeeze. "What can I do? How can I help?"

She loved that he wanted to help. Even more, he asked rather than deciding and doing whatever he thought would do the job. In all her relationships, she'd never had a partner do that. Not truly. "Just love me."

"You know I do."

"I do. And I love you." She took a deep breath, lifting her shoulders and letting them fall. "So much."

"I'm sorry I'm the reason you're stressed out."

"You're not. Meetings with the network execs are inherently stressful." Which was totally true.

"Yeah, but I'm the reason you're telling them no," he said.

It had felt that way at first. Like she was choosing between him and taking her career to the next level. But when push came to shove, the level they were offering was a step away from what she really wanted. With Bryce, but also for herself. She wanted a career where food sat front and center—cooking it, sharing it, making it more accessible to people. She hoped she could keep doing that on her show, but only if she could do it on her terms. "You're not. I am. And I'm not telling them no. I'm telling them yes with qualifications."

Bryce's features softened and he smiled. "I love you."

It was a little smushy and a little sentimental and she didn't even care. Well, cared but in a good way. Liked it. Basked in it. "And I love you."

"Enough to fix me a cup of coffee while I shower?"

She smirked. "Exactly that much."

She sent Bryce on his way and tried to work on the script for one of the upcoming episodes. She lasted about fifteen minutes, most of which she spent rereading every email she'd ever exchanged with Shauna, before calling Jada. Jada, who knew the meeting was scheduled for that morning, didn't even ask what the hell Chelsea wanted at 8:40 on a Tuesday morning.

"I'm telling you, you don't have anything to worry about."

Chelsea laughed. "I wish I could believe you."

"You should believe me. I'm very smart."

Smart or not, Jada also happened to be her biggest champion. It was great, having someone ready to sing her praises and pump up her ego at the drop of a hat. Unfortunately, it also made her less than reliable in moments like this. "You're smart, but you're also biased."

"Biased, schmiased. Your show is fantastic, your audience is solid. They're not going to cut you loose because you don't want to move to Charlotte and film forty weeks of the year."

"Yeah." A logical argument, one she'd made to herself and to Bryce. One Jada had made several times already. But she couldn't quite shake the fear that the rug could be pulled out from under her. A thanks but no thanks that amounted to a giant fuck you. Or worse, an ultimatum that forced her to say unequivocally that she'd choose love over career. Not that she wouldn't. She just didn't like having to be that person. She wanted to have it all, damn it. And despite the detente she'd managed to forge with Irene, a little part of her wanted to prove to Irene that she could.

"No, no. You're supposed to say, 'You're right, Jada. I should listen to you more often.'"

She laughed in spite of herself. "I'm going to save that for when they say yes."

Jada let out a not so subtle humph.

"In the meantime, I'll say thanks for the pep talk and comic relief," Chelsea said.

"I'll take that."

Since Jada was at Billy's, left to her own devices while he was getting his equipment ready for the harvest, they chatted for a while. It passed the time and gave her a semblance of direction for the script that she'd hopefully be able to tackle after her meeting ended. It did the trick, getting her safely to ten of ten—just enough time to pee and put on some lipstick so she didn't look like a corpse on camera.

Chelsea logged into the call, a little sad that Jada wouldn't be one of the faces on the screen. Shauna was already there, and Sylvia joined a few seconds later. Dave and Barb followed, and even though it was a virtual meeting, Chelsea would swear all eyes were on her.

"It's good to see you, Chelsea." Shauna sounded sincere.

Chelsea smiled, attempting to convey more calm than she felt. "You, too."

"So, you've taken some time to think," Shauna said.

The woman didn't mince words or waste time. Which she knew, but damn. "I have."

"And?"

"And as amazing an opportunity as it is, and as flattered as I am, I don't feel like relocating to Charlotte is something I can do right now, professionally or personally." She'd rehearsed the statement and it showed, but at least she didn't fumble the words.

"I had a feeling you might say that," Dave said.

Chelsea bit the inside of her cheek.

"Which is why I have an alternate proposal already prepared," Shauna added.

"Alternate proposal?" Chelsea swallowed the groan that threatened to escape. She'd gone from overly scripted to utterly clueless in under ten seconds.

"Go on," Sylvia said, making Chelsea wonder if she expected that or was simply better at rolling with it.

"Yes. Sort of a hybrid model." Shauna flipped a hand back and forth.

"Okay." The very fact that they were considering something else gave her an almost giddy optimism.

"We'd anticipated bringing in another permanent host, both for the stability of the show and because we assumed that would be the most appealing employment option. We were wrong." Dave gave a dumbfounded sort of shrug.

Were they talking about her? Or had they already had this conversation with someone else?

"Dave was wrong," Shauna said with a wink.

"Yeah, yeah." Dave waved a hand. "Anyway, the point is, Rocco said exactly what you said when we offered the spot to him."

A bubble of laughter escaped. Like, maybe she should be offended or disappointed or whatever that she hadn't been their first choice. But all she could feel was relief. Even though she didn't know exactly what they had in mind. "I'm intrigued."

Barb cleared her throat. "We'd like to continue the rotation model but make it more regular. One week of shows per month. You and Rocco will be our regulars and we'll bring in guest hosts to fill the gaps and test audience response."

It didn't take much in the way of mental math to calculate the commitment. "Three filming days a month."

Barb lifted a finger. "Technically every four weeks. With an option for future guest spots and holiday specials."

It sounded too good to be true. Time to drop her other bombshell. "Bryce isn't interested at all, I'm afraid. He'll do some appearances on my show, but that's all he's open to."

Shauna gave a flick of her wrist that said she'd suspected as much. "It was worth a shot."

She hated to put her vulnerability on display, but she needed to hear Shauna say it. "You're okay with that? With just me?"

Dave took that moment to jump in. "Chelsea, you're our star. You know that, right?"

Did she admit to not knowing that at all? Probably not. Especially with contract negotiations on the table. "Just making sure. I know Bryce makes quite an impression."

"Too modest." Sylvia rolled her eyes but laughed. "I'm working on it."

Both Dave and Shauna laughed. Shauna lifted a finger. "Promise that the next time we drag you to New York for something or other, you'll try to convince him to come with you."

She smiled, at the comment but also because Jada had been right all along. "I'll see what I can do."

CHAPTER TWENTY-NINE

Chelsea turned into the driveway of Bryce's parents' house with extra care, willing the cake sitting in the back of her hatchback not to slide. A glimpse in the rearview mirror showed the tall box exactly where she'd put it. She let out a sigh of relief and smiled.

"You seem especially happy today," Bryce said.

"Because I'm pretty sure my first attempt at a wedding cake arrived intact."

He laughed. "Sure."

"But also because it's Kate and Sutton's wedding day and weddings make me happy." Chelsea cut the engine and looked his way. "And because I'm in love with this really great guy and it turns out he's in love with me back."

Bryce's grin seemed to radiate as much joy as she had pressing against her ribs and vibrating through every muscle. "Those are both very good reasons."

"Plus I got to make a wedding cake. I never get to make wedding cakes."

Bryce rolled his eyes. "Only you."

"You complaining?"

"No." He leaned across the center console and kissed her with enough oomph that she wondered which of them would be wearing more lipstick when it ended.

"You have a little…" She brushed a thumb across his bottom lip.

"Worth it." He snagged a tissue and wiped most of it away. "Better?"

"But not great." She laughed. "Let's get this cake unloaded and I'll help you deal with it."

"Yes, ma'am."

Once they'd gotten it set up on the table in the backyard, Bryce went in search of Kate, and Chelsea popped into the kitchen to see if she could do anything useful. Kate's mom was a woman after her own heart, though, and everything was poised, prepped, and ready to be served when the reception began.

She did some mingling with the people she knew, as well as a few she hadn't yet met but who recognized her from the show. When the ceremony started, she took her seat and told herself she wouldn't cry. It lasted up to the moment when very pregnant Kate and adorably tearful Sutton exchanged their vows.

When they'd done, the minister guided them into the more scripted bits. "Sutton, do you take Kate to be your wife, to have and to hold, from this day forward?"

Sutton took a deep breath, seeming like she might burst with happiness. "I really, really do."

The minister gave an affirming nod before turning to Kate. "And do you, Kate, take Sutton to be your spouse, to have and to hold, from this day forward?"

Kate beamed. "I—oh, God."

Everyone froze, including Kate. Only Kate stood in a slightly hunched position, hand yanked free from Sutton's and pressed to the underside of her belly.

"Kate?" Sutton's newly freed hand went to Kate's shoulder.

"I just had a contraction."

Sutton's expression went from confused and concerned to sheer terror in under a second. "Oh. God."

Kate's water broke, adding a dramatic flair to the moment. Harper yelped. Sutton looked as though she might pass out. Kate, being Kate, took the whole thing in stride.

And then everything seemed to happen at once. Kate insisted on being pronounced spouses for life and the minister hurried to proclaim them so. Sutton helped Kate into the house to change clothes before heading to the hospital, and Kate's parents commandeered the DJ's microphone to assure everyone that the newlyweds might be cutting out early, but the party would go on.

Chelsea stood by, wishing she could do more to help but mostly in awe of how well everyone seemed to take the bride going into labor.

Bryce, who'd vanished into the house, returned. "I'm going to drive Sutton and Kate to the hospital. Could you go to their place and get some stuff for Kate? She says she can text you a list."

Chelsea nodded. "Of course."

"My parents are going to deal with a few things here and then follow us. Would you mind bringing Harper to her cousin's house before heading to the hospital?"

Harper appeared out of nowhere, like she'd been waiting for someone to mention her name. "I'm going to the hospital. Mama said I could."

It didn't take much to imagine the four of them crammed into one vehicle, Kate trying to reassure Harper on top of managing the pain and keeping herself from freaking out too much. "Why don't you come with me? You can help me pack a bag for your mom and then keep me company on the drive."

Harper's gaze darted to Kate—who was busy hugging people and telling them to enjoy the reception without her—before flitting to Bryce and back to Chelsea.

Bryce put a hand on Harper's shoulder. "You can change out of your dress, too. I promise the baby won't be born before you get there."

Chelsea didn't have enough experience with the ins and outs of giving birth to know whether he said that with authority or sheer optimism. Either way, Harper took him at face value. "Okay. Yeah. I know what she needs. And I know where the car seat is because we'll need to bring that, too."

She didn't have the heart to say, even best-case scenario, the baby probably wouldn't be coming home immediately. She locked eyes with Bryce, who seemed to be having the exact same thought. "That's a great idea," he said.

Harper nodded. "I'm going to go tell Mama and Sutton the plan."

Bryce nodded, too. "Give them both a big hug because you might not be able to see them until after."

Harper took off, looking a hell of a lot more like a little kid than the young woman she'd channeled as maid of honor.

"Thank you," Bryce said.

"Of course. She needs to be there, but she doesn't need to see everything."

"Or hear her mama cuss any more than she already does," Bryce said. Despite the humor in his words, worry practically radiated from him.

"It's going to be okay." She put a hand on his arm, like she might be able to channel more confidence through touch than her own shaky voice.

"It is."

She wanted to say more, to reassure even though her own anxiety about Kate, about the baby, spiked. "Now, go. The last thing we need is Kate giving birth in the back seat."

That broke the tension. "God, she'd never let us hear the end of it."

Chelsea kissed him hard and sent him on his way. She and Harper made their way through the throng of family and friends, stopping in the house long enough to grab her keys and purse. After packing a bag at Kate and Sutton's—and putting the still in its box car seat in the back—she made a quick stop at her place to change. After a moment of hesitation, she grabbed a pair of Bryce's jeans and a T-shirt.

For all that Harper was worried about her mama or the baby or missing things, she managed some teasing about how Bryce must sleep over pretty often to have clothes at her house. Chelsea had no illusions about what kids Harper's age knew, but she had no desire to hash out grownup sleepovers with her boyfriend's niece. Fortunately, Harper had more pressing things on her mind. She quickly shifted gears to double-checking they had everything they could possibly need, and then they were off.

❖

"What's taking so long?" Chelsea asked for the tenth time.

Bryce took her hand and gave it a squeeze, glad she was there even if she was impatient about it. "You're worse than Harper."

"Sorry." She looked at their joined hands, then into his eyes. "Sorry. I should be supporting you and I'm the one who's a train wreck."

"You're here. That's all the support I need." He chuckled at the cheesiness, then realized how much he actually meant it.

"What?" Chelsea bit her lip and frowned. "You think I'm being ridiculous."

"Nothing about you is ridiculous."

"I've just never been at a birth before. And it's so early."

For some reason, her nerves made it easy to steady his own. "It is early, but not dangerously so," he said.

"Are you saying that to make me feel better?"

"No. It's what Sutton and Kate told me on the ride here and what Google told me when I did frantic web searches waiting for you and Harper to get here." And he mostly believed it. Sure, the risk for complications was higher, but all the baby's major organs should be able to kick in at this point. Hopefully, the worst thing would be needing an incubator and extra oxygen for a little bit.

Chelsea nodded then seemed to make a point of changing the subject. He appreciated her efforts, especially the pains she took to keep his parents entertained. She even went down to the cafeteria in search of snacks, insisting Harper come along to help pick out good stuff. Time dragged but also flew—some strange sleight of hand that only hospital waiting rooms could manage.

At 2:08 a.m., Wren Adele made her way into the world, a little tinier than her parents and the doctor might have hoped, but otherwise none the worse for wear. Chelsea got shuffled in with the rest of the family. She'd always felt welcomed, but there was something about sharing middle-of-the-night hugs and laughter and tears that made her genuinely feel like one of them.

Bryce's parents said their reluctant good nights and headed home, Harper in tow. She and Bryce did the same, but not without taking their five minutes in the NICU before being shooed out for the night.

Chelsea didn't release her grip on Bryce's hand, but her free one came up and rested on the incubator. "She's so tiny."

"Only a little smaller than Harper was, actually. According to Kate, the doctor said she'd have been a chonk if she'd gone to term."

Chelsea regarded him with suspicion. "The doctor did not say 'chonk.'"

"You gonna be the one to call Kate a liar?"

He thought she might argue, but she merely smiled. "No. No, I'm not."

"Wise woman."

Chelsea's attention returned to the baby. "She's pretty perfect, isn't she?"

He couldn't have said it better himself. "Yeah."

They lingered another minute, but the nurse came and reminded them rules were rules, and they'd already been bent. They stepped outside the hospital entrance as a gust of chilly air whipped by. Chelsea took his arm and huddled closer. "Brr."

He held her against him. "There. That's better."

"What a day. You okay to drive?" she asked.

"Honestly, I'm wired. I'll even be okay if you want to nod off."

Chelsea grinned. "Not a chance."

Despite the assertions, neither of them had much to say on the ride home. It felt like a relaxed and happy sort of quiet, though, so he had no complaints. Because, as Chelsea had said, what a day. He drove to his house out of habit more than anything else, and Chelsea didn't complain. But when he pulled into the driveway and cut the engine, Chelsea made no move to get out. "What's wrong?"

She searched his face and hesitated long enough to make him antsy. "How immediately do you want your own?"

"My own what?"

Her shoulders dropped and she looked at him with exasperation. "Fantasy football team. Babies, Bryce. I'm talking about babies."

"Oh." Forget antsy. Full-on foreboding settled in his chest.

"I mean, obviously you want them. I knew that before. But seeing you tonight, with Wren? The when feels more relevant than the if."

"I do, but I swear I'm not in a hurry."

Chelsea folded her arms, her intensity seeming to hover on the edge of irritation. "Bullshit."

He did love that she didn't pull her punches. "Fine. I'd like to have them within the next decade so I can get them to high school before arthritis sets in."

She nodded but didn't shift her posture. "All right."

He hadn't settled on how to turn the question back on her before she got out of the car and booked it toward the door. Bryce scrambled to follow. "Wait, is that it?"

Chelsea stomped her feet. "Well, it answered my question. I'll happily answer any you have as soon as you let me in. It's freezing out here."

He unlocked the door but gave her a gentle poke in the ribs as she scurried past him. "I thought you were used to New York winters."

"Yeah, but all my real coats are in storage. Besides, this is a damp cold. It gets in your bones even when it's forty out."

He laughed at the emphatic tone. "Fair."

"So, you want to know if I want kids, right?"

Damn, the woman did not beat around the bush. "We should probably discuss it at some point. It doesn't have to be tonight."

Chelsea set down her bag and shed her jacket. Bryce got the sinking feeling he was in for a letdown. "I want them. I wasn't sure for a long time, but I am now. I'm not sure when and I'm pretty sure not yet, but I definitely want them."

The knot around his ribs loosened. "Oh."

She smirked and he had to fight the urge to kiss her. "You don't have to sound so surprised."

He shook his head, not sure how to convey the nagging worry in a way that didn't make him sound like a self-absorbed douche. "I didn't want to assume is all. I—"

She closed the distance between them and kissed him instead. "You're cute when you're flustered."

"You think?" he asked, not at all minding being teased.

"I do. You know what else?"

The look in her eyes told him all he needed to know. "What's that?"

"I love you."

He'd lost track of how many times she'd said it, but it got him every damn time. "I'm so glad. I love you, too."

She took a deep breath, blew it out slowly.

"But?" he asked.

"No but. Just working on a grand declaration here, and I didn't want to pass out."

"What's grander than I love you?" Other than her saying yes to the marriage proposal he'd already started daydreaming about, maybe.

"I want more."

"More." He did, too, but still wasn't sure their definitions of that lined up.

"I want a whole life with you. A home." She shrugged but her eyes went glassy with tears. "A family."

In that instant, his worries melted away. All that remained was the magical certainty that they wanted the same things. The rest was details. Fortunately, they knew their way around handling those, both big and small. They'd work it out and it would be fun and amazing and hard and adventurous and probably everything in between. And best of all, they'd do it together.

CHAPTER THIRTY

One year later

"Am I really doing this?" Chelsea looked to Jada for reassurance that she'd made the right decision.

"You are. And it's going to be amazing."

Jada probably would have said that either way, but Chelsea let herself believe the words. "Thank you so much for coming with me. I'm pretty sure I'd have chickened out if I'd been alone."

Jada slung an arm around her shoulders and squeezed. "Girl. I got you. Though I'm still not sure why you didn't want to bring your boyfriend for such a big day."

"Because I needed to do this on my own. Well, more on my own than having him here holding my hand." She chewed her lip. "I haven't actually told him yet."

Jada's eyes narrowed. "Why not?"

How could she explain in a way that didn't make her seem like an obstinate cow? "Because I need to prove I'm doing this for me, not him or even us. Plus I want to surprise him."

"Don't get me wrong, I don't think you need to run it by him first. And I have no doubt he'll be over the moon. I just thought you'd want to have this moment as a couple."

Forget obstinate cow. What she really didn't want to come across as was desperate and superstitious. "Because if I tie this decision to him and things go south, where would that leave me?"

"Do you really think things are going to go south?" Jada asked.

"I mean, my track record with relationships would imply it's a possibility." Though this one was her longest—and healthiest—to date.

Jada poked her in the arm. "Yeah, but most of the people you were with weren't good enough for you."

"Only one or two. Sometimes it was the other way around. Or mutual." None of which she'd been able to admit until after the fact.

"Still. Bryce is different. You're different."

She blew out a breath. Different as in happier than she'd ever been. "Still. I need this decision to be about more than sticking around for Bryce. And it is. I know it is. I just need the symbolism to back me up."

That finally got her a smile. "Like I said, I got you. Symbolically and otherwise."

"I really wish you lived here all the time."

Rather than rolling her eyes or making a comment about NYC forever, Jada gave an uncharacteristically sheepish shrug.

"What? What is that?" Chelsea asked.

"I'm a long way from even thinking the word 'permanent,' but I'm going to stick around for a bit."

Delight warred with disbelief. "Say more."

"I took a gig in New Orleans. It's a renovation show spinoff. Saving old houses, community development, that sort of thing."

"You're leaving me?" A lick of dread swept up her spine.

"No, you dork. I'd never leave you. It's a twelve-week job that should just fill the space between now and filming your next season."

She loved the idea of Jada staying local, of finding her own passion project to complement their work on the show. It seemed almost too good to be true. "Now who's not telling who their big news?"

"I signed the contract this morning. I was simply letting you have your moment before stealing the thunder."

Chelsea shook her head. "If you're staying here, you can have all the thunder."

Jada lifted a finger. "Around here. Not here here. I already scoped out a place in the Ninth Ward."

Of course she had. "It's within a hundred-mile radius. I'll take it. Tell me everything."

Jada did, save the interruption by the loan officer. Chelsea signed her name at least two hundred times, culminating in a handshake and a set of keys. She dragged Jada to the coffee shop next door to finish getting the scoop, then sent her on her way to meet up with Billy. Much like Chelsea didn't want her big decisions too tied to Bryce, Jada hedged questions about whether Billy influenced her in any way.

Though, even as she drew that parallel, the truth of both their situations was apparent. They were in love with local boys. And, it seemed, they were in it for the long haul.

❖

Chelsea smiled, eyes bright with what appeared to be a combination of excitement and nerves. "So, I may have made a very large, rather impulsive decision."

Bryce tried for an encouraging smile in return. "How worried should I be?"

She did that thing where she twitched her lips this way and that. "I don't think you should be worried at all."

"Well, then I'm not. I trust you." The funny thing was, he wasn't just saying it. He meant it. The fact didn't surprise him, but it didn't mean he wanted to take it for granted.

"Aw. Thanks, handsome. For the record, I trust you, too. Big impulsive decisions or otherwise."

He couldn't resist a smirk. "I'm going to remind you of that when I come home with a fishing boat."

"If you keep me in a steady supply of fresh redfish, I'll help you pick it out."

"I want to say be careful what you wish for, but I know I'd never spend that kind of money on something I'd only use a few times a year."

Chelsea nodded, as though filing away the details. "Well, I spent a crap ton of money, but I'm planning for it to get used every day."

He struggled to imagine something that fit the bill. A new car, maybe? That wouldn't be any of his business, though. He might have opinions, but they hadn't merged finances or anything, so they'd be the sort of opinions he'd keep to himself. Unless she asked, of course. "Are you going to tell me what it is?"

Her smile was sly. "I'd rather show you."

Showing involved driving somewhere, so he climbed into the passenger seat of her Fiat and dutifully closed his eyes when she told him to.

"It's not far," she said.

He noted the song on the radio so he could track time, but she put the car in park before it even ended. "Did we even go anywhere?"

"Well, we didn't leave town, if that's what you mean. Go on. Open your eyes."

He did and found himself staring at the old storefront of a restaurant that hadn't been anything since his childhood. "Is this the old Plantation Restaurant?"

"It was the old Plantation Restaurant. It's going to be something else entirely very soon." She lifted a finger. "Something with a less racist name, thank you very much."

A kernel of understanding took root. "Did you buy it?"

Chelsea gave him a look of terrified exultation. "I did."

"You're opening a restaurant." Even without all the pieces in place, he liked where this was going. It screamed words like *committed* and *invested*.

"I am."

With or without the details, joy swelled in his chest. "Chelsea, that's huge."

"The paperwork I just signed at the bank would indicate that's the case."

"I don't know what to say except I'm so happy for you."

She gave him a playful half smile. "You could also say you're willing to help."

"I'm absolutely willing to help. What do you need? What's the plan?"

"Well, today I'm hoping you'll walk through with me and make sure I don't have a panic attack and pass out."

He laughed, in awe of this amazing woman and the fact that she was in love with him. Wanted to be with him. "Deal."

At the front door, she fished a set of keys from her purse. Only her hands shook too much for her to get the right one in the lock. She held them out to him. "Apparently, I need help with this, too."

Inside, the space was smaller than he remembered. But without any furniture or fixtures, it still seemed cavernous. "I haven't been here since I was like ten."

She turned a slow circle. "No one has. The owner passed away and the building has been vacant ever since."

"Duchesne has been wanting for a good place to eat."

"That's what the bank said when they approved my loan."

A thousand questions swirled. Some had to do with how much Chelsea knew about getting a restaurant off the ground. Others were more fanciful, like what she wanted to call it and what kind of food she wanted to serve. But since she already seemed more than a little overwhelmed, he decided to go with his heart. "I guess that means you're planning to stick around."

She put her hands on her hips in a way that reminded him of Kate, and a little of Harper. "We've discussed this. I'd already decided to stick around."

"But this." He spread his arms. "This is a lot more permanent than, hey I really like you, let's see where things go."

"I more than like you." She put her arms around him, tilting her head back to look in his eyes. "We've discussed that, too."

They had. And it wasn't that he didn't believe her. It was, well, maybe he had a few doubts. Given his track record with relationships. Given hers. Given the seemingly endless opportunities that continued to come knocking. "You really want to stay, though. Not just for me."

"You're a big part of it. I'd be lying if I said otherwise. But yes, I do want to stay." She nodded slowly, looked around. "This is home."

"Home." He'd waited most of his life to hear a woman say that. Well, a woman he was in love with. And who was in love with him.

"I should warn you, this is probably going to turn out to be a crap ton more work than jetting off to Charlotte a few days a month."

"Are you quitting *The Dish*?" He didn't love her being away, but he'd sort of gotten used to it. And, if he was being honest, he'd grown especially fond of her homecomings.

Chelsea smirked and there was a glint of mischief in her eye. "Well, I can't exactly leave you alone with a baby a week out of every month, can I?"

They'd started talking about babies with more frequency. Weddings, too. But he'd held off on proposing until he could plan the perfect moment. "Only you would decide to open a restaurant as part of your plan to settle down and start a family."

She shrugged. "Settling down is relative, no?"

God, he loved this woman. "If this is your version of doing it, sign me up."

"Well, I was thinking it would be a great spot to have the wedding reception. After I get it all fixed up, of course."

"Of course."

"So, you like it?" she asked.

He loved what it symbolized, that it was something she wanted. "I do."

Chelsea turned a slow circle, lifting her shoulders and letting them drop. "I'm glad."

"I want to see every square inch and hear every detail of your plans." She angled her head. "Why do I feel like there's a but coming?"

It was his turn to smirk. "But I'm going to need you to come home with me first."

"Why? We're already here."

Happiness swelled in his chest and all the plans he had for orchestrating a perfect proposal vanished. "Because I want to ask you to marry me, and the ring is at my house."

Chelsea's mouth dropped open. "You do?"

"I've been wanting to for the better part of the last year. I was trying to come up with the perfect way."

She folded her arms, jutted her hip. "And this is what you settled on?"

"No, but I decided if I didn't hurry up and do it already, you might beat me to it."

"Oh, well, then. Sure." Chelsea nodded, grin wide. "Can we get a couple of hammers and a ladder while we're there?"

"Depends. You gonna say yes?"

She wrapped her arms around him then and kissed him long and slow. "For the record, I've been waiting."

Suddenly, the ring stopped seeming all that important, too. All he needed was the knowledge that Chelsea wanted to spend the rest of her life with him as much as he wanted to spend his with her. "Hey, Chelsea?"

"Yes, Bryce?"

For as long as he'd waited, it felt almost too easy. "Will you marry me?"

"Yes. Yes, yes, yes." She kissed him again. "But I definitely want that ring."

He grabbed her hand and pulled her to the door. "Not as much as I want to put it on you."

They got outside and locked up, but when they climbed back into her car, Chelsea paused. "Wait. Does this mean you're finally going to move in with me?" she asked.

They'd discussed that, too. Her house was bigger than his, not to mention outfitted for tapings of her show. She'd dropped a few hints here and there, but he'd always joked that he wouldn't sell his house until they were engaged. Not an insurance policy, exactly, but sort of.

"I'm pretty sure that was the arrangement," he said.

Chelsea took a deep breath and blew it out. Suddenly, she seemed unsure. Bryce took her hand again. "Is everything okay?"

She nodded, but when she looked at him, her eyes were glassy with tears. "I'm thinking how Jada always tells me I'm afraid to trust it when my dreams come true."

His stomach twisted. "And?"

"And it's going to be fun to prove her wrong once and for all."

"You deserve everything you ever wanted." He might not be able to give her all of it, but he damn well was going to try.

"I want you. The rest is gravy."

He didn't believe that, not literally at least. But he didn't need to. Chelsea was her own woman and she helped him be his own man. That was so much better than the cookie-cutter version of couplehood he used to think he wanted. So much more than he'd ever imagined. He pulled her into his arms and kissed her again. At the rate they were going, they weren't going to make it to his house. Not that he cared. He had everything he needed right there.

About the Author

Aurora Rey is a college dean by day and a life coach and queer romance author the rest of the time, except when she's cooking, baking, riding the tractor, or pining for goats. She grew up in a small town in south Louisiana, daydreaming about New England. She keeps a special place in her heart for the South, especially the food and the ways women are raised to be strong, even if they're taught not to show it. After a brief dalliance with biochemistry, she completed both a B.A. and an M.A. in English.

She is the author of the Cape End Romance series and several standalone contemporary romance novels and novellas. She has been a finalist for the Lambda Literary, RITA, and Golden Crown Literary Society awards, but loves reader feedback the most. She lives in Ithaca, New York, with her dogs and whatever wildlife has taken up residence in the pond.

About the author

Books Available From Bold Strokes Books

The Accidental Bride by Jane Walsh. Spinsters Miss Grace Linfield and Miss Thea Martin travel to Gretna Green to prevent a wedding, only to discover a scandalous passion—for each other. (978-1-63679-345-0)

Broken Fences by Jo Hemmingwood. Former army sergeant Seneca Twist has difficulty adjusting to civilian life until she meets psychologist Robyn Mason and has a place to call home. (978-1-63679-414-3)

Never Kiss a Cowgirl by Ali Vali. Asher Evans dreams of winning the National Finals Rodeo in Vegas, and Reagan Wilson wants no part of something that brings back the memory of what killed her father. (978-1-63679-106-7)

Pantheon Girls by Jean Copeland. Cassie Burke never anticipated the detour life is about to take when a meeting with a prospective client reunites her with a past love and reignites the star-crossed passion they shared twenty years earlier. (978-1-63679-337-5)

Roux for Two by Aurora Rey. For TV chef Chelsea Boudreaux and hometown boy Bryce Cormier, love proves as tricky as making a good pot of gumbo. (978-1-63679-376-4)

Starting Over by Nance Sparks. Jennifer has no idea if she can mend Sam's broken soul after the sudden loss of her wife, but it's never too late for starting over. (978-1-63679-409-9)

Three Wishes by Anne Shade. A magic lamp, a beautiful Jinni, and a cursed princess make for one unbelievable story. (978-1-63679-349-8)

Undiscovered Treasures by MJ Williamz. For Cyl and her friends Luna and Martinique, life's best treasures often appear when they're not looking. (978-1-63679-449-5)

Curse of the Gorgon by Tanai Walker. Cass will do anything to ensure Elle's safety, but is she willing to embrace the curse of the Gorgon? (978-1-63679-395-5)

Dance with Me by Georgia Beers. Scottie Templeton mixes it up on and off the dance floor with sexy salsa instructor Marisa Reyes. But can Scottie get past Marisa's connection to her ex? (978-1-63679-359-7)

Gin and Bear It by Joy Argento. Opposites really can attract, and as Kelly and Logan work together to create a loving home for rescue cat Bear, they just might find one for themselves as well. (978-1-63679-351-1)

Harvest Dreams by Jacqueline Fein-Zachary. Planting the vineyard of their dreams, Kate Bauer and Sydney Barrett must resist their attraction while battling nature and their families, who oppose both the venture and their relationship. (978-1-63679-380-1)

The No Kiss Contract by Nan Campbell. Workaholic Davy believes she can get the top spot at her firm if the senior partners think she's settling down and about to start a family, but she needs the delightful yet dubious Anna to help by pretending to be her fiancée. (978-1-63679-372-6)

Outside the Lines by Melissa Sky. If you had the chance to live forever, would you take it? Amara Rodriguez did, and it sets her on a journey to find her missing mother and unravel the mystery of her own heart. (978-1-63679-403-7)

The Value of Sylver and Gold by Michelle Larkin. When word gets out that former Boston homicide detective Reid Sylver can talk to the dead, the FBI solicits her help on a serial murder case, prompting Reid to assemble forces once again with Detective London Gold. (978-1-63679-093-0)

When It Feels Right by Tagan Shepard. Freshly out of the closet Marlene hasn't been lucky in love, but when it comes to her quirky new roommate Abby, everything just feels right. (978-1-63679-367-2)

The Fall Line by Kelly Wacker. When Jordan Burroughs arrives in the Deep South to paint a local endangered aquatic flower, she doesn't expect to become friends with a mischievous gin-drinking ghost who complicates her budding romance and leads her to an awful discovery and danger. (978-1-63679-205-7)

Lucky in Lace by Melissa Brayden. Straitlaced stationery store owner Juliette Jennings's predictable life unravels when a sexy lingerie shop and its alluring owner move in next door. (978-1-63679-434-1)

Made for Her by Carsen Taite. Neal Walsh is a newly made member of the Mancuso crime family, but will her undeniable attraction to Anastasia Petrov, the wife of her boss's sworn enemy, be the ultimate test of her loyalty? (978-1-63679-265-1)

Off the Menu by Alaina Erdell. Reality TV sensation Restaurant Redo and its gorgeous host Erin Rasmussen will arrive to film in chef Taylor Mobley's kitchen. As the cameras roll, will they make the jump from enemies to lovers? (978-1-63679-295-8)

Pack of Her Own by Elena Abbott. When things heat up in a small town, steamy secrets are revealed between Alpha werewolf Wren Carne and her human mate, Natalie Donovan. (978-1-63679-370-2)

Return to McCall by Patricia Evans. Lily isn't looking for romance—not until she meets Alex, the gorgeous Cuban dance instructor at La Haven, a newly opened lesbian retreat. (978-1-63679-386-3)

So It Went Like This by C. Spencer. A candid and deeply personal exploration of fate, chosen family, and the vulnerability intrinsic in life's uncertainties. (978-1-63555-971-2)

Stolen Kiss by Spencer Greene. Anna and Louise share a stolen kiss, only to discover that Louise is dating Anna's brother. Surely, one kiss can't change everything...Can it? (978-1-63679-364-1)

To Meet Again by Kadyan. When the stark reality of WW II separates cabaret singer Evelyn and Australian doctor Joan in Singapore, they must overcome all odds to find one another again. (978-1-63679-398-6)